**Issue 9
June 2018**

Heart's Kiss

Lezli Robyn & Tina Smith, Editors
Shahid Mahmud, Publisher

Published by Arc Manor/Heart's Nest Press
P.O. Box 10339
Rockville, MD 20849-0339

Heart's Kiss is published in February, April, June, August, October and December.

www.HeartsKiss.com

Pleaee refer to our website for information on how to submit material for *Heart's Kiss* magazine.

Available by subscription (www.HeartsKiss.com) or through your favorite online store (Amazon.com, BN.com, etc.).

ISBN: 978-1-61242-414-9

FOREIGN LANGUAGE RIGHTS: Please refer all inquiries pertaining to foreign language rights to Shahid Mahmud, Arc Manor, P.O. Box 10339, Rockville, MD 20849-0339. Tel: 1-240-645-2214. Fax 1-310-388-8440. Email admin@ArcManor.com.

Contents

D1514827

OPENING EDITORIAL

by Tina Smith

Ah, June. It's hard to believe it will be nearly summer when this lovely issue arrives in reader's mailboxes and is downloaded onto their ereaders. As I write this, it's raining and cold and windy, but I so look forward to the warmth kissing my skin like the heroes we read in our romances. Speaking of kisses, we have a deliciously sinful regency romance, "Five Wicked Kisses" by Anthea Lawson, *USA Today* bestseller and RITA® finalist.

Lezli and I worked hard to show you more delicious facets of this wonderful genre. Back by popular demand, we have another recipe from the kitchen of *New York Times* bestselling writer, Brenda Novak. Along with more non-fiction and the latest installment of You Read *That?*, in which Julie Pitzel takes on *Action or Romance: Why Not Both?* She reviews a recent survey which explains that romance is on the decline, calling foul since romance is woven into most major movies and entertainment and is part of what makes it successful. Julie also used the interrobang (a punctuation that combines the question mark and the exclamation point) in her article. Romance grammar geeks will love the break from traditional punctuation—and if there's anything we love at *Heart's Kiss* it's delivering the familiar with a new flare and twist.

We took care to pick scrumptious shorts that are every bit as sinful as an extra S'mores sneaked from the campfire. We absolutely loved the romantic suspense in "Hidden Treasure" by Sophie Mouette, the fairy tale retelling delights in "Goldilocks and Her Three Sisters" by Kay McSpadden, and the smart, determined heroines of Petronella Glover's near future astronaut series. We also have a bite sized flash fiction meet-cute, "A Fiery Reception" by Alia Mahmud. Lezli will also get cozy and chat with Beverly Jenkins, multiple award winning and *USA Today* bestselling author who has been a much-needed voice shaping multicultural awareness in the romance genre. If it's even more fiction you're after, then take a peek at the latest Recommended Reads from our review columnist C.S. DeAvilla.

However, it's not all fun and games when summer begins. We also have to say goodbye to good friends, if only a goodbye-for-now. Anna J. Stewart's last installment of her Warden series is in this very issue, "Warden of Fate." Like everyone else, I've been on pins and needles wondering what would happen to the last sister after the cliffhanger ending in "Warden of Sight."

So, grab a spot on the tree log in front of our campfire and wrap a warm wool blanket around you as we cater to your romantic fantasies. From paranormal, to historical, to contemporary of every heat level—we hope you find these stories as engaging and entertaining as Lezli and I have. Next time we meet, it will be nearly the end of summer and you will have to tell us about what adventures these months have taken you, dear reader. We are always available on Facebook and Twitter—we love it when readers tweet us photos of where they're reading our magazine. Thank you for being on this journey with us.

Beverly Jenkins is an American author of historical and contemporary romance novels with a particular focus on 19th century African-American life that she believes is often overlooked. This made it difficult to break into publishing because publishers weren't sure what to do with stories that involved African-Americans but not slavery. Jenkins was a 2013 NAACP Image Award nominee and, in 1999, was voted one of the Top 50 Favorite African-American writers of the 20th century by the African American Literature Book Club. In 2016 she was the recipient of the Romantic Times *Reviewers' Choice Award for historical romance, and in 2017 she was given the Romance Writers of America Nora Roberts Lifetime Achievement Award.*

HEART'S KISS INTERVIEWS BEVERLY JENKINS

by Lezli Robyn

I am delighted to be able to interview Beverly Jenkins, whose books are captivating a world on a precipice of change. While they are often set in years past, her books highlight the progress we need to make today to increase equality and acceptance of differences within the human race.

Lezli Robyn: You are known for writing about African American lives in 19th century, United States. But, most particularly, you have focused on writing about characters who were *never* slaves, weaving historical facts into your fictional depiction of what life was like in those days. In fact, your first three novels, *Night Song*, *Vivid*, and *Indigo* featured characters in positions equal to their white counterparts of the time. What made you focus on this part of African American history, apart from being able to create such strong and vibrant voices to represent their time?

Beverly Jenkins: I focus on African-Americans in equal positions to show the race's history is American history—not just African-American history. The contributions of people of color is often glossed over or given short shrift in our nation's schools. Documenting it in a novel is unique way to educate those who may be unfamiliar with the depth of the contributions.

LR: You write characters with such vivid attention to detail, helping others understand how a different way of life impacted the people of that time. How important to you is it to provide references for the historical facts you provide in your novels, to help ground your readers in the reality of that time period?

BJ: Providing references cements the truth and shuts down those who might think the history is made up.

LR: You are an advocate for increasing diversity in romance fiction. Books can have a profound effect on readers, helping them to experience, and hopefully understand more about, the ups and downs in human lives very different to their own. How important is it to for us, as writers, to promote equality, on and off the page?

BJ: This country is becoming more and more diverse with each passing day. Representation matters, and as younger readers age up, they will be looking for stories that reflect them. YA is way ahead of other genres in embracing this. Showing life through one lens is no longer going to be the default model. Romance and the rest of publishing is late to the party but, romance is having the much-needed conversation.

LR: You also write contemporary romances and have won numerous awards throughout your illustrious career for your books, including winning six Romantic Time Awards out of 8 nominations, as well as being a finalist for the prestigious NAACP Image Award for Outstanding Literary Work. Your most recent achievement, the RWA Nora Roberts Lifetime Achievement Award, in 2017, shows how accomplished you have been in your career. What was the first achievement/milestone you received where you realized you could have a career in this field, and/or that you were making an impact on readers?

BJ: My very first book, *Night Song*, let me know I could have a career by the way the readers embraced the story. As I stated in the last question, representation matters. That my books were added to college lit courses was further validation.

LR: Tell us about the your movie, *Deadly/Sexy*, and how it is an important venture for the romance field.

BJ: Siri Austin Productions is a small film company founded by author Iris Bolling. Hollywood and entities like Hallmark and Lifetime haven't shown much interest in African-American romance. Rather than wait for something that might never happen, Iris formed her company and filmed two of her own books. She's now branching out to green light other African-American romance authors and I'm blessed to be one of the first. She chose *Deadly/Sexy* one of my romantic suspense titles. Filming was completed in April and the project is now in post-production. I should have more news on what's next soon.

LR: If you had to pick *one* heroine from all your novels, across all your series, and *one* hero as your favorites, who would they be? And would you think they'd make a great couple if their paths had crossed between the sheets of the same book?

BJ: Hmm. Interesting question. I think I'd like to see how Raimond LeVeq from *Through the Storm* might pair with my lady gambler Loreli Winters from *Topaz* and *A Chance at Love*. There'd be fireworks, for sure.

LR: And lastly, what is next for you, for 2018? What do your readers have to look forward to?

BJ: What's next? The 9th book in my Blessings series will be available in late August. The title is *Second Time Sweeter*. I just signed a new 3 book contract with Avon for more historicals. The first is slated to debut next spring.

Copyright © 2018 by Lezli Robyn.

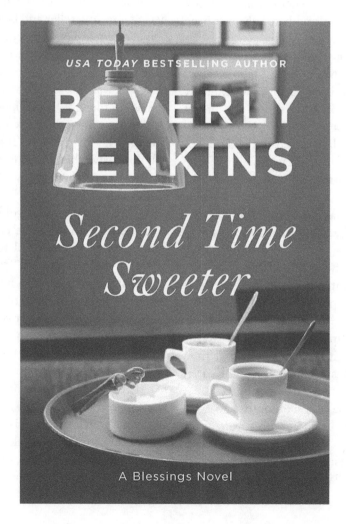

USA Today *bestselling author and two-time RITA nominee Anthea Lawson's books have received starred reviews in* Library Journal *and* Publisher's Weekly, *and she has been named "one of new stars of historical romance" by* Booklist. *Make sure to pick up her full-length spicy historical romances, available online at all digital retailers. Anthea lives with her husband and daughter in sunny Southern California. In addition to writing historical romance, she plays the Irish fiddle and pens award-winning YA Urban Fantasy as Anthea Sharp.*

FIVE WICKED KISSES

by Anthea Lawson

"He's watching you."

Juliana Tate did not need to turn around to know who her friend Henrietta was speaking of. There was, and had only ever been, one *he*.

Waves of heat raced just under her skin, and her heart tumbled abruptly in her chest. Their corner of the ballroom, chosen for its seclusion, was suddenly crowded with the hum of conversation and bright spikes of laughter.

She flipped open her lace-edged fan and wafted air across her cheeks. There could be no hint of reaction, no sign that the arrival of Robert Pembroke, the new Earl of Eastbrook, affected her. Since coming up to London, she had seen him on three occasions—and each time had done her utmost stay as far away as possible.

"You told me he was not invited." Her voice wavered, only the tiniest bit, but she knew her friend heard. "Hen, I depend upon you completely. You're the only one who knows."

Henrietta made an apologetic face. "He wasn't supposed to be here. But it's hardly the first time the Earl of Eastbrook has paid no heed to the social niceties. You know what they say about him."

Since ascending to the title six months ago, Robert had taken to life in London with a vengeance. According to the gossips, he had cut a wide swath through the ladies, leaving words like *seducer* and *scoundrel* in his wake. Juliana could well believe it.

Robert had always been handsome enough to break hearts, with his strong jaw, keen amber eyes, and auburn hair shot through with glints of fire. Not to mention a keen mind and wit. No doubt he was pleased to bring so many ladies of the *ton* to their knees, after years of being treated as unworthy, a shabby country cousin.

And Juliana had been the worst offender.

She plied her fan harder, trying to wave away the bitter memory. The past was done—all she could do now was move forward into an increasingly precarious future.

"Is he still looking?" she asked. It wouldn't be safe to turn around unless that penetrating amber gaze were focused elsewhere.

"His attention seems to have moved to Miss Snelling's bosoms. And there is so very much there to admire." Henrietta gave a disapproving sniff. "If her gown were any lower she might as well proclaim herself a melon-seller and be done."

Juliana could not help a quick glance down at her own, unrevealing gown. She had turned the seams and added new ribbons, but she feared it was evident that the gown was at least two seasons out of date. And it was not as though she had much to reveal, in any case.

Henrietta saw the look on Juliana's face. "Tsk." She took her by the arm. "It's hardly your fault that you don't have the newest fashions. You still make a lovely figure. Heaven knows I've envied your hair for simply ages. It's pure gold."

"A pity it's not actual gold. Though I suppose I could sell it." Things were certainly becoming desperate enough to contemplate it.

"No!" Henrietta gasped. "Promise me you won't."

Juliana raised a hand to her hair, a gently curling wealth of honey-colored locks that fell to her hips when unbound. It was her one vanity, though dark hair was currently in fashion. As were voluptuous figures—which made her quest to find a wealthy husband more difficult. But Henrietta had assured her that she could snare one within a fortnight, if she applied herself.

"Keep a watch out for Viscount Wrenforth," Henrietta said. "He seemed taken with you at the Cotteridge's musicale. Besides, he has a fine fortune, and is not *too* ill-favored to look upon. If one disregards the nose."

Juliana nodded. She had no time to lose. The debts were mounting, and there was almost nothing left for her to sell, her hair notwithstanding. Her jewelry now consisted of the strand of pearls about her neck and a single bracelet, and the walls of her suite were entirely bare of paintings. She would have to start in on the silver next, and it would become obvious that she wasn't simply selling her own belongings for a bit of extra pin money.

Once Society heard of her family's utter destitution, no one would want to marry her. She must be firmly engaged before that happened.

Letting out a quiet breath, she went with Henrietta, careful not to glace toward the ballroom doors. She could not bear to see Robert surrounded by the shimmer of colorful gowns and even more brilliant smiles, knowing she had long ago forfeited her place there.

Robert Pembroke watched as the slender figure in the blue gown moved out of sight—not that any of the ladies buzzing around him could tell where his attention was fixed. To all but the keenest observer, his interest appeared to be upon their laughing flirtations.

He could have his pick of the dashing widows and adventurous females. Since becoming the Earl of Eastbrook, he had never wanted for company in his bed. But tonight he would not choose any of the lovelies to dally with, despite their obviously-displayed charms.

No. His thoughts were on one woman alone—a woman with hair like sunlight and the lithe body of a nymph. A woman he had once thought he loved, until she had so cruelly broken his heart.

He had learned patience in the meantime, had waited four long years to claim revenge on Juliana Tate. Tomorrow, his retribution would begin.

"Miss Juliana, you have a caller. I have put him in the salon." The butler bowed and presented her the salver with a thick vellum card centered upon it.

Oh no. She did not need to pick it up to read the broad script. *Robert Pembroke, Earl of Eastbrook.*

Her lungs tightened and a tingle of nerves coursed up her spine. Robert. Here. In the parlor downstairs.

"Did he give you a reason for his visit? Is he here to see father?"

"He specifically asked for you, mistress."

Juliana drew in a steadying breath.

"Well then."

She raised a hand to her hair and quashed the foolish urge to change into a better gown. There *were* no better gowns, not since father had gambled away all of their money.

It was fashionable to keep callers waiting, but she had always preferred to face her problems head-on. She went downstairs and smoothed her hair one last time before pushing open the parlor door.

The room seemed suddenly very small with Robert in it, a tall, auburn-haired force of nature. She could not help but stare at him, the face she kept in her memory—chiseled cheekbones and mobile lips, hair on the long side of fashionable, and eyes lit with golden fire.

"Miss Tate." He was before her in two steps.

Before she could think to move away, he took her hand and bowed. His grip was firm and insistent.

She felt her pulse race as his attention traveled slowly over her body. His gaze lingered at her legs, her chest, her throat—where she could feel her pulse beating wildly—before he lifted his eyes to her face again.

"You are looking well." The look that accompanied his words shot a tingle up her spine.

Rake. Scoundrel. The words echoed through her body and she felt reckless heat rise in her cheeks. Was this truly the same Robert she had stolen kisses with in the apple orchard, four spring-times ago? Had becoming an earl changed him that much?

She pulled her hand out of his grasp. "Why are you here?"

It was altogether blunt of her, but she could not maintain her composure long enough to play the formal hostess with him. The only thing to do was discover what he wanted, quickly, and send him on his way.

She felt as though she were balanced on a swaying bridge over a chasm. To either side lay dangerous emotions—love, despair. One misstep and she would plunge over the edge.

"So abrupt, Juliana."

The sound of her name on his tongue made her dizzy with longing, with regret. She swallowed.

"Would you prefer I call you *my lord* and offer you tea? I'm afraid I cannot."

He gave her a hard look. "I'm glad to see the years haven't changed how you feel about me."

"They have not." She let her gaze slip from his. He would think she meant disdain, but she had never hated him. Never.

"My condolences on the loss of your mother." His voice was not particularly sympathetic. "You were in mourning for her a rather long time."

Did he suspect her mother's hand in what had happened? He had never liked Lady Tate—and the dislike had been mutual. In truth, her mother had detested young Robert Pembroke. Nearly as much as she had hated her own children.

"Yes," she said. "Father insisted on two years of the black."

Two years of formal mourning. At least the terrible misery of living with her mother had ended. Coming up to London this last month had been almost worse, however, once she had realized the desperate state of their affairs.

"Now you're out of mourning," Robert said, "and enjoying life in Town, I see."

"Not as much as you seem to be."

He leaned forward, with a twist to his lips—those sensuous lips that sent the ladies of the *ton* swooning. Juliana resolved not to think of his mouth.

"Indeed, I am," he said. "Being an earl has its advantages. In fact, I'm here to discuss one of those advantages with you."

Her breath caught in her throat. Was he going to suggest something scandalous?

"I'm sure I don't grasp your meaning," she said.

"Don't you?" He tilted one eyebrow up. "Your father seems to have gotten himself into a bit of trouble at the gambling tables. However, as we're such long-standing acquaintances, I took it upon myself to help."

"What has father done now?" She reached for the back of the settee, hoping Robert could not see her hands tremble. "What have *you* done?"

"You'll be relieved to hear that I've bought up his notes and paid off the creditors." He smiled, without a trace of warmth. "Your father's debts now belong to me."

"What?" Shock rippled through her.

This was dreadful. To have Robert, *Robert*, holding such power over them, after what she had done....

He captured her eyes with his own, and his expression sharpened to something predatory. Juliana felt like a wild doe cornered by a hunter. The beating of her heart threatened to drown out all other sound.

"I've spoken with your father," Robert said. "He has agreed that *you* can redeem the debt from me. For a small consideration."

"And what might that consideration be?" Juliana swallowed.

She would be ruined, utterly, if she became his mistress. It was a terrifying, exhilarating thought, and she thrust it to the back of her mind.

"I will hand over your father's notes, to dispose of as you like," he said. "After I take payment from you…of five kisses."

She drew in a sharp breath. It was not, after all what she had feared. What she had secretly hoped for. But of course, her father would never have consented to such a thing. Thank goodness her brother was safely away at school. She did not want him to know anything of this situation.

"Five kisses? How very forward of you, sir."

"Ah, Juliana. It is far less than I could have asked. Those debts represent a considerable sum."

It was true. Five kisses was a paltry payment, even with their reduced circumstances. Was it possible that Robert still cared for her, even after she had turned him away so cruelly? Had her hateful words faded in his memory?

She searched his expression, but there was no softness there, none of the eager yearning they had shared. No, she would be a fool to think that he had forgiven her.

"Why?" The word came out nearly a whisper.

"Because I can." His voice was hard.

"So, I'm just another bauble the earl can buy? A trinket to be played with and then discarded when you are done?"

The thought burned. He didn't even want her for a mistress, he merely wanted to toy with her, like a cat with a mouse under its paw. There was no warmth of sentiment in him. He only wanted revenge.

"Do you deserve better, Juliana?" His gaze bored into hers. "After heaping such scorn upon me, do you think I'd come to pay you court now?"

"My mother—"

"I didn't see her standing with a pistol at your back that day, making you say those words. You seemed convinced enough that I was unworthy of you. How did you put it? Ah yes…you said I was *no better than the dirt under your feet.*"

She dropped her gaze to the carpet.

How many nights had she lain wakeful in bed with shame burning through her? She had written to him, apology after apology—had tried to post the letters, but her mother had always intercepted them. The consequence of seeing her younger brother punished for her disobedience had put a stop to her efforts. But she still composed messages to Robert in her heart.

"I'm sorry," she said. The words came out nearly a whisper. "It was wrong of me."

"Juliana." He spoke her name like a cold stone. "Do you expect me to believe you feel remorse? You think that, now I'm the Earl of Eastbrook, all should be forgiven between us?"

"It's not because of that!" She lifted her head and met his gaze directly. "I don't care whether you hold a title."

It had been her mother who had cared—strongly enough to force Juliana to break all ties with Robert.

"What a remarkable liar you are." The coolness of his expression did not change. "Let's return to the matter at hand. Your debt to me."

She wrapped her arms about herself. It was clear he would never forgive her.

"I don't see why you'd even want to collect the debt in this manner, since you find me so contemptible. Can't I give you some other payment?" Though what, she couldn't imagine.

"Contemptible, but still beautiful." He reached out and ghosted a touch along the side of her face. "They call you the Ice Maiden, did you know that?"

She shook her head. Perhaps her friend Henrietta had heard but spared her the knowledge.

Would she even be able to find a suitor, with that name shackling her? She could feel all her plans col-lapsing. Nothing had ever come out right. Her past, and her future, lay in tumbled ruins at her feet.

What more damage could five kisses do?

"Very well," she said. "I will pay what you ask."

"Good." A slow smile spread the corners of his mouth. "Now, come sit down."

"I really don't—"

"Come." He took her elbow and steered her to the settee.

She perched at the edge, and he sat beside her, too close for any kind of comfort. She remembered kissing him—she *dreamed* of kissing him. Even if he no longer cared for her, it would not be dreadful.

Ah, if only she were the Ice Maiden in truth—cold and unfeeling. Instead, her heart was as vulnerable as a new rose, in danger of withering under the blight of Robert's disdain.

"I suppose…we had best begin," she said, holding herself stiffly away from him.

Soonest begun, soonest done, her old governess used to say. Juliana closed her eyes. It was too much to hope that he would simply kiss her cheek, but she tilted her head toward him nonetheless.

His low chuckle made her eyes open. He had not moved, except to extend one arm along the back of the settee. Despite his laughter, his expression was calculating.

"It's not as simple as you seem to think, Juliana. Let me explain exactly how you will pay this debt."

"What explanation do five kisses require? Take them and be done!"

His nearness was unbearable. She wanted to fling herself into his arms. She wanted to take to her heels and slam every door between them.

"No," he said. "Each kiss will require a separate visit. I'll take my first payment today and call upon you the next four Thursday afternoons to claim the remainder."

"I hardly think—"

"You agreed." He held her gaze. Flecks of amber burned in his eyes.

There was nothing she could say to that. She was entirely at his mercy. Her lips parted and his eyes shifted to her mouth. After a heartbeat, he shook his head.

"Give me your hand," he said.

"My hand?"

"Don't look so surprised. I told you we'll continue under my terms. I choose the placement of these most-expensive kisses."

She should not have agreed without determining what, exactly, Robert had been planning. But even had she known, refusal would have still been impossible. He had neatly trapped her.

"Placement of the kisses?"

"Yes." His gaze smoldered. "There are so many places on your body I could put my mouth. Five is hardly enough to make a beginning."

His words were so full of wickedness, she burned from hearing them. She stared at him, her heart pounding.

"Give me your hand," he said.

Slowly, Juliana extended her arm. He caught her hand, holding it palm-up. Keeping his gaze locked on hers, he set the fingers of his other hand at her wrist. Then, with exquisite slowness, he drew his fingers down. The movement sent sparks flickering along her nerves. His caress continued on to the warm hollow of her palm, his fingers drawing little circles that sizzled through her entire body.

"Is this necessary?" Her voice was treacherously unsteady. "I thought you were going to kiss my hand, not tickle it."

"Oh, I shall."

He turned her hand over, his grip warm and inescapable. Bending his head, he brought the back of her hand up to his lips. His lips were firm, and softer than she had expected, warm against her skin. Before she could adjust to the sensation, he flicked his tongue out, and she stifled a gasp.

Where his lips were warm, his tongue was hot. He parted his mouth, his tongue echoing the circling of his fingers, so that her whole hand was engulfed in swirling fire. She swayed back against the cushions, and he glanced up, satisfaction gleaming in his golden eyes.

It took her a moment to find her voice. "Are you quite finished, sir?"

"No." He turned her hand over, cupping it with his own. "Shall I read your fortune?"

"I have no fortune, as you are well aware."

"You have a wicked past, though." For a moment something flashed in his eyes. Then his expression hardened. "And you will pay for it, lovely Juliana."

She tried to pull her hand away. "I have paid enough, today."

"I think not." He would not release her, and truly, half of her did not want him to.

No matter their turbulent past, this had not changed—her body yearned for him, in ways she could scarcely understand.

Once again, he lowered his mouth to her skin. The heat of his tongue in the palm of her hand was astonishing, and incredibly intimate. He ravished her now, lacing his fingers through hers and spreading her hand wide, slipping his tongue in and out between her parted fingers.

The tips of her breasts tightened, and sensations she could not name swirled through her—heat and a curious discomfort. Despite her efforts at control, she knew he heard her breathing grow unsteady. She felt as though her entire being was there, throbbing in the center of her palm.

"That…was two kisses," she managed when he finally raised his head.

"No—merely the continuation of a kiss to your hand," he said. He folded her fingers over her palm.

"But…." She gazed into his eyes, seeing no room for argument. He had always had a stubborn nature. Once his mind was made up, there was no swaying him.

"Remember," he said. "I will return on Thursday."

She nodded, then cleared her throat. "The butler will see you out."

She did not trust herself to remain steady on her legs. Not with the aftermath of his kiss storming through her, the tangles of regret and desire knotted about her heart.

"Farewell." He gave the word an ironic twist as he rose and sketched her a bow. He did not look back, and the parlor door swung closed behind him.

Once she was certain he was gone, Juliana slowly opened her hand, as though something fragile and impossible rested within it. Robert's kiss, though it was not a lover's kiss.

Ah, she would pay a thousand times over for what she had done. If she had thought her life unbearable four years ago, after she had obeyed her mother and turned him away, how much worse would it be now?

To see him, to kiss him, and feel her heart breaking a little more each time. It was clear now why he had taken up Father's debts. It was to punish her. By the time the Earl of Eastbrook was finished taking his payment, their fortune would be restored.

And she would be reduced to nothing.

Robert leaned back against the cushioned seats of his carriage and smiled. That had gone very well, indeed. In fact, he'd been surprised—and gratified—by how quickly Juliana had responded to him. Beneath that reserved exterior of hers, passion simmered. And now that she'd revealed it, however inadvertently, he meant to use that passion to his own ends.

The first kiss had affected her better than he'd even dreamed. Though she had tried to conceal her reaction, her body betrayed her—her rapid heartbeat, her parted lips. It was only a short distance from arousal to desire, from desire to obsession. He would not call it love, that bitter word that curdled in his mouth.

Obsession would do well enough, though women and raw youths preferred to paint over the starkness of overwhelming passion, calling it by sweeter, more sentimental terms. Beneath the rosy haze lay harder truths. Love did not exist.

He'd learned that lesson. Juliana would, too. And no matter what name she called it, he would bring her to her knees. He would make her fall in love—or at least infatuation—with him, using all the means at his disposal. And then he would break her heart, just as thoroughly as she'd broken his.

Juliana Tate. Damnation, but she was still beautiful, with hair that could make any man yearn to sin. His fingers tingled at the thought of unpinning it, seeing those honeyed waves cascading over her shoulders and down her back. The image of Juliana clothed only in the golden veil of her hair was delectable.

The door of the carriage swung open, a waft of cool spring air interrupting his carnal imaginings.

"My lord," the footman said, setting the steps.

Robert nodded his thanks. Before him rose the imposing façade of the Earl of Eastbrook's town house. His house. He took little pleasure in it—the death of a good man had brought him here. The title and wealth were simply the means to an end. Juliana's downfall.

It had taken him the better part of a year to mend his shattered heart. That year had changed him from a dreamy-eyed youth to a man. He had learned that women lusted for him, and he had honed that power. Not until his cousin had died, leaving him the title, had he begun to think he could claim revenge on Juliana.

Her apology had been unexpected. Not genuine, of course—he'd be an utter fool to believe that. Still, he'd thought it would take her longer, by the third kiss perhaps, to offer a show of remorse.

Of course, it was on account of his new title. She'd inherited her mother's grasping nature. Robert stalked up the stairs, not pausing as the butler opened the door. He made his way to the dark-paneled study. A fire burned on the hearth, warding the spring chill from the air.

One of the maids had brought in a spray of apple blossoms. The sight kindled an icy rage within him. Snatching the white-petaled boughs from their vase, he threw them onto the coals. They hissed and smoked and then, at last, burst into flame.

Just as he had burned out the memory of Juliana, white petals caught in her hair, laughing in the apple orchard.

He would bring her low, make her suffer as he had suffered, and then he would be free. Only four kisses stood between him and the future.

"Miss Tate is expecting you, my lord," the butler said to Robert one week later, taking his hat and gloves.

The man led him to the same room as before, a parlor with striped wallpaper and a decided lack of ornamentation. Juliana was standing behind the settee, her arms folded at her waist. She was wearing the same drab dress as last time.

Did she think to try and put him off with unattractive clothing? Her hair spoiled the intent, however. The honeyed strands were twisted into an awkward coil at the back of her head. His fingers itched with the desire to pull her hairpins out and let that golden cascade tumble freely down.

"Good afternoon," he said.

"My lord."

She made no other concession to his title, no dip of a curtsy, not even an inclination of her head. So proud and intractable. But he would bring her to her knees—figuratively speaking.

And literally? His cock stirred at the thought of Juliana, hair unbound, on her knees before him. But no. That was not how one wooed a woman, even if he intended to break her heart in two at the end.

When he rounded the settee, she began to move away.

"I refuse to chase you about the room, Juliana," he said, catching her arm. "Stand still."

She swallowed, and he could see her pulse fluttering at her throat. Despite her icy demeanor, she was not unmoved by him. He intended to unsettle her even more.

"Very well." She tilted her cheek to him, as she had done before. "Kiss me and take your leave."

"Dear Juliana." He slid his hand down to the curve of her waist. "I told you, it's not that simple. Turn around."

He placed his other hand on her other hip and rotated her until she stood with her back to him.

"Really, sir." She tried to take a step away, but he held her firmly in place. "I don't see—"

"My kisses, to take as I please. As we agreed."

She would see soon enough. He felt a smile curve his lips.

A shiver went through her—he felt it beneath his palms where they rested on the sweet curve of her waist. Slowly, he pulled her back until their bodies were nearly touching. Awareness thrummed through him. That delicious, scant inch of space that separated them—the anticipation of touch, preceding the actual moment.

The pale skin of her neck looked smooth as cream satin. He could hardly wait to taste it.

He bent his head, inhaling the scent of orange-flower water drifting up from her hair. Slowly, so that she could feel the heat of his breath, he dropped his lips to hover at the delicate indentation of her nape. Feather-light, he brushed his mouth across her skin. Her stifled gasp made heat flare up in him.

Pressing his lips more firmly to her neck, he nibbled his way to just beneath her ear. Her pulse beat wildly beneath his mouth, though the rest of her remained still as glass.

"Delicious," he whispered.

He raised one hand and pulled gently at the neckline of her dress, exposing her collarbone. Just there, a tracing of the tongue, hot and smooth against her skin. He swirled delicate circles back up toward her ear, and another tremble ran through her.

It did not take long for him to locate the hairpins restraining the glorious mass of her hair. He pulled them out, one by one, and let them land, unheeded, on the carpet. All the while, his lips mapped the arch and curve of her lovely neck.

One strand of hair came free, landing on her shoulder. Her hand flew to the back of her head, but it was too late. Robert pulled out the last pin, and her hair tumbled down in all its golden glory.

She whipped around, her blue eyes hot, her face flushed. "How dare you!"

"What?" He kept his tone light, amused, though the sight of her arousal made a dark tide stir inside him. "I can ravish your neck, but woe betide any man who touches your hair?"

It lay over her shoulder, gleaming like sunlight. He reached for it, he couldn't help himself, and ran his fingers through the soft waves.

Narrow-eyed, she pulled her hair out of his grasp.

"Kisses are one thing," she said, "but I did not give you leave to wreak havoc on my coiffure."

"You prefer to leave that to your lady's maid? She's doing a terrible job of it, I must say. That style doesn't suit you."

"It's none of your concern." Juliana tossed her hair back behind her shoulders. "You've collected your payment for the day, my lord. Now I must bid you farewell."

She had always been beautiful when in a temper. Not that her beauty was any excuse for her past behavior. Still, he enjoyed cracking the façade of the Ice Maiden.

Knowing it would unsettle her, he went down on one knee and swept up the errant hairpins scattered on the carpet. He glanced up and gave her his scoundrel's smile.

"Shall I re-pin it for you?"

"No!" She took a step back, then held out her hand. "My hairpins, if you please."

He rose and considered the bits of metal in his hand. "Perhaps I'll keep them."

Her eyes widened, a flash of something like desperation moving through them. "Give them back. Please." The last word was strained.

Was she really so destitute, that she could not afford to replace a handful of hairpins? He thought back to the magnitude of her father's debts. Well, perhaps she was. And she deserved it.

Truly? a voice inside him whispered, *she deserves to be penniless and afraid?*

"Here." He thrust the hairpins at her, then spun on his heel and stalked out of the room.

Damn it.

Juliana was cold and cruel. She deserved no sympathy from him.

None whatsoever.

Thursdays shadowed Juliana's entire month. Two had passed, and on the whole, she wanted the next to never come. Yet late at night, while memory kept her wakeful, she wished the days would hasten forward.

If only her mother had not been so cruel, so fixed upon the importance of Juliana wedding a title. Then she and Robert might have married—and she would now be a countess. The irony was bitter in her mouth and might-have-beens scorched her heart.

On Wednesday, Henrietta paid her a visit.

"Juliana—you look so pale! Come, ring for tea and we'll have a cozy chat in your salon."

"Not the salon." She said the words too quickly, but the air there was too full of Robert's presence for her to be comfortable. It would be impossible to sit and talk to Henrietta, with the memory of Robert's kisses hot upon her skin.

"Very well," Henrietta said, one eyebrow tilting up.

She handed her hat and gloves to the butler and gave Juliana a keen look. There would be no escaping Hen's questions, and truthfully, Juliana was relieved that there was *someone* she could tell.

"We'll go up to my rooms," Juliana said. "There's no fire in the salon hearth today."

Indeed, they could barely afford coals to heat the bedrooms. Juliana had told the remaining staff how desperate the situation was, but reassured them she was taking steps to remedy the situation. The butler, the housekeeper, and the maid were staying—at least for now. Sadly, the cook had gone to another family. The housekeeper was taking over kitchen duties, with rather dismal results.

Henrietta settled on the window-seat in Juliana's room, then gave her a searching look.

"You've cried off all invitations this past week," she said. "Whatever are you thinking? There's no way you can catch a husband if you spend all your time hiding."

"I...." Juliana trailed her fingers down the slightly dusty curtains. "My circumstances have changed."

"What? How?" Her friend leaned forward and studied her. "You certainly don't look happy about it."

"Father's notes have been bought up. We're safe from debtor's prison." She wet her lips and turned to stare out the window.

"Oh?" Henrietta's eyebrows climbed. "His debts were paid...by whom?"

"Robert Pembroke, Earl of Eastbrook." Juliana clutched the curtains in one hand.

"Heavens! That certainly changes things. Let me think." Henrietta leaned back, pursing her lips. "I presume Robert has paid you a visit?"

Juliana nodded. How could she explain the knots of fear and desire twisting inside her?

"Is that why you've abandoned the pursuit of a husband?" Henrietta asked. "Does he have intentions toward you?"

"No! Not...in the way you mean."

Her friend sat up straight, shock widening her eyes. "Don't say he's forcing you to be his mistress! What a dreadful, horrible—"

"Hen, stop. I am redeeming father's debts, yes. But it is only for five kisses."

"What! Forcing you into kissing him! I cannot believe the effrontery of the man." Henrietta shook her head. "You ought to know that five kisses may *seem* harmless, but look at where they could lead."

"I know it." All too well. "So far, I have not kissed him—he has kissed me."

She tried to ignore the heat that flashed through her when she thought of his mouth on her. The tips of her breasts tightened and she folded her arms across her chest.

"Juliana. Just because you share a past, doesn't mean—" Henrietta clearly was about to launch into a lecture when the maid knocked at the door.

"Tea, mistress."

"Come," Juliana called.

She engaged Henrietta in chitchat about the balls she had attended recently as the maid set the tea things out. Finally, the girl finished and left the room.

"Tea?" Juliana moved to the small table and poured out a cup.

Henrietta surveyed the table dubiously.

"Whatever are these?" She poked at a plate of lumpy brown items.

"Scones." Juliana tried to smile. "I know, they look dreadful, but with plenty of jam they are edible. The housekeeper is not the best cook, sadly."

Henrietta took a sip of tea, then regarded Juliana steadily over the rim of her cup. "Be sensible, Juliana. You may not have creditors turning you out on the streets, but you're certainly not out of financial difficulty. It's imperative you find a wealthy husband."

"I suppose." She dropped a lump of sugar into her cup and stirred.

The swirl of liquid was like her own thoughts—going round and round but leading nowhere. Henrietta was right. It would do her no good to stay at home. Her father was certainly not going to be of any help—it was up to her to restore the family's fortunes.

"The Caswell's ball is Friday evening," Henrietta said. "Viscount Wrenforth will be there, and he is your best hope. You must attend. Oh, and do leave off stirring your tea. I'm quite certain the sugar has dissolved, and the noise is making me peevish."

Putting Henrietta in a peevish mood was something to be avoided at all costs. Juliana quickly set her spoon down and took a sip. "As usual, nothing but pearls of wisdom fall from your lips."

"Hmph," Henrietta said, but she couldn't hide her smile. "A pity we can't string them into a necklace for you to sell. That would nicely solve all your problems."

"A rich husband will have to suffice. Viscount Wrenforth is pleasant enough, despite his nose."

Henrietta nodded. "His annual income is *much* larger than his nose. It's all a question of comparison."

Indeed, that was part of the problem. Viscount Wrenforth did not compare at all well when measured up against Robert Pembroke. She gave herself a mental shake and forced herself to take a bit of scone as penance.

"Very well," Juliana said. "I will attend the Caswell's ball on Friday."

The memory of Robert might haunt her past, but she must look to the future.

The next Thursday, Juliana was again waiting for him in the parlor. She stood at the window, and despite the drab dress she wore, the light silhouetted her pert breasts. Robert smiled. He had plans for those breasts.

He closed the parlor door behind him, then prowled over to where she stood.

"Watching for me, Juliana?" he asked.

"Hardly. I would not still be gazing out the window, were that the case."

She did not turn her head to look at him, which he found amusing. It was a sign of how deeply he was beginning to affect her.

He came up behind her, where she stood, unmoving. Letting his breath feather against the side of her neck, he spoke. "Your hair is styled as deplorably as ever. Let me take it down for you."

At that, she did take a step away, keeping her back to him. "Unless you are planning to kiss my hair, it will remain as it is."

"Mm." He followed and set his hands at her waist. "Tempting…but it's not your hair that I plan to ravish today."

A tremble ran through her—imperceptible, if he hadn't been touching her.

"You have kissed my hand," she said, "and my neck—what is next? My elbow perhaps? My knee?"

He let out a soundless laugh, then drew one finger down her arm to the crook of her elbow. Her skin was warm and soft, and she drew in a breath as he made a lazy circle there with the tip of his finger.

"You were jesting, but the hollow of the elbow is very sensitive. As is the back of the knee. Had we more kisses, and time, I'd begin behind your knee and kiss my way up."

He slid his palm down the side of her thigh, half-expecting her to bolt out from under his caress. But she stayed, her breath quickening. His prior study of seduction was bearing fine fruit.

"I'd let my lips explore," he continued, "along the delicate skin of your leg. Until I reached the most sensitive spot on a woman's body. Do you know where that is, Juliana?"

She shook her head, ever so slightly. The scent of orange-flower water wafted from her hair.

"Here." He moved his hand, letting it brush lightly over the sweet place between her legs.

She gasped, then, and pulled away. When she turned to face him, her cheeks were pink with outrage, and arousal.

"You are scandalous! How dare you—"

"Don't fear. The secret place between your legs is safe from my kisses." He winked, shamelessly, roguishly. "For today."

Her eyes widened. Excellent. He'd planted the seed of an idea that would no doubt devil her—the anticipation of his final kiss. When he at last kissed her there, at her center, when he made her gasp and writhe and explode with pleasure, then his victory would be complete.

He would be branded on her soul, and she would never be able to escape the memory.

"Sit," he said, gesturing to the settee. "It will be more comfortable for both of us."

"Will you hurry and get this blasted kiss over with?" She pretended nonchalance, when she clearly was feeling anything but, and perched on the cushions, folding her arms. "I've far more important things to attend to this afternoon."

"Mm." He sat next to her. "I have every intention of making you forget those things."

She lifted her chin, and said in a haughty voice, "I truly doubt that, Lord Eastbrook. But by all means, proceed."

Despite her words, he could see her pulse fluttering wildly. He leaned forward and slowly drew one shoulder of her gown down. She let out a breath, and uncrossed her arms, but said nothing more.

Good. He was done with talking. There were other, better, uses for his mouth now. He continued to pull her gown down, revealing the white fabric of her chemise. Her skin was pale, and smooth as satin. Slowly, he folded her chemise back, revealing the pert slope of her breast.

"Robert," she whispered.

"He paused. Do you wish me to stop?"

"Would you, if I asked?" Her voice was low, breathy.

He would not force her, no matter the terms of their bargain. He was not such a cad as that. If he frightened her, then this seduction would be for naught. She must be a willing participant—however much she might deny the pleasure he gave her.

"I would." Not that he was pleased at the thought. But, no matter what had happened between them, he still considered himself a man of honor.

Indeed, he had never thought the kisses would go quite so far—or that Juliana would be so responsive, her chilly demeanor so quickly burning away under the heat of his touch.

She blinked, as though considering calling a halt, and he felt a sudden lurch of panic. If she said no, what would he do then?

She met his gaze. "I will not break the terms of our bargain. You…" She swallowed. "You may continue."

"With pleasure." His… and hers.

He gently tugged her chemise further down, exposing her entire, sweet breast. Her nipple was dusky pink and beginning to tighten. Oh, but he would make it stand up, a taut bud of desire. Despite the urge to caress her with his fingers, he controlled himself. He wanted her to feel keenly the warmth of his mouth, the wet coaxing of his tongue.

Slipping his hands around to brace her, he dipped his head and took the peak of her breast between his lips. She let out a gasping sigh, and he felt tremors race through her. With his tongue, he lapped at her nipple, encouraging it to stand. Her body did not need much coaxing—in moments she was taut.

He continued to kiss her breast, alternately flicking his tongue against her nipple, then drawing it into the warmth of his mouth. She moaned, and her body betrayed her yet again as she arched her back. He risked a glance at her face—her eyes were closed, her cheeks flushed, her lovely lips parted. The sight of her arousal fired his in return. Damnation, but she was lovely.

Slowly, he moved one hand down to the place between her legs. She did not seem to notice, except to breathe more deeply. It was warm there, heated from her desire. He gently rubbed the cloth of her dress, sending her arousal higher without shocking her. It was like breathing on the embers of a fire, stoking it until it could not help but blaze up. He was patient—and he did not want her to burn up, not quite yet.

At last he pulled back, removing his hand and his mouth. She lay there a moment, eyes still closed, her entire body a sigh. Her nipple was still tantalizingly alert…but no. He was finished, for now. Despite the vision that flashed through his mind of her lying in his bed, her golden hair spread gloriously about her.

She opened her eyes. A disarming softness showed in her expression, then quickly fled as she sat upright and pulled her gown back into place.

"That makes three," she said, scooting awkwardly away from him. "I will see you next week, sir."

"Doubtless." He stood. "Good day. And…pleasant dreams."

Her eyes widened, and he let out a low chuckle. Two more kisses, and Juliana Tate would never be the same.

"You dance quite well, Miss Tate." Viscount Wrenforth smiled at her as he guided her off the Caswell's dance floor.

"Thank you, my lord. I've always enjoyed the quadrille."

A pity the viscount was not lighter on his feet—she had narrowly avoided having her toes crushed. It seemed he attributed her quickstepping out of his way to skill and grace, rather than self-preservation.

"Would you…" the viscount cleared his throat. "Would you like to see the conservatory? Lord Caswell was telling me about a new orchid he has acquired."

Juliana studied Viscount Wrenforth a moment. Was he hoping to snatch a moment alone, or were his intentions more of a scientific nature?

"Are you botanically inclined, my lord?"

The tip of his large nose turned pink. "No, no. I simply thought ladies enjoyed flowers…but no matter, if you aren't interested—"

"Oh, I am! I'd be delighted to view the orchid with you."

This was a very good sign. If she managed the next half-hour correctly, she'd be well on her way to securing a proposal from the viscount. And, truly, there was nothing objectionable about the fellow. Scores of young women would be pleased to trade places with her.

She took the viscount's arm and let him lead her to the side door of the ballroom. Across the way, Henrietta widened her eyes and gave Juliana a significant look, then caught her aunt's elbow, turning their chaperone away from the sight of Juliana and Viscount Wrenforth departing the ballroom.

It was quieter in the hallway, the thick carpeting muffling their footsteps. Juliana shot a sideways glance at the viscount. Had she misjudged him? He didn't *seem* the type to whisk a young lady into an unoccupied room and have his way with her, and there was no gossip to suggest he was a scoundrel.

Not like other gentlemen of her acquaintance.

"You're frowning, Miss Tate. Is everything well?"

"Certainly." She pasted a smile on her face. "Do tell me more about Lord Caswell's orchid."

Oh, that was foolish. She should be asking questions about *him*, drawing him out, making him feel as though he was the most pleasant of company. That was how one managed a gentleman.

"I don't know much about it—only that it is new. And white, apparently. He could talk of nothing else at the Club today, and encouraged everyone to come admire it at the ball this evening. Ah, here we are."

The viscount opened a door decorated with a large cut-glass panel and ushered her inside. Warm, moist air enfolded her, and Juliana sighed. Warmth was becoming a luxury, now that they were being so careful with the coals at home.

If she were a clever girl, all that was about to change.

"Tell me, Lord Wrenforth." She squeezed his arm slightly. "What are your interests? I find myself fascinated to know."

"You do?"

The tip of his nose turned pink again, either with pleased embarrassment or because of the heat. It was too bad—the viscount needed nothing that drew attention to his overlarge proboscis.

"Yes," she lied. "Horses, perhaps? Or literature?"

She and Robert had lain under the apple trees, reading Shakespeare and Keats to one another. With a silent curse, Juliana folded the memory and shoved it to the back of her mind.

"Actually," the viscount said, "I don't read much. But I am rather fond of dentistry."

Juliana blinked at him. "As in…teeth?"

"Don't worry." He patted her hand, where it lay on his arm. "Yours are quite passable."

"Um." She could not think of an appropriate reply. "Oh, look—that must be the orchid!"

She quickened her steps toward that glimpse of white, grateful for the distraction. The viscount hurried to keep up with her as she brushed past an array of large ferns. She arrived at a low dais, where the flower in question sat in isolated splendor in a large blue-glazed pot.

It was, without question, the ugliest bloom Juliana had ever seen—protuberant and pallid, at the end of a long bare stalk. The thing almost looked more like a fungus than a flower.

The viscount came up beside her, and they stood for a moment, regarding the orchid.

"It's very…white," he said at last.

"Whiter than teeth," Juliana said, then instantly regretted it. "The petals are so, um…." She could not bring herself to assign an adjective to them.

"Well." Viscount Wrenforth glanced about, then took a step closer. "I'm very pleased you came to view it with me. Although you are lovelier than that orchid."

Considering the flower in question, it was not much of a compliment. Still, she gave him an encouraging smile.

"Thank you, my lord."

It was clear he was thinking of kissing her. Juliana leaned toward him and widened her eyes.

After a tense second, he came even closer and dipped his head. She let out a silent breath of relief, though his large nose grew even larger as it approached her face. Juliana closed her eyes and tilted her face up. Their noses bumped together for an unfortunate moment. Then his lips landed on hers, warm, if a bit unfirm.

He did not enfold her in his arms or kiss her as though he craved the taste of her mouth. Juliana shifted, trying to give him encouragement, but it did not seem to help. The cold tip of his nose pressed distractingly against her cheek.

"Excuse me." The voice was chilly, and all too familiar. "I hope I'm not interrupting anything important."

Heart sinking to her toes, Juliana opened her eyes as the viscount pulled away. She was relieved the kiss was ended—but that was the only good thing about the interruption. Biting her lip, she turned to see Robert Pembroke, arms folded, standing on the far side of the hideous orchid. His features were controlled, but temper sparked in his amber eyes.

"Eastbrook," the viscount said, blinking rapidly. "Have you come to see our host's flower?"

"No." Robert did not take his gaze from Juliana. "I will escort Miss Tate back to the ballroom. Carry on, sir."

It was a clear dismissal.

"I, er…" The viscount glanced from Robert to Juliana, then back again. "I see. Good evening, then. Eastbrook, Miss Tate."

He inclined his head in farewell, then turned and hurried away. She did not know whether to be thankful or dismayed that he had capitulated so easily. The ferns swayed closed behind him, and then she was alone with Robert Pembroke. Again.

"What were you doing with Wrenforth?" Robert asked, circling the orchid. His voice was cold.

"I think it was clear enough." She held her ground. "You are not the only gentleman interested in kissing me. And at least *he* has honorable intentions."

Robert made a sound like a low growl. "Stay out of his company."

"I shall do no such thing! I would thank you to stay out of my business and stop scaring off my suitors. Viscount Wrenforth is a perfect gentleman in every way."

Not to mention her only hope for pulling herself and Father from the brink of destitution.

"Perfect gentlemen," Robert said, "do not lure young ladies into conservatories and steal kisses."

"Oh, and I suppose a scoundrel like you would know all about such things."

Her words were meant to be tart but came out a bit breathless. Robert was standing uncomfortably close, staring down at her with a possessive expression on his handsome face.

"Indeed," he said. "I do know about such things. Allow me to demonstrate."

He took her by the upper arms and, before she had time to gather her wits, drew her against him. His touch was firm, but not so hard that Juliana felt trapped. One quick wrench and she could have been out of his grasp—had she wanted to free herself. Her treacherous heart beat so loudly she expected the nearby ferns to tremble from the force of it.

Then his mouth descended over hers, and she closed her eyes. His tongue traced a wicked line along the seam of her lips. Sparks whirled through her and, despite herself, she let out a little sigh. This,

this was the kind of wicked kiss that lured young ladies into conservatories.

His lips coaxed hers open, and then his tongue dipped into her mouth. Oh heavens—this was nothing like the lovely, fumbling kisses they had shared four spring-times ago. A taste of the wild and forbidden seared along her senses. This was plundering and surrender, the hot twining of desire whirling between them. She clutched his shoulders, trying to keep the heady sensation from pulling her under.

His hands moved restlessly over her gown, one large palm coming up to cup her breast. The peak tingled from his touch, then tightened even more when he swept his thumb across the sensitive point. With his other arm behind her, he pulled her close. The heat of him seared along her entire body. His thighs were tautly muscled, pressed against hers, and there was an unmistakable bulge between his legs. It gave her an odd thrill of power, to know that she affected him so.

Then Robert deepened the kiss, his mouth demanding over hers, and she was lost.

There was no ball, no conservatory, no London night spread out darkly behind the glass. Only this—two bodies locked in an embrace, hardness against softness, mouths melding into sweet fire.

Long moments later, he broke the kiss. She blinked up at him, trying to catch her breath.

"That…that's four," she said, her voice unsteady.

The hint of warmth in his eyes was instantly extinguished. "We had best return you to the ballroom. It wouldn't do for people to gossip about what a lightskirt you've become, Juliana."

Stung, she pulled away. "I can find my way back alone, thank you."

"No." There was no room for argument in his tone. "I wouldn't want you to wander into any more trouble. After you, milady."

He waved at the fern-shrouded pathway. Squaring her shoulders, Juliana marched forward, far too aware of Robert behind her. Her body still sparked and hummed with the aftermath of their kiss.

What a disaster. This evening was not turning out at all as she had hoped.

Robert scowled as he stalked down the steps of the Caswell's mansion. He couldn't leave that damned ball fast enough. Curse him for giving in to the impulse to attend—though clearly Juliana needed looking after. She was asking to be ruined, going off with Wrenforth like that. Although, admittedly, the viscount was not the ravishing kind.

Still, if anyone was going to ruin Juliana Tate, it would be him. *He* had saved her fortunes, and she owed him dearly for that. Bedamned if he was going to let another man take the prize. As soon as he returned home, he was going to pen the viscount a letter, warning him well away from Miss Tate. He had no doubt Wrenforth would comply.

How dare that huge-nosed fellow put his hands on Juliana, let alone kiss her? Robert was half-tempted to call him out. But no—that would only add to the titters and raised eyebrows that had met their return to the ballroom. Not that the *ton's* gossip mattered to him. He had only one goal.

Robert balled his hands and strode on, little caring that the wind whipped his coat fiercely behind him. It matched his mood well. A bit of driving sleet would have added the finishing touch. A pity it was May.

Wrenforth had made him waste one of those tremendously expensive kisses. Robert had plans for those five kisses, each one mapped out to ensnare Juliana's senses. But no—his careful seduction had been overturned by the primal instinct to possess.

Revenge was a damned complicated beast.

No matter, he still had one kiss left. Despite the wasted opportunity this evening, he had no doubt of the outcome.

It would only take him one more afternoon to finish cracking Juliana Tate's heart into a dozen pieces.

"Juliana!" Henrietta rushed down the hall and gave Juliana a hug, under the disapproving eye of her butler. "Your hat and pelisse are simply soaked. Come to the drawing room, and I'll ring for tea immediately."

"I left in such haste, I forgot my umbrella," Juliana said. "I didn't think coming up the walk would make me so wet."

As if to punctuate her words, rain spattered heavily against the sidelights on either side of Henrietta's mahogany front door. It was one of those spring days filled with sudden squalls—one moment the sun peeking cheerfully out from behind silver-limned clouds, the next, dark and ferocious rain pounding the cobblestones.

In the drawing room, Henrietta pulled two chairs up to the hearth and insisted Juliana take the closest one.

"I'll not have you catching a chill here, and wasting away like some tragic heroine," her friend said.

Juliana laced her icy fingers together. Although she was nearly sitting in the coals, no heat penetrated the cold that gripped her.

"I'm afraid I'm headed in that direction in any case," she said. "The tragic heroine, I mean. I received a letter today from Viscount Wrenforth."

She swallowed, fear a heavy lump in her chest. Henrietta would know what to do—her friend could always be relied upon for some kind of solution.

"Goodness." Henrietta's eyes widened. "Has he heard the gossip, then?"

Juliana shivered. "What gossip? And that reminds me—why didn't you tell me the *ton* calls me the Ice Maiden?"

"I knew it would only wound you. Besides, there's no truth to it!"

"Truth has very little bearing on what the scandalmongers say—you know that as well as I." Juliana frowned at her friend. "Now, what current gossip are you referring to?"

"I'm afraid they're saying that you are…er," Henrietta bit her lip, "dallying with the Earl of Eastbrook."

"Dallying? You mean, that I'm his current paramour?" Juliana dropped her gaze to her hands. "I suppose it would appear to be the case—though I've told you Robert holds me in no regard. It is nothing more than revenge. A payment of debts owed."

She knew that was true. Why, then, did her foolish soul try to believe otherwise?

The blood was finally returning to her fingers, making them sting fiercely. Now if only her toes would unthaw. And her heart? She only wished it were frozen as solid as the gossips claimed.

"But tell me." Henrietta leaned forward. "What did Viscount Wrenforth say in his letter?"

"Oh, Hen." Juliana blinked back the sharp sting of tears. "He said that I should not misinterpret his attentions, and that while he found me admirable, he would prefer to do so from a greater distance. He

wished me well, and farewell—all in four miserly sentences."

"Blast it." Henrietta handed over her handkerchief, then pursed her lips in thought. "Viscount Wrenforth is an unfortunate coward. You are better off without him. Truly, it was a narrow escape. Just think of being wedded to that nose for the rest of your life."

Juliana wiped her eyes. "If only his character was as strong as his nose. I'm quite certain he let Robert run him off with no protest."

"Well then, we will simply have to come up with another plan."

"I don't think I can snare a husband, with the gossip circulating that I am Robert's mistress." She wadded Henrietta's kerchief between her hands. "Viscount Wrenforth seems proof enough of that."

Henrietta gave a short nod. "Then there is only one thing you can do. If Robert Pembroke is going to be so careless with your reputation, you must negotiate new terms."

It was the last Thursday. The last kiss.

Robert strode into the Tate's town house, anticipation firing his steps. The culmination of his revenge lay within his grasp. He dismissed the hollow feeling that hovered just behind the thought. Of course he would be slightly adrift, after striving for so long toward this one goal. But the thrill of victory would carry him through.

He entered the parlor, closing the door firmly behind him. Juliana was waiting for him—but instead of standing warily behind the settee, she was sitting upon it. Her hair was loosely bound up in some style that looked vaguely Grecian, and her gown had been altered to a more flattering cut.

"Robert." She inclined her head, light sheening over her golden hair.

What had happened to the stiff, unyielding Juliana? Yes, the kiss in the conservatory had been incendiary, but it hadn't changed anything between them.

Or had it? Did Juliana now fancy herself in love with him? Triumph flashed through him. He had won.

"I…." She wet her lips. "Sit down. Please. We have something to discuss."

He waited a moment, just to show he wasn't hers to command, then lowered himself to the settee. The length of his thigh pressed against hers, but she did not shift away.

"I don't intend to waste my time today in talking," he said.

Her cheeks flushed a delicate pink. "I'm well aware that my debt is not yet paid. But, Lord Eastbrook, I must ask. Is your intent to ruin me completely?"

"Ruin you? No."

He wanted Juliana in pain, brought low—but not in a literal sense. Reducing her to poverty or destroying her social standing had never been his aim. He wanted her to suffer exactly as he had. Nothing more, nothing less.

"Are you quite certain?" She let out a dry laugh. "Your association with me is not going unremarked. Perhaps you require more than five kisses, after all."

"Are you accusing me of lying?" He kept his voice even, though his temper spiked at her words. "I assure you, once I have taken this final kiss, I will be done with you."

"You may be finished with me, but the *ton* will believe you are just beginning." She raised her chin and stared him straight in the eye. "You have frightened off the only suitor I had, and no more will be forthcoming."

"Don't tell me Viscount Wrenforth was truly essaying for your hand?"

"Of course he was!" She narrowed her eyes. "Do you think I'm that unworthy? And now…now my family is ruined. He was my only chance to make a match that could have saved us."

"*I* saved you."

"You did not. You only kept us from debtor's prison. All our money is gone, Robert. We have nothing." She dropped her head, despair clear in the curve of her shoulders.

"What about the estate, the rents?" An odd, hollow feeling beat through him. Had he misjudged so badly?

Juliana's family had never been tremendously well off, but their property had brought in a tidy annual sum. Nothing compared to the holdings Robert now had, as earl, but certainly enough to keep the Tate family quite comfortably.

"Father mortgaged everything." Her voice was nearly a whisper. "We have until the end of the month, and then even this townhouse will be gone."

Damnation. He should have investigated more closely when he'd bought up her father's debts. His gaze went to her hands, clasped so tightly in her lap that her knuckles were white.

This was not the victory over Juliana he had wanted.

"Take me, Robert." She raised desperate eyes to him. "I'm ruined in the eyes of the *ton*—you heard the gossip at the Caswell's ball, as well as I. Now that Wrenforth has flown, no one will believe…." She swallowed. "Make me your mistress."

"No!" The word was out before he could even consider it.

Her face went pale and he caught the sparkle of tears in her eyes before she turned her head away.

Bloody hell. His temper flared again, but this time at himself. His grand schemes of revenge had gone farther than he had ever wanted. Instead of evening the scales between them, he had, indeed, ruined Juliana.

"This was not what I had intended." He grated the words out. "Consider your debt paid."

He rose, and she looked up sharply, misery still etched on her face.

"You can't simply leave," she said.

There was nothing else he *could* do. Surely some solution would come to him—but not while his thoughts were tangled with the sight of her.

He could not even bid her farewell. Victory turned to ashes in his mouth as he strode out of the parlor. He collected his hat and gloves from the butler, then stormed out onto the walk.

He was brought up short by the sight of an umbrella pointed directly at his midriff.

"Halt right there, Robert Pembroke," a shrill voice said.

A young lady dressed in violet stood before him. She looked vaguely familiar…. Ah yes, the Brightstone girl, Juliana's bosom friend. Possibly the only person in London who knew of their previous acquaintance.

"Miss Brightstone." He tipped his hat, then tried to move past the point of her umbrella.

"You, sir, will remain here until I've said my piece." She brandished her umbrella at him.

Robert took a careful step back. "I pray it's short, then—I'm required elsewhere. Miss Tate would doubtless be glad of your company. She's a bit overset."

He supposed he could make a dash around her—but that was undignified behavior for an earl. He might as well hear what Miss Brightstone had to say.

"Whatever you have done to Juliana," the young lady said, "she is blameless."

"I think not." He bit the words out.

"You're being a complete fool." She glared at him. "Why would Juliana scheme to break your heart? She was terribly in love with you. I dare say, she still is."

"Her parting words to me four years ago indicated otherwise."

"You don't think her dragon of a mother had anything to do with that?" Miss Brightsone stamped her foot.

"Even if she did, Juliana could have shown some spine! We were planning...." He checked himself. How much did Miss Brightstone know?

"To run away together, yes. And Juliana would have, too, except that her mother caught wind of it. But do you know who bore the brunt?"

Robert shook his head. So far, there was nothing in Miss Brightstone's story to make him change his mind about Juliana's faithlessness.

"Her brother." The young lady lowered her umbrella. "Her younger brother, who was locked in his wardrobe—his wardrobe!—without any food, until Juliana broke it off with you. Their mother would have starved him for days. The sound of his crying was horrible." She met his gaze. "Do you really think Juliana should have abandoned her brother in order to run off with you?"

"I...didn't know. Blast it! She could have told me."

His memory of the past was suddenly tilted—all the things he had thought true now cast in an odd, sideways light. Had Juliana loved him, after all? Had his revenge been built on a lie?

"She could not have told you—not and kept her brother safe. You had to believe completely that she was done with you, or her brother would pay the consequences, over and over. Their mother...." Miss Brightsone looked away. "She was not a pleasant woman."

His heart gave a bitter lurch. "Juliana was quite convincing."

"She had to be. Oh, try and understand what it was like for her! Her heart broke as much as yours did. Maybe even more."

Robert shook his head, trying to settle his thoughts into some kind of order. Only one thing was clear—he must see Juliana again, immediately. He spun on his heel and headed back toward the front door.

"Wait!" Miss Brightstone cried.

He ignored her, ignored the butler's startled expression as he strode past, and flung open the parlor door.

Juliana looked up. Her eyes widened—clearly she had been weeping.

"Robert!" She scrambled to her feet, a handkerchief clutched in one hand. "What are you—"

"Why didn't you tell me?" He took her by the shoulders and searched her expression. "Juliana—if I had known you still cared for me four years ago, I would have crossed fire to be with you. I would have slain dragons."

She swallowed. "My mother...was a dragon in truth. But, how did you find out?"

"I met Miss Brightstone coming up the walk." A chill moved through him. Had she been a minute later, he never would have known, and Juliana would be lost to him. Forever. "You should have told me."

"Secrecy is...a difficult habit to break." She bit her lip. "We had to keep silence on so many things, my brother and I. There was nothing you could have done, Robert."

"I would have taken you away from there."

"And my brother, too? And supported us, and hidden us? I know you would have tried—but I could not have asked it of you."

She was right. He let out a frustrated breath. The youth he had been would have fractured under the burden. Resentment would have grown up like weeds in the garden of their love, until it was a bitter, choking tangle.

"Why didn't you tell me, once your mother was dead?"

"You hated me." She turned her face away. "And I could not blame you for it. Besides, you wouldn't have believed me."

"I believe you now."

He did. The past had righted itself, and now shone with a clarity he had never known. What was done could not be undone—but the future lay, suddenly full of promise, before them.

"Juliana—we wasted four years." He wanted to pull her to him and kiss her senseless. "The day you turned me away, I was coming to ask you…."

For a moment that young man lay just beneath his skin, striding up the blossom-filled lane, a simple gold ring in his pocket and a heart full of nothing but light.

"I know." She sounded breathless.

He took his hands from her shoulders and slipped the heavy signet ring of the Earls of Eastbrook from his finger.

"Bedamned if I'm going to waste another moment—or risk losing you again." He went down on one knee on the threadbare carpet and took her hand. "Juliana Charlotte Tate, will you do me the very great honor of becoming my wife?"

"I…." Her eyes were bright with unshed tears. "Oh Robert—I will!"

He slid the ring onto her finger and closed her hand over it, then rose and gathered her tightly to him. The scent of orange-water was suddenly the happiest smell in the entire world. He dipped his head and inhaled deeply, letting the golden crown of her hair tickle his face.

"There is one thing," she said, her voice muffled against his coat.

"Yes?" He loosened his embrace so that he could look directly at her.

"The matter of a final kiss." Her cheeks flushed a becoming pink. "That is, I believe there is one more payment owed. In a certain…place."

He nearly laughed out loud. So she *had* been thinking of his mouth there, between her legs. Ah, but he was going to seduce her for years to come.

"I see you are going to be a delightfully wanton wife."

"Actually, since I have no dowry, I'm afraid I must owe you kisses for that as well." She smiled up at him, a light of mischief in her eyes. "How many, do you think? Five hundred?"

"Five thousand, at least. And I owe you that many in turn, in penance for nearly ruining you."

Her brows rose. "Are you saying I may have my wicked way with you? I may lead you into conservatories and kiss you senseless?"

"I expect nothing less."

"Ten thousand kisses…" She laced her fingers behind his neck and pulled his head down toward hers. "I think we'd best begin right away."

Their lips touched, and for a moment he smelled apple blossoms. Something in his soul stilled, the bitterness of four years dissolving in a rain of white petals. He would never grow weary of the taste of her. His Juliana—at last.

Copyright © 2012 by Anthea Lawson.

Kay McSpadden writes novels, plays, newspaper columns, and poetry, but she has a special love for short stories. Her story "Why Women Moan in Bed" won the Norman Mailer Fiction Prize, and she was a finalist in the Tennessee Williams Literary Festival for her story "The Proxy." Her stories "The Alien" and "The White Cat" appear in the anthologies Orphans in the Black *and* Once Upon a Quest. *A collection of her newspaper columns on education was published as* Notes From a Classroom, *and her children's book of classic stories is* A Child's Book of Virtues.

GOLDILOCKS AND HER THREE SISTERS

by Kay McSpadden

She expected the airport to be busy before Christmas, but this was crazy. The long walkway to Concourse C was jammed with slow-moving crowds—harried businessmen with cell phones to their ears trying to dodge strollers and toddlers tethered to their parents, aloof twenty-somethings picking their way down the moving sidewalk, everyone else buffeted along like waves crashing into the already jammed waiting areas by the gates. She should have made the drive to Sea-Tac instead of flying out of Portland. Larger airport, more direct flights. But the traffic. Seattle traffic at rush hour. At *any* hour. No, that wouldn't have been worth it. She reshouldered her bag and looked around for a place to sit.

If there was an unoccupied seat, she didn't see it. People were hunched over or slung back, winter coats folded on their laps, rolling carry-ons standing sentry at their feet. A row of teenagers sat on the ground along the far wall, each one looking at a phone.

She walked the perimeter of the waiting area and gave up. The food court would be less crowded. She might as well go there now and grab something from the paltry choices. That a foodie town offered such miserable fare was a crime, really. Never mind that she was a food writer for a small independent weekly. Even the blandest palate would have been offended by the cardboard pizza and indeterminate Asian stir fry in the PDX food court.

At least she was tired enough that she might be able to sleep on the plane. A nervous flier, she usually didn't try, but the red-eye to New York was six hours at least. Even a semi-doze would help. She needed all the energy she could muster to face her sisters at the holidays.

When she was a baby and her hair sprouted from her head in blond ringlets, her older sister Pippa dubbed her Goldilocks and the name stuck. Her real name was Greta, a fusty old-fashioned German name she never liked and rarely used. She signed contracts, negotiated a car loan, introduced herself to new acquaintances as Goldie Bayer. If Social Security was still solvent when she retired, there'd be hell to pay and paperwork to sort out. She didn't care.

"I know it seems like a long way off," Pippa told her the last time they spoke on the phone, "but you need to give serious thought to your future *now*." Like most of their conversations, it was a one-sided lecture about what Goldie needed to do. Finish graduate school. Find a better job. Get married and settle down. Something. She imagined her older sister saw her as a child lost in the woods.

"The world isn't kind," Pippa warned. "The wolves will eat you up."

Pippa only had three years on Goldie, but seemed much older. Their parents were killed when a patch of black ice spun their car into a guardrail two days after Christmas, while Pippa was a senior in college. She didn't return for her last semester, took a retail job in a local discount store, and made sure the two youngest sisters, Marta and Bebe, 16 and 14 at the time, got up every morning and went to high school. Goldie had just started her freshman year at State and offered to drop out to help. "Don't be ridiculous," Pippa told her. "You'd be useless."

Goldie limped along and finished up a half-hearted journalism degree while Pippa was promoted to store manager and eventually to corporate headquarters as an assistant to the CEO. By the time Bebe left for college, Pippa was running her own athletic wear startup and living in a Brooklyn neighborhood so gentrified that even the junk food in the corner bodegas was organic.

No matter where they were or what they were doing at Christmas, the four sisters always converged on Pippa's apartment for a few days. At some point there was the obligatory drive together to the cemetery, more wistful than sad as their memories of their parents dimmed. They ambled awkwardly among the graves and told stories that began with remember when. Later they had a drink in Pippa's kitchen—bourbon or the kind of expensive vodka Pippa's husband preferred—and grew quiet.

This year Pippa's calls began early in October.

"You're coming, right? I need you to help me in the kitchen. The food prep always falls on me and it isn't fair."

"It wouldn't fall on you if you weren't so bossy." Goldie angled her phone between shoulder and cheek and pulled the tab on a can of Diet Coke.

"Carbonated drinks leach calcium from your bones," Pippa said. "They cause osteoporosis. What are you drinking? I hear you drinking something."

"Apple juice," Goldie said. "Chill out. I'm not going to get osteoporosis at 32."

"You're laying the foundation for your old age now. You have to plan ahead."

A sudden noise on the other end of the line—a clatter and slam—and Pippa said something indistinguishable. Probably scolding her twin boys for running through the apartment. Or for eating a cookie between meals. Or chastising her husband about something: A light left on in an empty room, the dog's leash not put back on the hook by the door. Pippa the taskmaster, the rule-maker, the stern hand at imposing discipline.

"When are you flying in? You aren't waiting until the last minute to get here," she said.

The familiar accusations again—that Goldie had forgotten her family, that she thought only of herself. No matter that coming home was an expensive day-long ordeal of airports and turbulence. Pippa would send her money if she asked. She and her lawyer husband spent more on a single meal out than the price of a plane ticket.

But the price to Goldie would be astronomical—her sister's not-so-gentle reminder at odd times about the debt, the sidelong glances that meant Pippa had judged her and found her wanting.

Her two younger sisters were more forgiving and easier to be with. Marta was an elementary teacher in Jersey, short and pillowy and inclined to spontaneous

hugs, like a young version of Mrs. Santa Claus. Bebe was stick thin from smoking, her hair a different vibrant color every time Goldie saw her. She and her girlfriend lived upstate on a farm where they made pottery they sold from a converted dairy barn.

"You should leave Oregon and move to our place," Bebe told her. "We have plenty of room. It's the best life ever."

Both Marta and Bebe offered to meet Goldie at the airport. It was both touching and annoying that they treated her like something delicate. "It's just that you'll be so tired," Marta told her. Bebe was more zen. "I like airports," she said. "All that energy. It keeps me focused."

But it was Pippa who picked her up in a new Land Rover, a car so unsuitable to driving in New York that Goldie eyed her normally sensible sister with suspicion.

"A cab would have been easier," she said, as Pippa pulled out into the line of traffic.

"I have a place I want to show you." Pippa made a vague motion with her hand at the window and Goldie knew better than to question her further. She sat back and watched the familiar landscape of Jackson Heights roll past.

In some ways she'd never left the East Coast, the way the apartment buildings and row houses of Queens and Brooklyn still felt more familiar than the hipster craftsman homes and bungalows of Portland. Perhaps if she bought a house in Oregon she'd feel more connected to the area. Responsible for a yard. The person who took care of a broken water heater, a blown fuse, a loose piece of siding.

She'd grown up with her sisters in a ramshackle two-story house her grandfather had built in Sheepshead Bay. It was the perfect place for a kid—Coney Island in the summer, skating at Rockefeller Center in the winter. In the stories she told of her childhood she mentioned those two iconic landmarks and was rewarded, every time, with the listener's eyes widening in recognition and envy.

Pippa pulled the Land Rover off the busy highway and started down a warren of smaller streets.

"Is this Red Hook? I thought we were going to your house."

"I told you. I want you to see something."

A left, a left, a right—Goldie sighed and threw up one hand. Pippa slammed on the brakes and backed the Land Rover into a parking spot in front of a boarded up warehouse. "Well, what do you think?"

Goldie shook her head. "Think about what?"

"This place. This building. It's affordable right now, but if you wait—"

"I thought you liked your apartment. Isn't it close?"

Pippa let out an audible sigh. "Not for me. *You!* You need a place to live. A home. A friend of mine is flipping this place into nice-size apartments and mixed-use retail and he asked if I was interested in investing. The neighborhood might not look like much now, but it will. See that row of brownstones at the end of the street? The last one just sold for three million. That's *before* the renovations. *Before.* This place isn't going to cost anything close to that. At least, for now it won't."

So this was the reason Pippa wanted to drive her home from the airport. The same old pitch about returning to the nest, the hard sell about coming home.

"I have a home," Goldie said. "It's in Portland."

"That's not your home. That's a detour. A way station. You need to settle down somewhere real. This could be it." She held up a key. "Let's at least go take a look, since we're here."

There was no use arguing with Pippa when she was in this mood. She was as inflexible as cement, as immoveable as a wall. Goldie sighed again and opened the car door.

Pippa kept up a running patter as she led the way through the old warehouse. The solid foundation, the oak laminate floor, exposed brickwork, a view on one side, and above all, the potential—Goldie half listened, wanting a drink. None of her sisters understood why she had moved so far away, as if her choice was a personal insult.

"You know I can't afford it," Goldie said when they were back in the car and on their way at last. "That's beyond my budget."

Pippa said nothing until she parked the car in the garage near her apartment. "People afford the things they want," she said.

"Are you hungry?" Marta held out a plate with a piece of pie as soon as Goldie stepped into the house. "I know it's early, but pie is always good."

"Give her a chance to get inside," Pippa said. Marta grimaced and bobbed and pulled the plate back.

That was just like her, eager to please, to feed, but squelched by any criticism.

"It's okay," Goldie said. "I am a little hungry."

"If you don't want apple, there's lemon. And pumpkin, but I know you don't really like that. Unless you've changed? Do you like pumpkin pie?"

From the corner of her eye Goldie caught a flash of color. A man she'd never seen before came up behind Marta. He was tall and dark, with thick unruly black hair that he raked back from his face with his fingers. His smile was as white and toothy as a Pepsodent commercial. Marta glanced back and said, "You need to meet Wolf."

Wolf reached out and Goldie hesitated a moment before taking his hand. His palm was calloused and rough—not unpleasantly so, but surprising in someone so…pretty.

"Wolf? Like Wolfgang Amadeus Mozart? Are you a musician?" She looked down at her hand and Wolf released her fingers.

"Like Wolfgang Puck the chef. My parents liked to eat." He flashed his very white incisors again.

"You've told that joke before."

Wolf laughed.

"Wolf made the pies," Marta said. "He sells them at Bebe's stand."

Goldie felt a moment of confusion. She'd assumed Wolf was Marta's guest—boyfriend? Colleague? Lost lamb? Marta was forever bringing people to their Christmas gatherings, strangers who needed a meal or a place to stay. His connection to Bebe threw Goldie off. "You live…upstate?" she asked.

"For now," Wolf said. He took the plate with pie from Marta and handed it to Goldie. "I'm thinking of moving back to the city. I used to work for Jacques Torres. I could probably talk him into a job again."

"The chocolate guy?" Goldie's eyebrows rose. Jacques Torres was a master pastry chef whose Brooklyn chocolate shop was internationally known. If Wolf had worked for him—

"Try my pie," Wolf said. "I think you'll like it."

From the distance Goldie heard Bebe's voice. "Everybody likes Wolf's pies! They fly off the shelf like magic!"

Despite Pippa's complaint that the bulk of the food prep always fell on her, Marta was the real cook in the family. While Goldie ate Wolf's pie— Granny Smith apples, not too sweet, with an unexpected but not unwelcome hint of lavender in the glaze—Marta chatted away and organized the kitchen into stations. She put Pippa's twins and Wolf in charge of decorating gingerbread cookies, handed leaf lettuce to Pippa to wash and tear, and sent Mark, Pippa's husband, to the grocery store for a list of forgotten items. Bebe—whose girlfriend had gone to her own parents for the holidays—held court from a stuffed chair in the corner, coffee cup in hand, calling out directions and encouragement to everyone else.

The afternoon rolled on, golden and buttery and with a hint of spice in the air. Slowly people started to drift away—first the twins, who stayed long enough to eat two cookies apiece, and then Pippa and Bebe, and finally Marta, who wiped the counters a second time before declaring that she needed a nap. Goldie wasn't fooled. This was her family's careful manipulation of something between her and the handsome visitor. She was embarrassed—and amused—and not a little titillated when she and Wolf brushed arms as they kneaded pizza dough for the night's meal.

"You've done this before," Wolf said, nodding as Goldie flicked flour onto the countertop.

"Lots of times," Goldie said. "I'm not a bad cook, you know. Not trained-pastry-chef good, but decent."

"I thought you were a writer."

"I am. I write a food column for the *Portland Mercury*. You probably never heard of it."

"I've heard of Portland. That's in Maine, right?"

She gave him a mock glare. "You better watch it, or I'll have Pippa throw you out. You won't have a place to sleep tonight."

"About that," Wolf said, "where *am* I sleeping tonight?"

A ribbon of cool air flickered up Goldie's spine and she shivered like a child waiting a turn on a roller coaster. What exactly was he asking?

Bebe wandered into the kitchen. "If you want to wash up, let me know. I have the key."

"What are you—"

"Pippa's neighbor down the hall was going to Airbnb his place out while he's away this week, but Pippa bought him out instead. Hallelujah, I say. I

don't mind sleeping on Pippa's couch, but I didn't invite Wolf here to have to."

"I'm confused," Goldie said. "Who's staying in another apartment?"

"Well, not me. You. And Wolf. That way you can get to know each other better. Ah, look at her, Wolf. I've embarrassed her."

"Yes, you have," Goldie said, grabbing Bebe by the wrist and tugging her out of the kitchen behind her. "I don't even know this guy! He's *your* friend. *You* share the apartment with him."

Bebe threw up her hands. "Hey, fine with me. I thought you'd like a nice bed for the night, but if you prefer an air mattress on the floor in the twins' room, that's up to you."

Goldie let out an audible sigh. Her fussiness about sleeping was well-known and often mocked by her youngest sister, who unlike everyone else, could get a good rest anywhere, anytime. "Alright, alright, but you tell him—"

"What? That you snore? That you're a cover hog? You aren't sharing a bed, Goldie."

Goldie opened her mouth to retort, but Bebe beat her to it. "Unless, of course, you *want* to."

The knocking on the door the next morning was persistent and loud. One of her sisters, no doubt, telling her to come for the annual Christmas Eve breakfast blow-out. She'd gone to bed reasonably early the night before—she and Wolf saying awkward goodnights almost as soon as they locked the apartment door—but she'd had tossed and turned until finally slipping into a restless series of dreams where she was lost or alone or in some vague sort of danger.

Before she could untangle herself from the bedsheets, she heard the rattle and clink of the locks being undone. Wolf, then, beating her to the front door.

She tried to sit up and sneezed. A cold, probably caught on the plane…. Or was it too soon to get symptoms if she caught a bug only yesterday? Perhaps she caught it at the hairdressers then, when she'd gone to trim her unruly curls a few days ago, to spruce herself up for this trip. Reaching around for her glasses on the side table, she sneezed again, harder. The room began to swim, and she lay back on the pillow.

She heard her bedroom door open. "Aren't you up, yet?"

Not one but all three sisters stood in the doorway. Goldie could see Wolf peering over Bebe's shoulder.

"Start without me," she said. "I don't feel so good this morning."

Pippa crossed the room and put her hand on Goldie's forehead. "You do feel hot. You might have a fever."

Goldie shivered. Pippa's fingers were chilly, uncomfortable, and Goldie shrugged her off.

Suddenly Marta's face loomed over her. "You look cold!" Marta clucked and fussed with the blankets, pulling them up and tucking them in. "Do you want some coffee?"

"I just want to go back to sleep."

"Maybe if you sit up, you'll feel better." Like all of Pippa's suggestions, this one sounded more like a command. Goldie tried to muster the energy to argue but Bebe stepped in.

"Let's leave her alone," she said. "She'll get up when she feels like it."

"Well—" Pippa said, clearly not convinced.

From the doorway, Wolf spoke. "I'll keep an eye on her. I'm going to stay here anyway, to do my baking."

"You don't have to. There's plenty of room in Pippa's kitchen," Marta said. A rustle, a pinch—something passed between Bebe and Marta—and Marta added, "But that's a good idea. We won't get in each other's way when I make lunch later on. That's good. Great!" Goldie saw her meet Bebe's glance.

A moment more and the sisters were gone. Wolf appeared again, this time leaning on the bedroom doorframe. "Tea? Something hot?"

But Goldie shook her head and closed her eyes. She really did feel dreadful, as if a heavy wet blanket had been folded into her sinuses. Before she knew it, she was asleep.

The next time she woke up, the light had shifted, and she was hungry. She raised her head slightly and the room didn't swim. Progress, then. With the palms of her hands she shoved herself upright until she was sitting against the headboard.

"Sleeping Beauty!" Wolf tapped twice on the doorframe and walked in, a steaming mug in his hand. He set it down on the bedside table and then hovered over her, arms crossed, as Goldie smoothed her hair from her face.

"What time is it?"

"Close to noon, I think."

"You should call me Rip van Winkle." She picked up the mug and sniffed. "What is it?"

"Nothing fancy. Euthanasia tea."

"Wait—What?!"

Wolf uncrossed his arms and laughed. His hands and wrists were speckled with flour and dough. Despite her stuffy nose, Goldie could smell cinnamon and nutmeg in the air.

"That's what my little sister calls it. It's echinacea. And some lemon verbena. It'll help your cold."

"You know that's not proven, don't you? The studies are inconclusive."

Wolf's eyebrows flew up. "Seriously? You mean I've been drinking this crap for nothing?"

Now it was Goldie's turn to laugh. "Well, maybe not for nothing. I didn't say it *didn't* help. I said the studies were inconclusive. That's not the same thing."

"You like to be precise, don't you?"

"Don't you?" She took a sip of the tea and let it slip over her scratchy throat. It did seem to help, studies or no studies.

Wolf nodded. "Bakers have to be precise. Chefs—not so much."

That was true. For the past two years she'd interviewed and observed dozens of artisan bakers and chefs, people so dedicated to their craft that they often had difficulty talking about anything except food. The bakers were careful, calculated, exact—even the most creative ones. Kitchen scales and thermometers were their tools of choice. The savory chefs were a more dangerous breed. Freewheeling, free-spirited, they came and left the Portland food scene with such regularity that Goldie had coined a term for them—Snapchef, because they disappeared almost as soon as they arrived. She'd learned to be skittish around them.

Goldie took another sip of tea. "So, you have a little sister."

Wolf moved closer and sat on the edge of the bed. "Two sisters. One older, one younger."

"You're a middle child, too? Too bad."

"I disagree! There's always someone to blame, no matter what happens."

"And no matter what, you're faultless."

"Exactly."

This was just the kind of flirting that made Goldie feel lonely afterwards—bantering and light but with a hint of seriousness underneath.

"And yet," she said, "I think my sisters are much more trouble than yours."

"What do you mean?"

"I mean—this. The way they've thrown us together. Trying to make something happen. I'm sorry about that. You had no idea why Bebe was really inviting you."

She could feel her face flushing as she spoke—from fever or embarrassment—but it felt like a necessary speech, a way to square any loose ends. She hazarded a glance at Wolf's face. He was staring at her oddly, a hint of a smile on his lips.

"You think that's funny?" Goldie said, more than a little confused. "I'm apologizing about the ambush—"

"I knew why Bebe invited me. I'm not some innocent lamb being led to the slaughter. She's always talking about you—her amazing sister, living an exotic life on the West Coast. Her accomplished sister who writes, who has ventured further than anyone else in the family. They're proud of you."

Goldie set the tea down and snorted. "They're worried about me, you mean. They aren't proud. Pippa's trying to get me to buy an apartment in Red Hook, Marta thinks I'm wasting away and need to eat more, and Bebe.... Well. You know Bebe. She lives in a world of her own."

"You can't blame them for wanting to have you closer," Wolf said.

Goldie shivered, violently.

"Oh, hey," Wolf said, standing up. "Let me get you some lunch. Feed a cold—"

"Starve a fever," Goldie finished. "I never did understand that saying."

"It means," Wolf said, whisking the tea mug from the bedside table, "that food can cure anything."

He crossed the room and then turned back at the door. "Food, and euthanasia tea."

She was feeling well enough to join everyone for dinner at Pippa's—all of whom insisted she not miss Christmas Eve because of the fear she would get any of them sick. Armed with a thermometer in case her fever returned, she sat ensconced on an overstuffed chaise lounge in the living room, a blanket tucked up under her chin. Through a large open archway into the dining area she watched her splendid family orchestrate the meal—the children seated first, the adults hovering over their plates to cut and chop, then the sisters bobbing up and down between courses to gather salad plates and reissue new forks.

Wolf made her a plate of food piled so high that she kept knocking things off onto her lap. He returned from the dining room with a second plate, this one for himself.

"Oh, you don't have to keep me company," Goldie said. "I'm perfectly content in here by myself."

"I'm not doing it for you," Wolf said, pushing lock of hair from his eyes. He pulled a straight back chair next to the chaise lounge. "I'm doing it for me."

"Now you're lying. It's not nice to say things you don't mean."

Wolf leaned so close that she could see that his eyes were the color of dark tea. "I never say anything I don't mean."

Goldie tried not to flinch. "What big eyes you have, Grandmother."

Wolf laughed and batted his lashes. This was flirting on a dangerous level. Goldie felt her cheeks grow hot.

"Wrong fairy tale, I think," Wolf said. "There's no wolf in that story of Goldilocks and the bears."

"The Bayers, you mean."

"The four Bayers. Hmm. Something's not quite right about that."

More laughter, and Pippa wandered in. "What are you two up to in here?"

Goldie and Wolf exchanged a look and said nothing.

"I see," Pippa said after a moment, "that I'm not needed."

Christmas Day was a blur of gifts opened and discarded into growing piles, a turkey paraded and applauded and denuded to the breastbone, hot chocolate and coffee and cake, and one of the twins plunking out *Good King Wenceslas* on the portable keyboard, hauled into the living room for the occasion. After the afternoon trip to the cemetery, the silent toast back home again, Goldie was begging off to go to bed before an early flight in the morning. She hugged her three sisters and made her goodbyes now, while everyone was still clear-eyed and willing to let her go.

Wolf followed her down the corridor to the neighbor's apartment.

"You don't have to leave the festivities just because I am," she said, wrestling with the key. Another wiggle but the lock didn't give. She pulled the key out and started over. Behind her, Wolf seemed willing to wait forever.

It was one of the things she decided she really liked about him, his ability not to jump in, not to try to rescue her, not to dictate what the narrative would be. Refreshing, actually, not to have a masculine hand reach out for the key, no voice instructing her on what she should do. She tugged the key up and down and was rewarded with a distinct click.

"Got it," she said, pushing open the door.

"I never doubted you," Wolf said.

"You'd be surprised how many men do," Goldie said. She tossed her purse on the credenza and flopped into a chair. Wolf stood for a moment before settling in the opposite chair, lanky and halfway in shadow.

"You know," Goldie said, "I really don't know anything about you."

"You know the important stuff. I bake. I'm a middle child like you. I have sisters—like you. I'm looking for something—like you."

"What do you mean?"

"I want the same things you want. A place that feels like home. A job that feels worthy. Someone to share it with."

"I never said I wanted all that."

"You didn't have to. Your sisters did."

Goldie rolled her eyes. "My sisters don't know what I want."

"They know you're looking for something. They might not understand exactly what, but I do."

"After knowing me for what—a couple of days?" Goldie said, starting to get annoyed. "I have a home, I have a job, and I'm *not* moving back to New York."

"I don't think you should," Wolf said. He sounded sincere and Goldie felt a twinge of disappointment.

"Well, good. I'm glad you agree. It's been nice meeting you, but I'm heading to Portland in the morning and I doubt we'll see each other again." She stood up and extended her hand, a gesture that made her feel silly as soon as she did it. Wolf stood up, too, and looked down at her hand, bemused. Carefully, slowly, he leaned forward, closed his big, dark eyes, and kissed her softly on the cheek.

"Invite me to Portland," he whispered into her ear. "I hear it's a great place for a pastry chef."

Goldie's heart hammered so loudly that she wasn't sure she heard him. "You don't need my permission to come to Portland."

"What about an invitation?"

Goldie looked down at her hands—anywhere to keep from looking at Wolf's face. "You don't need that either," she said. She turned and headed to the bedroom, pausing in the doorway. Without turning back around, she added, "But you have it, if you want it."

The Uber was early, and she was in the airport in record time. No traffic to speak of, and the weather was clear and cold. She'd seen no one on her way out—not even Pippa, who often got up before dawn to go running on the Promenade. Wolf's door was shut, and though she was tempted to knock, she hadn't. Better to stop this here and now. She was perfectly happy as she was—living an unencumbered life of her own, without someone else deciding what she needed.

And yet…. And yet, her sisters weren't wrong.

When she got back to Portland, she'd get in touch with a realtor and see what was on the market. Move out of her rental, put down some actual roots. And she'd call her friend who worked at the daily paper, see if they were hiring. Maybe it was time to move on to more serious journalism, writing about something more substantial than artisanal smoked meats and trendy bars. Maybe download a different dating app, or go to an audition for a play, or sign up to canvass neighborhoods before the next election. Something to meet people. Get involved.

Wait to see if Wolf showed up.

Well. She hadn't wanted to give that serious thought, but there it was. He would love Portland. Laid back and hip, but exciting in its own way. Different from the stuffy restaurant scenes of Boston and Philly, and even New York. More willing to experiment. More open to the journey.

She got to her gate, to see a man with a familiar mop of dark hair and unrepentantly wolfish smile lounging in one of the chairs, phone plugged into a charging pole, his feet resting on his backpack.

"How?" she all but spluttered, shocked.

"I'm on stand-by. I might not make this plane, but I have a confirmed seat on the next flight. Thought I would keep you company until you fly, at least."

Butterflies erupted in her stomach. "But—"

"I know, I know." He brushed his hand through his hair, a little nervously, then grinned. "I'm impulsive. I thought I would come visit—just for New Years. Just to see if I would like it."

She took a deep breath and smiled. He was making a leap of faith.

If he was willing to try out Portland, she was willing to try out a new kind of happily ever after.

Copyright © 2018 Kay McSpadden.

Jessica Valdez began writing at the age of thirteen, after reading Gone with the Wind *and falling in love with romance. Finding inspiration in the small things in life, her words are enriched by the people she feels lucky to call her family and friends. Jessica lives in her hometown, in Amish-country, Ohio, with her two white pups and her fiancé. She has a deep love for her Irish roots and believes that everything good in life comes from hard work and determination.*

YOU HAD ME AT "HELLO"

by Jessica Valdez

Abigail Chase looked up as her brother walked into the room.

Dorian Chase scowled at her. "Abbie! How many times have I told you, you can't do everything you want? You can't slug every guy that says 'Hi' to you. That's the fourth time this month that I've had to pay a guy off to *not* press charges on you." He raked his hand through his hair.

Abigail laughed. "Well, what should I do? I thought I have an obvious resting bitch face. I can't help it if they don't take the initial hint."

Her brother's face turned red. "Why don't you try keeping your ass at home and study? You go out every night to bars, and at bars you're going to get hit on." Dorian sat down in the chair next to her. "Abigail, you are going to graduate from college, from law school, in six months. Please start taking this seriously. Mother and Father would be turning in their graves if they knew you were acting out like this."

Abigail stood quickly. "Do not bring them into this. And, like you have any room to talk, Dorian. Last I checked you've enticed four different girls into your bed this month. Why don't you try keeping it in your pants for a change?!" She turned and began to stomp away.

"Abbie, wait." Dorian rose and began to follow her. "Abbie…come on, stop."

She halted and waited for him to catch up to her.

"Look, if you insist on going out, please, just don't hit anyone. Maybe give one of them a chance—you might find one of them is worth something."

"I'll think about it. You know I haven't had good luck with men." She grimaced, thinking of that one guy who had tried to go too far. Her hand fisted.

Abigail left her brother standing in the hallway as she went down the hall to her room.

That night she looked at herself in the mirror. She heard a knock and Dorian opened the door.

"I have to go into the city tonight. Will you be okay?"

"I've spent the night alone before, Dorian. I am a grown woman."

"Just be careful, okay? Maybe you should stay home tonight."

"Dorian, stop doing that. I can handle myself."

"That, baby sister, is exactly what I am concerned about." And with that, he shut the door.

She finished getting ready, let her pitbull, Horatio, inside her room, called a cab to take her across the city, and opened the door to O'Malley's bar a half an hour later, stepping inside. She saw her friends sitting in the corner. As she started to walk towards them, someone bumped into her.

He turned quickly and said, "Sorry about that, luv. Are you alright?"

She looked at him and glared. "Yes, but you should watch what the hell you are doing."

"Aye, I should. But, you don't have to be rude about it."

"You're right, I don't. But, such is your fate from me. Fuck off." She turned away from him and walked towards her friends. She sat down and ordered a drink.

Her best friend of many years, Natalia Thomas, raised an eyebrow at her antics, looking over at her. "What did Dorian say today?"

"Normal Dorian things, of course."

"You going to calm down some?"

Abigail picked up the Guinness her friend had bought her and smiled. "Probably not."

Natalia shook her head and began to speak to one of their other friends.

Abigail watched them, feeling an odd pang of jealousy. Their parents felt no need for them to get degrees and become professionals. They just had to be beautiful and happy. She was ashamed to realize that on some level that lifestyle appealed to her—no more leaving her comfort zone to navigate the cut-throat legal field....

Dorian was right: she should not have gone out. All she was doing was wallowing.

At least she had not hit anyone...*yet*.

Abigail downed the Guinness, stood up, muttered something about feeling tired and the need to cram for an exam, and stepped back out onto the street. Natalia followed her out to see her off safely.

"Will Dorian pick you up?" Natalia asked.

"No, he went into the city tonight, so I'll be going home alone."

"Will you be okay getting home?"

"I'll grab a cab. Go on now. You should go home, too. I know your Mom worries when you're not home by three."

Natalia hugged her and walked away to hail a cab.

Abigail turned as she heard a man exit the bar behind her. She recognized the guy that bumped into her from earlier. She now noticed he was tall—even taller than Dorian, who stood six foot two inches tall. His black hair and blue eyes matched her own and his arms muscles flexed as he gestured toward the parking lot down the street.

"Do you need a ride?"

"If I did, I wouldn't take one from you. I saw you watching me earlier and that's creepy, in case you didn't know."

"Come on, luv. Just to let me apologize, I'll drop you off home and that will be the last you'll see of me."

Abigail saw Natalia climb in a cab and shook her head.

He shrugged, "Suit yourself," and put his hands in his pocket, strolling off in the direction of the parking lot.

She turned as she heard the door again. An obviously drunk man stumbled her way with seeming purpose. What is it with men tonight, she wondered. She looked away, towards the street—giving him the literal cold shoulder, hoping he would get the hint—but she soon felt his hand on her arm.

He was definitely *not* reading her body language well.

"You alone tonight?"

Abigail pulled away from him and turned to reply, ready to sock him one if he became too insistent.

She heard a motorcycle pull up. "Come on, luv, we'll be late."

She swiveled to see the tall hottie from earlier. He held out his hand.

"We have an early start tomorrow." He told her, gesturing for her to get on the bike.

She took a deep breath and rather than risk the fight that could ensue with the drunk man behind her, she took the rider's outstretched hand and climbed on the bike behind him.

He nodded to the drunkard. "You okay?"

The inebriated man nodded and stumbled away.

"You didn't have to do that. I don't need rescuing," she told him.

"Aye, I am sure you don't. Alas, my bike was feeling very chivalrous." He handed her a helmet. "Safety first, babe."

"Okay, but don't try anything funny."

"I won't."

She pulled the helmet on her head, told him her address, and put her arms around his waist. He hit the accelerator and they pulled away.

She felt her pulse racing as he pushed the throttle harder and the bike pushed forward. The wind whipped her hair in her face, stinging her eyes. She tightened her grip around his waist and rested her head on his back, blocking out most of the wind. She sighed deeply and held on tight.

There was no small talk—the wind ripped away any sound.

By the time she arrived her hair was in knots, but she felt exhilarated and climbed off the bike when he stopped by her front walkway.

"You have a nice house."

"My parents build it for us."

He raised an eyebrow, a twinkle playing in his eye. "Aren't you a little old to be living with your parents?"

Abigail's bitch face was earning its reputation. "I don't live with my parents, I live with my brother. My parents are dead."

"Dammit, I really am fucking this up, aren't I?"

"If you're aim is to annoy me, then no, you're doing great."

He hopped off the bike and turned to her. "No, that's not what I'm trying to do."

"I don't even know what the hell your name is. You haven't even told me that."

"You haven't exactly been forthcoming yourself, luv."

Abigail heard the heaviness of his Irish accent and could not help but to smile to herself, remembering the way the voices of her childhood used to sound.

"Why do you keep calling me that? You sound like you're from Ireland or something when you do that."

"My Dad was Irish, yes. My mother met him while she was on a trip to Dublin."

"Oh, sorry." She blushed slightly and looked over to her house and then back at him. "Guess I'm the one being rude now."

He extended out his hand. "I'm Declan."

She took his hand and shook it. "I'm Abigail."

"Nice to meet you, luv."

She motioned towards the house.

"Would you like a beer before you head back? It's the least I could do. You did give me a ride home, even after I was a bitch to you."

"And I saved your virtue from the drunk vagabond."

Her familiar ire returned, and she glared at him, half-heartedly. "I could have handled him myself."

He grinned unrepentantly, his blue eyes shining as the outside lights came on when they approached the door. "You're not afraid to invite a stranger into your house?"

"I can handle myself," she repeated, with a grin of her own. "Besides, I keep a 9mm. I'll just shoot you."

She let him into the house, down the hallway towards the kitchen.

He watched her walking in front of him, seeing that she had a confident stride and held her head high. He could tell through her tight jeans that she was well-muscled. She was impressing him in more ways than her spirited personality.

The lights came on as they moved throughout the rooms.

"This is a very nice house."

"My brother added some new technology after my parents passed, but we decided not to extend it. It's just the two of us."

They entered the kitchen and the light came on. She opened the fridge and pulled out two Coronas. She opened them and handed one to him.

He could not help but be curious. "Your brother in school?"

"No, those are my books."

He lifted up the front of the book and looked at the title. "Accounting law?"

"My brother is an accountant, I'm going to be a lawyer. Kind of a family tradition. Our father and his brother were accountants and lawyers."

"Is that what you really want?"

"Doesn't matter much what I want. My brother and I would have done anything our father asked us to do. He asked Dorian to be an accountant and he asked me to be a lawyer—so here we are." She took a drink from her beer. "What do you do?"

He took a drink and looked at her. "Whatever I can, I guess. I'm not a doctor or lawyer. I'm just a run-of-the-mill guy."

"A run-of-the-mill guy who offers rides home to girls?"

"Not normally, no, but you looked like you needed a ride."

She picked up her beer and turned. "Let's go outside."

She opened the double doors and led him out to the pool area. She sat down at a table and lit a cigarette.

He looked out at the view. "This is beautiful. You can see the whole city from here."

"It's why my father chose this spot. He loved the view, he could watch us sparring from his office upstairs and still felt he was away from the city. We were taught early to fight for what we wanted and defend what we had. Dorian learned swordsmanship and boxing. I took gymnastics and karate."

"Karate?" he asked, smiling.

"Yeah. My father wanted me to take ballet, I had a better idea."

He sat down across from her. "You don't strike me as the ballet type."

"No, I'm not."

They drank the last of their beers in companionable silence, she finished her cigarette—telling herself she will stop smoking, one of these days—and she motioned to him, asking if he wanted another. He nodded his head and she went into the house.

He leaned back in the chair and stretched. He breathed deep, feeling relaxed for the first time in a long time.

Watching him stretch from through the porch doors, Abigail felt her phone begin to vibrate and turned to pull it from her pocket. "Yes, Dorian?"

"I just wanted to make sure you made it home okay. I assume you went out."

"Of course."

"You're being more succinct with me than normal. What's going on, Abbie?"

"Nothing."

"Where's your bathroom?" she heard Declan ask behind her.

She turned and pointed down the hall. "Second door on the left." Her eyes followed him as he walked down the hallway. He had a strong form, a firm stride. She imagined briefly what it would feel like to be lifted into his arms as he kissed her. She felt embarrassed for her thoughts, but couldn't shake the image in her head.

"Abigail, who the hell is there with you?"

"No one, just some guy who gave me a ride. I offered him a beer to thank him." She didn't say for getting rid of the drunk pervert. Then her brother would *really* have been worried.

"You're actually *conversing* with a guy, rather than hitting him?" He sounded shocked. "You be careful. Don't be dumb."

"Wise words from a guy who fucks everything that walks past him."

"All right! Quit it. I hate arguing with you. Good night, baby sister. Get some sleep—*after* the guy is gone."

Dorian ended the call just as Declan came back in the room. She pocketed her phone, opened the refrigerator door and pulled out two more beers. She grabbed the bottle opener from the counter and opened them. She handed one to him and they walked back out to the pool area.

"Your brother?" he asked politely.

"Yes."

He sat down again, nodding thoughtfully, and looked at her. "So your name is Abigail, you have a brother, you are going to be a lawyer and you live in the hills. There has to be more to you than that."

"Sorry to disappoint you. That's pretty much who I am, in a nutshell."

"What the hell were you doing in Hell's Kitchen?"

"I'm sorry, I hadn't realized it was an exclusive part of town."

"It's not. It's just…your kind don't normally go there."

"'My kind'—what the hell does that mean?"

"Rich girls."

"Oh, I see. Now you think I'm just a rich girl?"

"Aren't you?"

She lit another cigarette and sat back in her chair.

"No, actually. I know my father gave us education opportunities some didn't have, but our parents worked hard for it. *We* worked hard for it. That front pathway you came in on—my brother and I poured that. That pool—we dug it. As teens, we cleaned every inch of this house, twice a week; we're still clean freaks. I'm not saying I know what hard times are, but I know what hard work is."

He held up his hands in surrender. "Okay, luv. I'm sorry. We aren't communicating well, are we?"

"I suppose we aren't. In your defense, I don't do communication well." She smiled. "That's why my father felt I should be a lawyer. I will argue anyone into the ground."

He smiled. "That is something I have no doubt about." Then he yawned. "Perhaps it is time to call it a night."

She agreed, surprisingly reluctantly.

She walked him into the house and to the front door and noticed that he was wobbling slightly. "Maybe you shouldn't be driving."

"You might be right. I'll call a cab, luv. I can come back for my bike tomorrow."

She hesitated, but then he swayed some more, so shook her head no. "Don't be ridiculous. We have an extra bedroom. You're about my brother's size; I'll get you something to sleep in."

"You really aren't scared, are you?"

"Of what, exactly?"

"You don't know me. I could be a killer for all you know, or a rapist—a serial rapist murderer." His last words came out slightly slurred.

"Well, I have to just comment that most men who are those type of people don't tend to brag about it while they are physically vulnerable. Also, like in several other places of the house, I have a gun in my room, beside the bed. My father did not raise me to be afraid and so I am not."

Abigail helped guide him into the bedroom, then darted into her brother's room for some clothes. She walked back into the spare room to see Declan removing his button-up shirt. She saw that he was well-toned and obviously worked out. She admired his arms for a moment and then cleared her throat.

He looked up at her, and she extended her hand, with the clothes in it, towards him. He reached out to take them and stumbled slightly. She moved forward and caught him.

"Okay, let's try sitting on the bed," she instructed him. After he complied, she motioned for him to put his arms up. He did as she asked and she pulled a T-shirt over his head.

"Okay luv, that's enough. Get out now. I'm not going to take my pants off in front of you."

"Trust me, you don't have anything I haven't seen before. I'm not exactly a virgin."

"No. I can do it. I promise, I don't need help. I have changed my clothes, mildly drunk, before. Go on now—get some sleep."

She turned and left the room. She grabbed the door handle and started to pull it closed. "Declan?"

"Yes, luv?"

"I also have a pitbull I sleep with, so don't get any ideas."

"Good to know."

She shut the door and walked down the hall to her own room. She was thinking to herself that maybe she should just invite him to her room and stop the madness she felt inside, but then reminded herself he was half drunk—she did not take advantage of inebriated men. One part of her could not help but be amused, however, that she obviously had a stronger stomach for alcohol than he did.

Abigail shook her head in bewilderment and opened her door. Her dog, Horatio, jumped down from the bed as she came in the room. She rubbed his ears and unlocked and opened her private sliding door to the backyard. Changing while her dog was outside, relieving himself, she then closed the door after he ran back inside. Sliding the deadbolt in place and turning off the lamp she had left on earlier in the night, she climbed into bed and Horatio jumped up beside her. She snuggled up to the dog and closed her eyes.

The next morning, Abigail felt Horatio stir and sat up. She saw her bedroom door swinging open and her Pitbull jumped down and barked. She had reached for the gun on her bedside table when she heard her brother's voice.

"Horatio, be quiet. Abbie, why the hell is there a motorcycle out front?"

She put her gun back on the table and glared at him. "You know, Dorian, you act like Mother raised you with no manners at all. What if I wasn't alone in here?"

He closed her bedroom door and sat down in the chair across from her bed as Horatio pawed at the private porch door to be let out. She rose and opened the door.

"So, *is* there someone else in the house?" her brother finally asked.

"You didn't notice that the door to the guest room is closed?"

"I didn't notice, probably because I don't care about closed doors."

"Do you care about anything, really?"

"I care about you. Now, why is there a motorcycle out in front of our house?"

"Declan—the guy that helped me out at the club— had too many drinks and I wasn't going to let him drive home, obviously. I am going to be a lawyer. I *do* have respect for the laws and human life, Dorian."

"So, that's all it is?" He raised an eyebrow as he looked at her, curious.

"Don't you have a meeting, or some shit, this morning?"

"It's Saturday."

"Don't you have some bimbo you are romancing today?"

He laughed. "No. I thought we could go see a movie or something."

"Brother/sister time?"

"Yes."

She opened the door and let Horatio back in the house.

"Feed my dog for me while I throw this guy out of the house."

"Take your time. I have to run somewhere real quick. Be ready by noon."

"Okay, okay. Go."

After she head the front door latch behind a departing Dorian, Abigail walked down the hall. She knocked on the spare room door and waited for a response. When there was none, she opened the door a crack to see if he was still sleeping. Instead, she heard the shower running in the adjoining ensuite and turned to leave to give him privacy, but then the shower shut off and she paused.

Curious, she turned back to look into the room. The bathroom door opened and Declan came out of the adjoining room. When she saw he wore nothing but a towel, she smiled.

He looked up and saw her and pulled the towel tighter around his waist. "I really needed a shower, sorry."

"No, its fine. Are you hungry?"

Tentative smile. "I could eat."

She saw that he was moving closer to his clothes. "I'll give you some privacy."

She started to shut the door but he crossed the room and stopped her, wrapping his hand around the door edge. "Won't your brother be home soon?"

"He's already been home and gone. I will let you get dressed. I have to exercise and be ready to go by noon and Dorian has even less patience for waiting than I do."

His hand slid down the door to cover Abigail's hand. "You don't have to cook for me. I can just go."

She looked down at his hand covering hers. She felt like it was on fire and she slowly, reluctantly, pulled it away. "No, its fine. My Mother would have killed me if she knew I let a person leave our home hungry. She wasn't the type and I won't be either. Get dressed."

"Thank you for the kindness. You really don't have to be so generous."

"Next time, I might not be."

"Next time? So, I *can* see you again?"

"I didn't say that." She turned and walked away down the hallway, unable to shake the butterflies in her stomach or the grin off her face.

Declan entered the kitchen and saw that Abagail was at the stove. "You always do the cooking around here?"

She nodded. "It's just the two of us. Trust me, you don't want Dorian cooking for you." She turned around with his plate in one hand and the egg flip in the other and motioned for him to sit at the counter.

He sat down and picked up his fork while she placed the plate in front of him. "You're not eating?"

"No, if I eat before working out, I'll throw up."

"Is that why you're wearing that outfit that shows off everything you've got?"

"If you think it does that, I guess."

"I got the impression from you last night that you do not like guys in close proximity."

"I don't know. Well, maybe…." She shook her head, as if to brush away the topic. "What's the point really? After I graduate, I'm going to Boston to live. I'm taking over for my uncle who is the lawyer in the family from the older generation. My brother feels my skills will best be used there."

"You don't look like you agree with him."

She shrugged and turned around to the sink to wash the dishes she had dirtied.

He stood, went around the counter, and came up behind her. "I would like to see you again."

Abigail stopped what she was doing and turned around. She noticed how close he was and she retreated until her butt hit the counter. "Declan, back up."

His eyes grew more serious. "Do you really want me to back up? I will, if you do."

She bit her lip, frustrated, not sure what she wanted. She should say goodbye and be done with it. But…she wanted him.

He noticed her indecision and stepped closer to her. "Why are you like this?" he all but whispered, as if trying not to frighten off a skittish deer.

"Like what?"

He reached out and gently put his hand on her shoulder. "Do you not want me to touch you?"

She looked at his hand and then back at his face. "I didn't say I didn't want you to. I just don't see the point. Like I said, I'm going to Boston when I graduate. What's the point of one night stands? I'm not one for meaningless sex. I take a lot more convincing than most girls, I'm sure."

He smiled. "What if I said I don't want meaningless sex either?"

She rolled her eyes. "I'm sure *all* the guys from the club use that line—to get into bed with us girls. Hell, my brother might use it."

"So, it's about me convincing you, then?"

She smiled and put her hand on his chest. "If you really think you can."

He pulled her to him and leaned down to kiss her. She tensed up and he stopped. "What's wrong? What happened?"

She shrugged. "A lawyer at a firm I was interning at. I hit him before he could kiss me, but he groped me before I could knock him out. I just don't trust men now."

"You can trust me."

She laughed out loud. "Yeah, right."

'You can." He traced a finger down her face, gently cupping it. "Can we try this again?"

She nodded.

He leaned down again and kissed her slowly at first until she relaxed against him and her mouth parted. She felt his other hand move to her shoulder. Her hands moved to his hips, pulling him closer to her, and he moaned until his hands slid down her arms to cover her hands and he gently pulled them away.

She broke free of their kiss. "Why did you do that?"

"Abigail,"—he raised his hand and smoothed her curls away from her face—"you can't control everything, luv. You're going to have to let someone else take the lead at times."

Declan waited for her answer: "I'm willing to try that."

He took her by surprise by leaning down and scooping her up in his arms. "Which room is yours?" he all-but-growled at her.

She laughed. "What makes you think I'm going to let you in my room?" She wriggled in his arms, almost as if to absentmindedly free herself.

"Easy, luv. I don't want to drop you."

He began heading toward the bedrooms.

She looked up at him as he reached the hallway. "End of the hallway, last door on the right."

He strode down there with spring and a sense purpose in his step, as if she didn't weigh a thing, and pushed the door open.

Within a seconds he had laid her on her bed and was kissing his way down her neck. Another few seconds later he was introduced to a growling pitbull, wrapped up in blankets, newly awoken from his morning nap.

"I'll happily go to my grave today, just to have you one time," he told Abigail, wryly.

Abigail laughed and pushed him off her to coax the dog out of the room.

She walked him outside as he made his way over to his bike.

He leaned down and kissed her. "So, can I see you again?"

"Maybe…I will think about it."

"How will I know if you want to? You didn't give me your phone number or even your last name."

"But I will be going to Boston soon," she pointed out.

"Maybe…maybe not. You don't seem overly enthused by the idea. Why not scout out the options at law firms here in town?" He leant into his bike, placing his hand over his heart, sighing dramatically. "Besides, you assured me you were not into one night stands—or meaningless sex. You are not saying you lied to me and took advantage of me, are you?"

She laughed and held her hand out for his phone, adding her digits into it before returning it.

"Until next time," he promised her, his eyes twinkling.

She grinned and he kissed her again, this time with the promise of future delights—if she stayed.

He climbed on his bike and put on his helmet. He started the motor and pulled away down the drive.

She smiled to herself and went back in the house, to shower before her brother arrived home.

Dorian came through the door, just before midday, and yelled for her, telling her they would be late for the movies if she didn't get her butt moving.

She came into the living room, putting her earrings in.

"I see you're alone now."

"I told you I would get rid of him."

"You aren't snapping at me. Why?" Dorian's eyes widened in realization. "You slept with him, didn't you?"

"Oh, shut up. What the hell do you expect me to say?"

"I'm actually surprised. Normally guys don't get past "Hello" with you."

"I know." She picked up her purse and looked at him, smiling. "There was something different about this guy."

Copyright © 2018 by Jessica Valdez.

*Author of the 4-star (*Romantic Times*) novel* Cat Scratch Fever, *and* Out of the Frying Pan, Possessed, Undressed, and in a Mess, *and many short stories, Sophie Mouette is the brainchild of two widely published authors of erotica, romance, and speculative fiction. The two halves of Sophie—Dayle A. Dermatis (aka Andrea Dale) and Teresa Noelle Roberts—met almost three decades ago at a writers' conference. Talking nonstop, they closed down the hotel bar and went somewhere else to keep on talking. They still are…. For more information, visit their website at* SophieMouette.com.

HIDDEN TREASURE

by Sophie Mouette

When Brenda was a girl, her widowed mother had worked at Frogmorton House and, promising always to be good, Brenda had been given the run of the estate. She never touched any of the antiques as she wandered through the folly of a Germanic castle, pretending she was a princess in the turreted tower and believing that the narrow servants' staircase was a secret passageway.

When she was older, she fell in love with the romance between railroad magnate Winthrop Frogmorton and Austrian Henrietta Ströbel. Henrietta had claimed the Adirondacks reminded her of her beloved Alps, so Winthrop commissioned her a castle of their very own.

By the time she hit college, Brenda was beyond notions of girlish romance and obsessed instead with history, particularly the Victorian era of upstate New York. When she finally returned and took on her dream job as curator of Frogmorton House, it had been her idea to have the staff dress appropriately, to give visitors the full experience of the *schlöss*-like manor.

She'd never admit aloud that one of the reasons she'd hired Sean as a security guard last month was because she guessed he'd look mouthwatering in a proper Victorian policeman's outfit of dark blue wool.

She'd been right about that. Oh, had she ever been right.

Now, as the lights flickered ominously, she looked up from the computer screen, aware that she hadn't been seeing the membership newsletter in front of her. She'd been fantasizing about Sean again.

Still, she automatically hit Save, just in case they lost power. The battery backup should mean she wouldn't lose anything, but you never knew with computers.

She slipped off her narrow black-rimmed glasses, surprised to see how dark it had become. Had she been woolgathering that long? Somehow, not surprising when it came to thoughts of Sean.

They'd gone to the same high school, but she'd been bookish and involved, and he'd been distant and sporty and a little shy, his bangs always tumbling into his eyes when he ducked his head.

Now his silky black hair was shorter, but tousled and untamed on top. He'd enlisted after high school, he told her when he started work at Frogmorton House, and by God, now that he was out, he was growing his hair again.

He was no longer shy, no longer a boy. His shoulders had broadened; his brilliant blue eyes held depth and experience. His grin was roguish, his stride confident.

And Brenda appreciated all of that. A lot.

She also appreciated the way his wool pants snugged over his tight asscheeks. Her hands itched to cup the muscled curves, pull him close....

Shaking herself back to the present, she flipped on the antique banker's lamp on her desk and glanced at the clock, certain it would be time to close up the House and head home to her thermal lounging pajamas, leftover homemade pizza, and her Welsh Corgi, Mort.

But it was only 3 p.m.

She glanced out the window. All day they'd had menacing grey clouds, as ominous a sign as the flickering lights. She'd known they were due for a storm, and by all accounts it was going to be a humdinger.

She just didn't expect the world to be white already.

The snow swirled down in gusts and eddies, the flakes dancing like manic fairies. She couldn't even see the evergreens just outside the window.

The lights flickered again, this time going completely out for a few seconds before returning. Brenda saved the membership newsletter file again, copied it onto a flash drive, then shut the computer down. It had been an excruciatingly slow day already,

and in this weather they weren't going to get any more visitors. Best to close early and get out before the roads got too slippery.

She grabbed the walkie-talkie off the desk. "Sean, this is Brenda."

No answer.

"Sean? Pick up, please."

She gave the walkie-talkie an exasperated shake. Cell phone service was seriously dodgy in the Adirondack Mountains as it was, but Frogmorton House was nestled in a little valley that defied the reach of any cell tower. Sean should have his walkie-talkie on...

She'd just have to go find him.

Not that seeking him out was such a bad thing. Brenda slipped her burgundy velvet fitted coat over her deep green wool and cashmere dress, glad for the extra warmth—Frogmorton House was drafty even in the height of summer and today's storm was rattling the beautiful but ill-fitting windows, the glass wavy from over a century of excruciatingly slow gravitational slide.

She smoothed the velvet down the molded line of her torso. Even on quiet days like this, when time dragged and she didn't get to share her passion for Victoriana with another soul, her job still thrilled her. How many people got paid to hang out in a castle and wear a glorious late-Victorian outfit, complete with corset, to work?

Plus, a well-made corset was incredibly comfortable. Not to mention the pleasing way it nipped in her waist and plumped up her breasts.

She'd definitely noticed Sean ogling her cleavage.

Sean could ogle her cleavage any time. Do more than ogle, if it came to that, which she hoped it did.

During his interview, his sensual lips had curved into one of his roguish grins when she mentioned the required policeman's uniform and the formal butler's outfit he'd don when he helped at fundraisers.

"Bonus," he'd said. "Halloween every day. I always loved...trick or treating." His tone was light, but his voice deepened suggestively on the last words and hit straight between her legs. She felt herself flushing and bit back an urge to offer all sorts of treats (and an assortment of tricks), right on the spot.

Thank God Hank, their bookkeeper, had been looking down at Sean's résumé at that moment; his proper elderly brain would have caught fire from the looks shooting back and forth between them.

The heated glances and flirtatious remarks had been piling on ever since. But they simply hadn't had time to do anything about it. First hosting the series of Victorian Christmas teas for the local school kids, and the holiday fundraising cocktail party (Sean had portrayed the kind of butler who'd have had real Victorian matrons consorting with the lower classes in a heartbeat), and then getting the house undecorated, and getting year-end thank-you letters out in time to make the IRS happy, and trying to sort through the Whitney bequest…

Plus all the maintenance issues that kept Sean busy because, admit it, a lot of the time there wasn't a lot for a security guard to do except just be there, but the house itself could devour all your time if you let it. And like Brenda, Sean would let it.

One more reason she liked him. The house was important to him, too.

She left her office, which was in the parlor off the foyer, so she could hear when tourists arrived.

Frogmorton House's pale stone hearkened to its Austrian and German inspiration, and it had round towers and clusters of narrow windows and a meandering, wandering layout that didn't make a whole lot of sense, really. The unconventional design made the House seem vaster than its two-stories-plus-basement-and-unfinished-attic. From the outside, it looked like it should be the setting for a ghost story or a Gothic tragedy, but Winthrop and Henrietta had lived into chubby, philanthropic old age, surrounded by a passel of children and grandchildren who, unusually for the era, had all survived to adulthood. The place was homey as well as grand, with a large nursery and elegantly framed children's drawings proudly displayed next to the Sargent portrait of Henrietta.

Brenda loved the place with an unholy passion.

She found Sean emerging from the basement into the kitchen. His dark hair was mussed—then again, it always had a mussed look to it, like he'd just crawled out of bed, and that was a lovely image because then he'd probably be naked—and a few cobwebs clung to the crisp navy blue wool of his uniform. The brass buttons shone as if he'd just buffed them, though.

"There you are," Brenda said. It was sort of a stupid thing to say, but for a moment there, the spicy smell of his aftershave had glued her tongue to the roof of her mouth. "I was trying to reach you, but the damn walkie-talkie…"

"Needs new batteries, I think," he finished with an apologetic smile. "I'll pick some up tonight. But if you wanted me to check the fuse box, I just did. Replaced the fuse for the left tower, but the rest survived the power surge okay. Fuses. Sheesh. You wouldn't have an electrical upgrade scheduled any time soon?"

"It's tricky with a historic house—and expensive." She shrugged. "Maybe after we reslate the roof so it stops leaking into the Birch Bedroom." Frogmorton House was luckier than many small museums—some of the numerous Frogmorton descendants had inherited Winston's generous spirit and knack for business—but money was still a constant struggle.

"Maybe we should check out the Birch Bedroom. Make sure it's not snowing in there?" Sean raised one heavy dark eyebrow in a way that would have done a movie star playing a wickedly naughty hero proud. If Brenda had any doubts that his mind was in the gutter—and she didn't, because hers had descended right along with his—his smile made it clear he wasn't thinking about protecting the William Morris wallpaper or the delicate dressing table.

"Oh, no," she blurted. "That bed frame's already damaged."

Oh God. She felt her face suffuse with heat. Had she actually said that aloud?

Yes, and despite the rush of mortification, she couldn't say she regretted it.

Not from the look on Sean's face, which had gone from flirty-but-work-safe to something that wasn't safe anywhere, and certainly not at work. Especially not when your workplace boasted seven bedrooms, six of which had sturdy, comfortable, downright decadent Victorian beds.

Heat coiled from her flushed face, tickled her nipples, spread down to her sex, which pulsed in appreciation of the images racing through her mind. Her. Sean. One of those Victorian beds—not the one in the Birch Room, which was only a single anyway, but maybe the grand canopied Frogmorton matrimonial bed….

Her lace-trimmed silk drawers caressed her thighs as she shifted nervously back and forth, rubbed against her suddenly damp and sensitive cleft. The corset held her like an embrace.

Her nipples felt like they were drilling through the now-confining corset.

Sean took a step forward.

The lights flickered again as the wind let out a howl like a tortured soul.

In the brief darkness, Sean's arms slipped around her, pulled her close.

His lips brushed hers. Soft, an inquiry, but with the promise of so much more behind them. He smelled good, like bay rum and something slightly musky that she thought was just him.

They'd kissed once before, back in high school when Brenda had been inexperienced and she guessed Sean had been, too. He hadn't gone to the prom, but crashed the party by the lake. Of course there'd been drinking. At some point she'd turned on the log where she sat and he'd just been *there*, and their lips had touched, and then he'd eased back and for a moment she saw the fire reflected in his eyes, and then he was gone.

He kissed like a man now, and she was woman enough to appreciate it.

She had a dim memory, however, that she'd come to find Sean for reasons other than snogging him, but damned if she could remember what they were. She'd been thinking about his sculpted mouth for a long time, and it felt just as good on hers as she'd imagined.

Better, even.

The lights came back on all too soon, though, and with it, some semblance of reason.

Damn.

She licked her lips, aware of how provocative the action was by the way Sean's nostrils flared. "Uh… don't know if you've noticed, but the snow's coming down pretty hard. I'm declaring us closed on account of bad weather."

Suddenly serious, he nodded. "Plan. Do you want to ride back into town with me? At least if we get stuck, we won't be alone."

Brenda's Outback was fine in snow, but he did have a point. Being alone out there if something went wrong would be Not Good. If it had been anyone else, she might have suggested he just follow her so they could keep an eye on each other—get both cars back to town, all that.

But she liked the idea of a ride home with Sean. More to the point, she liked the idea of asking him in once they got there, and having him meet the dog, share the pizza, maybe open a bottle of wine—and see if they could build on the promise of that kiss. "Sounds good. You lock up the back. I'll grab a few things from the office and meet you out front."

Brenda made sure everything was shut down, changed the message on the answering machine to say they were closed, and grabbed her flash drive. The one thing she'd wanted to get done this afternoon she could do at home just as easily (assuming she didn't let Sean sweep her off her feet, that is).

Very little of what Mrs. Whitney had left the house was directly useful—some Victorian-era family photographs and papers and a few nice pieces of furniture. But some of the more modern stuff looked like it might be collectible and she'd been combing eBay and other auction sites, looking for information.

Good God, that wind was terrible. She swore it wasn't just rattling the windows, but penetrating the stone walls.

Then she looked out the window.

Damn.

The world was a solid wall of white.

She went to open the front door. It opened a crack and then stopped. Too much snow piled in front of it.

Double damn.

"I think we're stuck."

Sean's voice made her jump. He'd snuck into the room; when she turned, she saw he was in his stocking feet, as if he'd left wet, snowy boots in the kitchen. Snow clung to his pant legs, all the way to his thighs.

Normally the idea of snow on the irreplaceable and already worn peacock rug would trigger her anal-retentive tendencies, but it was hard to get into full preservationist mode while staring at Sean's thighs—the snow was almost up to his crotch. The carpet had survived several generations of Adirondack winters, when various Frogmortons had presumably tracked in snow on a regular basis. It could handle a little more.

"You can get out through the kitchen door," he added, "but the snow's knee-deep—or worse—already. We could dig my Jeep out, but we're not going to get far. Even if they're keeping up with the main roads, no one's touched Frog Hollow."

She picked up the house phone. "I'll call the plow guy. Maybe he can push us up on the schedule. Assuming his cell phone's working." Frog Hollow Road was private, more like a long driveway than an actual road, and they had arrangements with a neighbor with his own plow to keep them dug out.

The plow guy answered his cell, all right—from the hospital, where his wife was in labor. ("Great timing, eh? I can already see this kid's gonna be trouble.") He had back-up, but she had a day job to get home from and her own plowing clients to hit. "Best make some coffee and get…"

A loud crackle made Brenda jump and hold the phone out from her ear as if it was a live mouse.

When she moved it gingerly back to her ear, it was dead.

Well, wasn't this interesting? Snowed in *and* incommunicado.

On one hand, poor Mort was stuck home alone—she just hoped he'd have the courtesy to do his business on the tiled bathroom floor when he got desperate. (Or better yet, that the next-door neighbor who'd walked Mort for her when she was working late would be clever enough to notice she hadn't made it home and come to the poor dog's rescue.)

On the other hand, she'd daydreamed about spending the night in the romantic old mansion. Spending the night in the romantic old mansion with a devilishly handsome man was an even better idea.

Especially a devilishly handsome man who'd already kissed her once and showed every sign of wanting to kiss her again. And more.

Oh yeah, especially more.

The next gust of wind was so hard she half expected the stained glass window sporting the Frogmorton utterly ridiculous faux coat of arms (which included, perhaps unsurprisingly, a frog salient, or leaping) to blow in. Which would be a shame. Fundamentally tacky it might be, but it was part of the house's history.

"It's warmer in the kitchen," Sean suggested. "And that's where the coffee pot is."

"And the food. We might as well use the microwave before the power goes out. Because face it, the power *is* going to go out."

Sean took her hand. "Oooh, I'm scared of the dark. Will you protect me?"

"Jerk." She smacked him playfully on his ass (his very fine ass). But she didn't let go of his hand while she did it.

And when he took advantage of that fact to reel her in for another kiss, she decided that inconvenience and potential carpet-cleaning and all, being snowed in was just fine with her.

His lips were warm, but his cheeks were cold from his foray outside, a contrast that made Brenda shiver with delight.

The first kiss had been tentative. Questioning. This one started that way, too, with feather-light brushes and tiny flicks of his tongue against her lips like snowflakes against bare skin, only hot.

Brenda was more than happy to encourage him to the next level.

She threaded her fingers into his hair, which was damp from the snow, and boldly deepened the kiss, meeting his tongue with hers and then dipping farther, between his lips, to find the sweetness beyond.

A sharp intake of breath. His body tensed. Then he leaned in, his fingers massaging the muscles just inside her shoulder blades as he pulled her closer.

This version of the kiss sent tingles right down to her toes and back up to where they mattered the most.

The lights flickered again, actually going out for enough time to plunge them into darkness, where the only thing that existed was the feel of him touching her, mouth to mouth, chest to chest, thigh to thigh, and a delicious hardness of his pressing against the softness of her lower belly.

Power restored itself, with no promises of how long it would remain, or whether the next time would be The Big One. It took all of Brenda's willpower to pull away from Sean enough to say, "Um. We'd better get something to eat while we still have electricity."

Sean's grin was fiendish, and they were halfway to the kitchen when it occurred to her that he'd interpreted "something to eat" in an entirely different way from how she'd intended it.

It was her turn to grin. Oh, she liked the way his mind worked.

❖

When Jeremy whined "It's *co-old*" for the third time, it was all Clyde could do not to undo one of his snowshoes and smack it into his friend's kisser.

"It's not that bad," he said for the third time. "I heard once that when it's really cold, it can't snow. All this snow means it's not really cold."

"I don't get it," Jeremy said. "It snows in winter, and it's cold in winter. Snow is cold."

Clyde didn't understand it, either, but he'd lived in the Adirondacks for all twenty years and three months of his life, and he'd noticed that sometimes it was colder when it wasn't snowing, so cold the hair in his nose froze up.

It wasn't *that* cold right now, a fact for which he was quite grateful.

The snow fluffed and fluttered around them, and poofed up beneath their snowshoes. Their breath lingered in the cold air like pot smoke in the shed behind the high school.

"It's not my fault you didn't dress warmly," he snapped, finally giving in to his exasperation. He regretted it almost immediately when he saw Jeremy's face fall.

Still, he couldn't keep from adding "Like I told you to."

"I didn't know it was going to be this *far*," Jeremy protested.

Apparently Jeremy had thought they'd be driving to Frogmorton House, as if they were going to make a triumphant entrance and demand the property that was rightfully Clyde's.

Clyde didn't think that would go over well with the people who worked there.

"It's no farther than the deer blind on the other side of Cascade," he pointed out.

Jeremy heaved a sigh. "But we have *beer* stashed there."

"I will buy you a case of Pabst when we get back, I swear," Clyde said.

A smile crossed Jeremy's wind-red face. "Really?"

"Cross my heart," Clyde said.

Mollified, Jeremy started off again. Really, the long underwear top and down vest and jeans should keep him warm enough while they were moving. Clyde felt almost too hot in his own layers, which included a checked red-and-black hunting shirt and thermal socks his grandmother had given him last Christmas.

God rest her soul.

Then again, it was all his grandmother's fault he and Jeremy were out in the middle of the woods right now.

She may have gifted him with thermal socks, but she'd denied him his birthright, and as God was his witness, he was going to claim what was rightfully his.

Before or after he pitched the whining Jeremy into a ravine.

❖

Sean put on a pot of coffee to brew while Brenda explored the fridge and cabinets for something resembling a light supper. The rich aroma made her mouth water as she set out her findings.

Bagels and cream cheese left over from a Chamber of Commerce breakfast. A frozen pizza stashed by Sean in case of a dire lunch emergency. Energy bars and green tea drinks. A handful of ketchup packets—not at all useful right now. A tin of instant hot chocolate with mini-marshmallows. (Possibly dessert.)

Best of all, far back in a cupboard, a dusty bottle of decent champagne left over from some long-past benefit. Brenda tucked that into the fridge for later.

She'd always believed in thinking positively, and positive thinking right now included the idea that by the end of the evening, they'd have something to celebrate.

From the pantry she dug out a pair of the nothing-special-but-looked-properly-historic heavy silver candelabra they used for parties. Soon candles were flickering over on the counter, making the kitchen both cozy and romantic. She hadn't intended that.

Okay, maybe she had. Just a wee tiny bit.

Sean had his flashlight at the ready, too. But when the power went out for good, they didn't reach for the flashlight. They reached for each other.

The candle flame sent Sean's cheekbones into sharp relief, made his eyes just that much deeper before he pulled her in for another kiss.

First little nibbles on her lower lip that made her shiver with delight, but set a fire deep inside her. Shivering but hot. Nice.

Her lips parted, and his tongue brushed the inside of her mouth, exploring the surfaces, sparking more delicious sensations.

Once again, she laced her fingers in his hair, holding him as if he might escape. Not that he was showing any sign of wanting to escape.

Sean kissed away from her mouth to her ear (which made her giggle, even though it tickled in a very, very sexy way), to her throat, until his lips were brushing against the handmade lace ruffle just at the base of her throat.

Sean found an extra-sensitive spot on the side of her neck, half-hidden by lace. When she moaned, he seemed to decide that lace and a little bit of wool were tasty enough as long as he could reach her through them.

More shivers. More fire. Throbbing nipples and a pussy that pulsed in time with her heart.

Pure need.

Damn, why wasn't she wearing her ball gown? Sure, she'd have been freezing with her arms and cleavage bare, but it would give him so much more skin to touch and kiss. She pressed herself against him, trying desperately to feel more of his body. It wasn't easy through layers of skirt and petticoat—she'd gone for the layered effect because it was both authentic and warm, but damn, right now she was regretting it. As much as she was regretting her authentically high neckline.

Her hands slid down his broad back to his ass, cupping and gripping it, pulling him closer so she could push herself against the hard bulge in his crotch.

Not enough. Not nearly enough.

He slipped a leg between hers and still it wasn't enough contact.

It wasn't just the fabric in the way, although that was a problem. She wanted to feel his skin. No, she wanted him *inside* her skin—inside her, yes, but under her skin too, and she under his.

At the very least, she wanted to start unbuttoning his crisp uniform jacket—but she'd have to pull away to give herself room to work, and that would mean less delicious contact.

Decisions, decisions.

"Too many damn clothes," Sean said, barely lifting his mouth from her skin. "I love the way you look in the Victorian outfits, but they get in the way."

"They do come off, you know."

He pulled back enough that Brenda could see his face. His grin was even more wicked by candlelight. "A little at a time, though. We've got all night, and I'm getting off on seducing the lady of the mansion… who quite likes slumming it with a policeman."

She resisted the urge to note that in the Victorian era, *slumming* referred to counterfeiting.

Resisting had less to do with actual thought than with the way Sean's big hands slipped her velvet coat off her shoulders and then went to work on the tiny buttons on her bodice.

He paused to run his fingertips lightly over the top of her breasts, where they swelled over the corset. She gave up on thinking altogether and just felt.

Clyde stopped. Jeremy went right on by him before he realized it, and stopped as well, scootching backwards carefully.

"What is it?" Jeremy asked.

Clyde jerked his head, indicating forward. "There it is." As if Jeremy couldn't see it.

Dusk had fallen. The air was the midnight blue of twilight, when everything seemed possible. Around them, the wind was the only sound. The snow still tumbled down.

In the gloom, the house loomed before them like something not out of a bucolic Christmas movie. Clyde had expected to see some lights on, even after the staff left, but the entire place was menacingly dark. He was glad he had a Maglite in his backpack.

"Whoo-ee," Jeremy said. "Crazy-lookin' place, ain't it?"

Since the land around Frogmorton House was owned by the museum trust, there was no hunting on the premises, but their usual hunting grounds skirted the area, so they were familiar with its bulk.

Even though hunting season was long past, Clyde had brought his shotgun, just in case. Never know when you might come up against a bear, grumpy at being woken early from its hibernation.

"Guess they went home early," Clyde said. "Better for us, anyway. Won't have to wait."

Jeremy rubbed his hands together, his ski poles dangling from straps around his wrists. "Can't wait to get my hands on some treasure."

Clyde tossed him a silver flask. "I'll drink to that," he said.

❖

Sean moved from the left nipple to the right, drawing it into his mouth, making her arch so he could take more in. The bereft left nipple puckered in the cool air, pressing against the slightly damp linen of her corset cover. He didn't let it get cold for long, though, tweaking it between his thumb and forefinger.

Tit for tat—or was that tit for tit? Brenda pinched his nipples, which stood out dark behind the not very Victorian, but eminently practical white t-shirt he wore under his uniform.

True to his word, he was taking his time. Her dress was open to the waist, but he decided he liked the lace-trimmed corset cover and had worked her breasts above the corset without taking it off. And while her skirt was pushed up, showing off her silk drawers—she was perched on the kitchen counter at this point, with her legs wrapped around Sean's waist—he wasn't rushing to get the drawers or his pants off, either. (Although, thank goodness, he'd taken off his gun belt—that had been a little distracting.) Never mind that he was hard as a steel rod, threatening to pop the fly buttons on his trousers, and never mind that her drawers were so drenched in the crotch that they must be transparent, or that they were both trembling with want.

When was the last time someone had taken the time to explore her this way? Never, not that she could remember—and Brenda was damn sure she'd remember it.

Remember being this aroused, this sensitized, so much so that Sean's breath on her skin felt like a touch. Remember being this wet and open and needy. Remember her sex pulsing around emptiness, yearning to be filled. Remember reaching for a fly with an achingly hard cock behind it and being turned away with a playful reproach and a passionate kiss.

Her mother always said patience was a virtue.

And in this case, Mom was right—up to a point. But damn, if Sean didn't pick up the pace, she might catch on fire.

"I want to be naked with you," she whispered, running her hand down his chest and taut belly to his fly. One of the relatively few brain cells that wasn't focused on her rising need pointed out that there might be a better location for doing so than where they were. Someplace with soft surfaces and warm blankets. "And not on the kitchen counter, either."

"Spruce Bedroom?"

The master bedroom with the fully made-up bed, very comfortable bed including an impressive, if perpetually dusty, embroidered velvet coverlet and canopy? "Hell yes." The sheets were Irish linen, still sturdy despite their age. And if by chance they destroyed them, well, it would be a shame, but they had an entire closet full of similar sets.

Before she hopped down from the counter, he cupped her mound at last, and that pressure was almost enough to drive her over the edge.

Almost. Not quite. "Please?" she moaned, feeling ridiculous to beg but needing it so badly that she didn't care.

His grin grew. He looked like a fox, or maybe it was just foxy. Delicious, in any case. "I like hearing you beg."

Brenda writhed under his hand. "Please. Pleasepleasepleaseplease…"

He started circling his fingers, slowly but with just the right pressure. "Yeah. That's it. Perfect…so close…"

She took a deep breath, sensing that within seconds she'd need it to scream.

And in that instant of silence, they heard the distant sound of shattering glass.

She might have thought she imagined it, except that it was followed immediately by the shrill droning of the burglar alarm.

❖

Jeremy jumped back as if the house had bitten him. He started to run—and promptly fell down because in his panic, he forgot he was wearing snowshoes. It would have been hysterical except for the alarm screaming at them.

"Clyde! There's an alarm!"

"Asshole. Of course there's an alarm. And you just tripped it by breaking the window."

"Then how were we going to get in?"

Honestly, he'd been hoping that there wouldn't actually be an alarm, but he wasn't about to admit that. But he did have a plan. He reached into his pocket. "I have instructions! How to disarm an alarm system."

"Really? Where'd you find that?" In the last of the fading light, Jeremy finally looked interested.

"On the Internet. You can find all kinds of shit on the Internet." It occurred to him belatedly that he'd never tried them out and they might be just as fake as the boobs on a porn site.

What the hell. The window was broken anyway, the alarm was going off. Might as well just crawl in the window the old-fashioned way. If the alarm was sending a message to the police station, well, the cops couldn't get there before morning at least, and by then they'd be long gone. They could just ignore the noise.

He propped his rifle against the wall and leaned down to remove his snowshoes. Then he shimmied out of his backpack and tossed it inside before clambering in after it.

It was, of course, pitch black inside, but he got the flashlight on just as Jeremy fell through the window and landed with an audible thump.

"Just a broken window," Brenda said, hoping Sean would put any quiver in her voice or shake in her hands down to sexual frustration.

Which was definitely part of it. Whatever this emergency was, the timing couldn't have been much worse. Although maybe it wasn't all bad. She'd probably feel even more anxious if every nerve in her body wasn't too busy screaming for relief to register the influx of fight-or-flight hormones.

"It's really windy," she added. "Probably a branch or a roof slate or something blew through." She was buttoning every third button of her bodice as she spoke. Getting them all would take way too long, but she'd be damned if she'd face down an intruder—or even deal with a simple, drafty, broken window—with her tits hanging out.

"Let's hope." Sean fastened the gun belt around his hips, grabbed his big flashlight, then gave her one last quick, hard kiss. "You stay here. I'll go check."

"No way. I'm going with you."

"I'm the security guard. It's my job."

"And it's my museum, dammit."

"Your museum?" He glared at her, his thick eyebrows drawing together. He did *fierce* awfully well for someone with such a gorgeous smile. But not well enough to make her back down.

"I'm responsible to the board for anything that happens…and I know this place like the back of my hand. Better than you do." She took a deep breath and decided to admit to the truth. "And if I have to sit here alone, I'll go nuts. I'll leave any tackling of burglars up to the person with combat training, but I can't just sit here."

Sean nodded. "Good points, all of them. Let's go." He headed for the main door.

She shook her head as she grabbed the candelabrum. "Servant's hallway. If there's anyone in the front rooms, we can surprise them coming that way. And shut off the damn alarm while we're at it."

They'd made it to the front of the house. Clyde poked his head in one room, but it was being used as an office, and he didn't see his target.

"What are we looking for again?" Jeremy asked.

Something resembling a brain in your head. Clyde gritted his teeth. "My grandmother's writing desk. You remember, the one that used to be under the window in her living room."

"I don't remember," Jeremy said, as if he hadn't sat in that living room a million times eating Clyde's grandmother's homemade peanut-butter thumbprint cookies like he was one of those starving kids from Africa.

"It was kind of a reddish wood, with carving along the front—roses or something. Stood about this high." Clyde held out his hand, palm down. "She usually had a vase of fresh flowers on it, and a framed photo of my grandfather."

Jeremy squinted. "Okay," he said finally, reluctantly, as if he maybe didn't really remember but he didn't want Clyde to get angry.

At Christmas a few years ago, Grandma had gotten tipsy on eggnog and told Clyde something very, very important.

She'd told him the desk contained a special treasure.

When he'd asked what sort of treasure, she'd smiled a smile he'd never seen before (and even though he couldn't quite explain why, it kind of squicked him out) and patted him on the head and told him he'd understand one day. And Clyde had taken that to mean that she'd be giving the treasure to him.

Then she'd upped and croaked and left everything to Frogmorton House, including the writing desk—which, as far as he was concerned, they could keep—and the treasure she'd promised him.

"We'll split up," he said, because Jeremy had done one thing right and remembered to bring a flashlight of his own. "You go upstairs; I'll look down here. Look for anything that looks like the desk I described. We'll meet back here in—" he checked his watch "—fifteen minutes."

He felt compelled to add, "Don't break anything else. Don't even touch anything," as Jeremy clomped towards the stairs.

He shone his own flashlight left and right. Right seemed to be the dining room, and he doubted the desk would be in there. Left, then.

At the top of the stairs, he heard a bang and an "Owdammit!" from Jeremy. Then Jeremy's faint voice wafted down, "S'okay! Didn't break anything!"

Clyde went left.

❖

As Sean fiddled with the alarm box, Brenda leaned out the broken window, careful not to brush against a fragment of glass. "They came on snowshoes," she announced. "Two pairs. There's a rifle out here, too."

"Good to know they didn't bring it inside," Sean commented into the blissful silence left when the ringing stopped.

"They could have another one," Brenda said. She stepped back, her shoes crunching on the glass. She was pretty sure the window hadn't been an original, but she was still pissed off that the slobs had broken it.

"We'll cross that bridge when we come to it."

They continued on. At the end of the servants' hallway, in the dining room, Sean signaled a halt.

Brenda halted all right. She felt a little ridiculous with her long gown and her candelabrum, like the ditzy heroine of a vampire movie.

At least she wasn't going to make the ditzy-vampire-movie heroine mistake and run off on her own. Face it, neither the master's in history nor the certificate program in non-profit management had covered How to Deal With Intruders.

"Flashlight," Sean whispered, making almost no sound at all. She had to lean in to hear him, which brought back the scent of—oh God, *herself* on his fingertips. The reminder of her arousal made her clit tremble again.

"What was that?" she whispered back, sure she'd heard something.

"Voices. Couldn't hear what they said. I think you're right: there's two of them."

"Good odds," Brenda said, even though she wasn't sure she was a match for one of them. She'd been desperately trying to remember the self-defense course she'd taken in college. That had been a long time ago, and she and her friends had spent most of the time ogling the instructor.

Why hadn't she paid attention? Nobody said she'd actually *need* that information being a curator.

"Stay behind me," Sean said. In any other circumstances she would have gladly done so just to look at his ass, but now she actually paid attention to the matter at hand.

They crept through the dining room and entered the foyer just in time to see a faint light moving away from them, towards the sitting room and library.

Sean had loosened his jacket so he had easier access to his gun, but he left it in its holster. Brenda hoped he wouldn't have to use it.

She was appalled that someone would break in. Yes, the place was brimming with antiques, but most of it was heavy furniture. The knickknacks were all discretely marked and everything, down the silver, was obsessively categorized and photographed. If the thieves tried to sell anything, they'd get caught, no question about it.

Sheer mindless vandalism, then? It wasn't out of the question, but it didn't make a whole lot of sense. They usually had problems on the 4th of July or around graduation time, when stupid kids got stupid drunk and came up with stupid plans.

Surely nobody was stupid (or drunk) enough to want to come out here in the middle of winter, on *snowshoes,* just to smash things up.

The snowshoes, Brenda decided, meant they'd planned this.

That made her even madder. She felt like a mother partridge puffing up to protect her young.

Although didn't mother partridges pretend they were wounded to draw predators away from their chicks? Might not be a bad strategy here, if it came to be needed.

Following Sean, she was impressed at how smoothly he slipped through the rooms. Victorian decorating called for a lot of furniture to be jammed into small spaces—and don't even mention the knickknacks and lace and frippery. It was all utterly lush and romantic, but it made it hard to walk in a straight line.

Sean moved like a panther, lean and silent. And Brenda knew where every stick of furniture was placed better than she knew her own apartment.

The man (she assumed it was a man) they followed, on the other hand, had neither of their skills. He wasn't crashing into things, at least, but he was moving slowly and bumping into the occasional side table, chinking the curios and ornaments against each other.

At this rate, they could have followed him blindfolded, just from the noises he was making.

They caught up with him easily in the vaguely leather-scented library, which had looped them around almost back to the foyer. Brenda had the vague sense that they could have just waited for the perp to come back to them, but it was too late to contemplate that now.

"Freeze!" Sean shouted.

Brenda jumped. She pressed a hand to her pounding chest as the thief whirled and his hand shot into the air. His flashlight made crazy patterns on the ceiling.

"Don't shoot!" he said.

"What are you doing here?" Sean demanded, training his own flashlight on the thief's face.

Wait a minute…. Brenda stepped from behind Sean, squinting in the gloom.

"*Clyde?*" she said. "Clyde Whitney, is that you?"

Clyde started to bring his hands down, but Sean's sharp "Hey!" made him re-think that. "Yes ma'am, it is."

"What in God's name are you *doing* here?"

Sean shot her a look that clearly said, *Who's in charge here?*, but she ignored him. The situation was back in her territory now.

"It's Clyde Whitney," she told him. "His grandmother left Frogmorton her things when she passed. I know him from when I subbed at the high school. You graduated two years ago, isn't that right, Clyde?"

"Yes ma'am."

"So why *are* you here?"

"The things my grandmother gave you," he said. "She wasn't supposed to give you everything. The treasure was supposed to be mine."

Treasure? "What treasure?"

"In the writing desk. She *told* me."

"I'm sorry, Clyde, but I think she was mistaken. She gave us a detailed listing of everything she was donating, and she didn't say anything about something being in the desk."

Clyde let his hands drop, not threateningly, but as if he'd forgotten he'd been caught. "But—"

And that's when they heard the voice behind them. "Clyde, I think I found it! It's in the big bedroo—Oh, crap."

The speaker loomed right behind Brenda. Without thinking, she turned and nailed the stalker across the head with the heavy silver candelabrum.

The young man blinked once, then crumpled to the floor.

Most of the candles went out, but one dislodged and went flying. With a shriek, Brenda dove after it, stomping out the flame before it caught anything alight. She winced at the thought of wax on the hardwood floor, but she knew several different secrets to removing it.

Then, in the near-darkness, she ran her hands over the candelabrum to check for any dents or nicks. It may have been an everyday one, but it was still a part of Frogmorton House.

"Nice job," Sean said, admiration in his voice.

She straightened her coat. "Thank you."

Sean gestured to Clyde. "Come on."

Clyde's eyes widened. "Where are we going?"

"You two can cool your heels in the basement until morning. The cops won't be able to get here 'til tomorrow, and we can't let you go off tramping around the countryside."

"What about my treasure?"

"There's *no* treasure," Brenda said.

"But—"

"But we'll check the writing desk, just in case. Okay?"

"Okay." Clyde's shoulder's drooped.

Sean made Clyde help him lug the half-conscious and moaning Jeremy to the basement. Brenda grabbed an armful of wool blankets from the linen closet. It would be chilly down there, but they wouldn't come near to freezing to death. Then she closed the door with more force than was strictly necessary, and firmly turned the key.

In the light of the freshly burning candelabrum, Brenda found the secret compartment in the back of the writing desk within minutes. Sean whistled his admiration.

"I never thought to check for a false back," she said. "Hello, what have we here?"

She drew out a packet of papers, tied with a red ribbon and smelling of cedar and lavender.

She examined the envelopes. "They're letters," she said. "From Mr. Whitney to Mrs. Whitney, and vice versa."

"Love letters?" Sean said with a chuckle. "Grandma's secret treasure was her love letters? Aw, that's sweet." Then he smiled, and it wasn't the roguish, flirty grin that Brenda had come to lust after. It was a softer smile, still sexy as hell, but almost…wistful.

So, naughty Sean was a closet romantic? Brenda told herself firmly it was too soon to obsess about the ramifications of *that* bit of information—although they could be very nice ramifications—and filed the knowledge away for future reference.

She'd meant to take a quick glance at the letters, then put them away and get back to more interesting matters, but the first few lines she read intrigued her so much that she kept reading, not even bothering to sit down.

"Oh my. Not just love letters. *Steamy* love letters. Listen to this." She scanned the letter until she found the passage that had caught her eye.

"'I miss you. All of you: your eyes, your laugh, your toes, that mole on the back of your leg, your beautiful breasts, your round little bottom, and every other bit of you. But right now, I really miss being inside you, feeling you so tight and wet and hot around me. When I get home, I'm going to kiss every inch of you, from your forehead to your cute painted toes'—hmm, seems Mr. Whitney was

a bit of a foot fetishist—'and then I'm going to lick you until you beg to fuck me. But I don't just want to fuck you. I want to make love to you. I want to make love to you so we can't tell where I end and you begin.'"

Brenda looked up. Sean's eyes were shining, dark blue and wide.

"Hot stuff," he said. "As long as I don't think about Mrs. Whitney playing bridge with my grandmother, at least."

"Let's not go there, okay?" Brenda laughed. "God, Clyde would die, knowing we're reading his sweet old grandparents' smutty letters. Hell, knowing his grandparents *wrote* smutty letters."

Brenda shuffled through the papers. "Here's another good one. 'I know I'll be home in a week. I may even get home before this letter gets to you. But a week's too long. When I'm alone in my hotel room, I take out my cock and play with it, trying to pretend you're touching me instead, imagining your hands, your lips, your sweet, greedy cunt. And I come. Oh, do I come. But even while I'm coming, all I can think about is how much better it is when I'm making you cry out and tighten around my cock. Do you touch yourself and think of me? I'm sure you do, because you're a naughty girl and that's part of why I love you so much, but write to me about it. That way, the next time I travel, I can read it and imagine you lying in the dark touching yourself and imagining it's me.'"

"Did she?" Sean asked.

"If he was half as sexy as he sounds in these letters, I bet she did. It looks like he traveled a lot on business."

"I mean, did she write him about it?" Sean had moved in behind her now and was reading over her shoulder while he unbuttoned her dress.

Brenda leaned back against him as she flipped through the packet. "Found it! 'You want to hear how I keep from going crazy while you're away? You want to know how much I miss you? I miss you so much that my fingers aren't enough sometimes. I can make myself feel good that way, but it's not the same without you inside me. I hope they're feeding you well in Indianapolis, because you're going to need your strength when you get back here.'"

"Lucky man. I bet he got a warm welcome home."

Sean pushed against her as he spoke. Even through her layers of skirt, Brenda could feel how hard he was.

It pretty much matched how wet she was getting again, between the steamy letters and Sean's hot body pressed against hers and the memory of their play down in the kitchen.

"It gets better. It got so bad that today I went to the market and found a cucumber about the right size. It wasn't the same at all, but filling myself up with something made it easier to think of you inside me. So imagine me so desperate for you that a cucumber looks pretty good. Imagine me pushing that cucumber in and out of me and calling your name and…'"

She stopped. "I actually can't read the rest because…well, it looks like he did imagine it. Often. This letter's pretty beat up."

Sean let out a shuddering breath. "Jesus, that's hot. Just knowing she was so horny and so far away must have made her husband crazy." He pushed her dress off her shoulders, forcing her to set the letters down on the desk so he could work the narrow sleeves down her arms. "Have you ever been that horny?"

She turned in his embrace, letting the dress slither off her hips as she did. "Not until tonight. And it's all your fault. Hope you're planning to do something about it."

Another of those rougish grins that made her insides quiver and melt. "I don't know…I kind of like the idea of watching you getting yourself off." He paused just long enough to get her concerned about the evening's plans, then added, "Sometime, if you'd be into it. Not tonight. Tonight I want to be inside you when you come. Want to feel you exploding all over my cock."

Brenda slithered the rest of the way out of the dress and got her petticoats and corset cover off in record time.

Sean stopped her when she was down to corset and drawers. "Let me look at you," he breathed. "Just for a minute. Damn, you look good like that."

She made a show of unpinning her hair, shaking it out so it tumbled around her shoulders. "No fair. It's cold. Besides, I want to see you, too."

"Fair enough." He opened his fly teasingly, one button at a time. The purple head of his cock peeked out the top of his purple briefs.

She couldn't resist. She sank to her knees and kissed it before working the trousers and underwear down.

Enough teasing. Enough playing. She wrapped a hand around the base of his cock and took him in her mouth.

Salty and delicious and just the right size, thick and meaty. Perfect to suck and even better to fuck.

Sean groaned as she moved her lips up and down his shaft. God, she wanted this moving inside her, filling her, making her scream. She wanted to milk him so he exploded inside her, wanted to come and come and come on this delicious cock, but damn, he tasted so good it was hard to resist continuing to suck.

He was the one, in the end, who pulled away. "Let me help you with the corset," he said huskily, "and get on the bed. I want to be in you."

She was already turning around so he could reach the laces, even as she teased, "I thought you liked the corset."

"I do, but I want to feel you. See you. The corset's sexy, but you're gorgeous."

It wasn't necessarily easier having him help with the corset—she'd gotten good at managing on her own and it seemed to be new to him—but it was certainly more fun.

Onto the bed then, with a mountain of covers pulled over them, the linen sheet cool underneath her and Sean lying over her. Like Mr. Whitney had promised his bride, he kissed his way down her body—suckling her nipples until she moaned and rolled her hips with need, exclaiming over the corset marks on her hips and belly and licking them "to make them better."

He reached the reddish curls of her mound, buried his face there, took a deep breath as if enjoying the bouquet of a fine wine. Brenda made a small noise, half crazy with arousal, and put her hand on his head.

She didn't think he'd needed the hint, but he certainly took it.

Brenda didn't have time to enjoy a full demonstration of Sean's oral skills, though—after the long tease and the hot letters, a few flicks of his tongue were all it took to send her into convulsions of pleasure.

There was a brief interruption while Sean fished a condom out of his wallet. (She was amused—and a little relieved—to catch him checking the expiration date on the packet. He might be sexy as hell and a big-time flirt, but he hadn't needed the "just in case condom" in a while.) Even with the interruption, she was still twitching with aftershocks when he repositioned himself between her legs, the head of his cock pressing against her pussy.

He'd said he enjoyed hearing her beg, hearing her admit just how much she wanted him. And since she did want him, and the hotter she made him, the hotter she got, and so on, she opened her legs a little wider, rolled her pelvis, looked into those amazing blue eyes, and whispered, "Please. Please fuck me."

"Sure you wouldn't rather have a cucumber?" He pressed against her as he said that, teasing at her already sensitized clit with his head.

She smacked him on the ass. To her surprise, the yelp he let out sounded awfully happy. "Sounds like you liked that."

He shook his head, a bemused look on his face. "I think I did. Who knew? We'll have to talk about that. Later. Much later."

He pushed into her slick pussy, just the head at first, giving her a few seconds to appreciate how thick he was, how delicious he felt there, how much she wanted to feel more.

Wonderful as the long teasing had been, she'd have to be superhuman to be patient any longer. She raised her hips, grabbed his ass, said "Now," and gave him a push all at once.

"The lady desires something?" he purred, and slid the rest of the way in.

He froze, buried to the hilt inside her. His eyes widened, looking impossibly bluer in the flickering candle light. His mouth opened. He looked like he was striving to make the perfect clever, wicked remark, but couldn't find words.

Then he started to move.

Oh God, did he start to move.

He was like the blustery weather outside, fierce and elemental and inexorable. He was howling like the storm and cutting through all her defenses like the wind cut through the walls. He was wild and dangerous and beautiful as the snow. But he wasn't cold. In the freezing room, he was fire, and she was burning with him.

After his earlier delicacy and restraint, he was letting himself go crazy now. Each stroke jarred her to the core, but in the most pleasurable way, raising her up off the bed and throwing her down again. Each stroke touched someplace new, someplace wonderful, sending another wave of icy-hot ecstasy out to drown her. The storm was raging and she was raging, gouging at his back and ass with her nails, urging him to fuck even harder even though if he did he'd break her in two or at least break the antique bed.

She came, and it didn't end. Not multiple orgasms, because that implied stopping at some point and then starting again. This was one long spiral of pleasure, rising higher and higher without respite, without conclusion.

It was almost too much, but at the same time it wasn't enough.

It wasn't enough until Sean's face, already red, contorted to something beautiful but scarcely human, some god or nature spirit, maybe the face of the storm itself. "Yes! Brenda…" he cried and she almost didn't recognize her own name, but she recognized the way his muscles clenched and released, the way that even with the condom between them he seemed to surge into her.

They fell asleep tangled in each other and woke to early light peeking between the velvet drapes. Brenda crawled reluctantly away from Sean's warmth, wrapping herself in her velvet coat, to look out onto the white world. The snow had finally stopped, but it didn't look like they'd be going anywhere for a while.

Not that she minded (although she'd be happy when the police could come out and take charge of the two idiots in the basement—maybe she should toss them some bagels). Sure, the house was chilly, but she suspected she and Sean could find ways to keep warm. Something about watching her play with herself, for one, and something about spanking him, for another. They could probably make the spanking go both ways, because she was curious about being on the receiving end herself. So many possibilities—and for once, so much time.

And now, in the light, they could really see each other.

Brenda crawled back under the covers, snuggled close to him and kissed him on the shoulder. "Wake up, sleepyhead."

"I was awake. I was just about to roll over and grab you when you got up."

"It's a beautiful, cold, snow-covered day and it looks like we're stuck with each other."

"Aw, damn. Whatever shall we do?" He rolled over and grabbed her, and for a few glorious minutes there was nothing but his body, his mouth, and his clever hands.

Then he stopped, pushed himself up on his arms and looked down at her. "Brenda, I have a confession to make."

She froze. She couldn't tell if he was serious or not, couldn't read the dense blue velvet of his eyes, couldn't read what lay behind the sudden absence of his usual grin.

The silence lasted longer than she liked. Finally he spoke. "I applied for the job just knowing it was for a security guard."

Brenda nodded. It had been a blind ad; she knew because she'd written it, hoping to get at least a few applicants who weren't dreamy kids who just wanted to work at the "castle" and would fall apart at the first sign of a real problem.

"But I took it because of you."

Gulp.

"I had another offer, from a resort out by Blue Mountain Lake. Paid better and I could have lived onsite. But after I saw you again at the interview, I knew I'd have to take this job and then ask you out like I didn't have the nerve to do in high school."

"I refuse to believe you pined for me since high school."

The roguish grin came back. "Not exactly. But you intrigued me, and I thought about you. Wished I could go back in time with what I'd learned since then and sweep you off your feet—or at least really get to know you. So when I got a chance, I took it. Plus you grew up really nicely."

"You too." Brenda breathed an inner sigh of relief. "At least we both had ulterior motives. So I don't have to worry about a sexual harassment lawsuit?"

A snort. "No way. We're both adults, and we're *definitely* consenting. But, I do hope you don't mind if I ask my boss for sex every chance I get."

Brenda grinned. "Your boss will love that, especially if it means she can do the ordering around every now and then." She imagined making him go

down on her, in his butler's outfit, under her formal hostess gown, and all but moaned. "So what kind of, ah, duties do you want to perform this morning?"

He stretched. "I'm not sure yet. So many possibilities. I know—why don't you grab those treasure letters and we'll see if we find anything inspirational?"

Copyright © 2008, 2018 by Sophie Mouette.

Alia Mahmud has loved reading and writing since she was a child and is especially interested in the power of storytelling. She is a big fan of comic books and video games, and practices short-form improv on a regular basis. Though she often tries to seem cool and tomboy-ish, she has a secret sappy romantic side that she is happy to now share with you.

A FIERY RECEPTION

by Alia Mahmud

I gripped tightly as the fire engine swerved around the corner and screeched to a stop. In front of us, flames danced in the windows of a small apartment building. The fire chief spoke with the owner as we pulled out the hoses and began trying to douse the fire. After we had the hoses trained directly on the burning building, the chief gestured for me and a couple of other firefighters to search for anyone trapped inside.

We charged inside and divvied up the apartment building. I took the stairs two at a time to meet the firestorm head-on. Sweat drenched my body under my thick flame-retardant overcoat as the flames burned all around me. Axe in hand, I began to search the rooms, occasionally calling out, asking for responses. I had cleared most of the floor when I heard a faint moaning from a nearby collapsing doorway. Peering through the smoke, I saw no one. I was about to move to the next doorway to search when I saw a hand waving near the floor.

I rushed over and found a woman trapped underneath the rubble. I recognized her as the cute girl who went jogging past the fire station every day. I had always been too nervous to approach her, but now was not the time for nerves.

"I'm here," I told her, as I moved burning debris to reach her. "Can you move at all?"

"I…don't think so. My legs…" The woman looked at me, grimacing as she tried to pull her legs free.

"Alright, don't move. Let me see what I can do."

I knelt beside her to get a better view. It was bad. A large wooden beam had fallen over both of her legs. If she were lucky, she would end up with a broken bone or two. I dropped my axe and pushed on the beam, but it would not budge. I looked at the

woman, who stared at me in terror. I had to think of something else.

"Hold still," I commanded.

She nodded anxiously, raising her hands up to clutch a wriggling bulge in her sweater as I picked up my axe and stood. Before the woman could register what I was about to do, I swung my axe down on the beam. The wood splintered, but still held firm. I swung at it again, sending more splinters into the air. Just one more hit. I swung down with all of my might, and the beam split with a satisfying *crack*.

I slid the axe in my belt and pushed the shorter piece aside with my foot. Then I was able to lift the other half up and prop it against a pile of rubble. I pulled the woman free and lifted her up. She wrapped her arms around my neck and I held her close as I made my way through the apartment building. I leapt down the stairs and out the door just as a piece of the ceiling collapsed behind us.

I carried the woman away from the building. Now that the danger was behind us, I could feel her arms pull me closer. I held her tightly before laying her down on a ready-waiting ambulance stretcher.

She looked up at me, and for the first time I was struck by her eyes. I had never seen them up close before. They were beautiful, and the world seemed to slow down around us.

She pulled me closer to her and gently kissed me. "Thanks for saving me," she smiled.

I was about to tell her it was my pleasure when her sweater started moving again. I looked down, confused, as she coaxed a little kitten out of it.

She must have seen my expression. "She's only nine weeks old. She would never have made it."

"What's her name?" I asked.

She held up the squirming orange bundle of fur. "I hadn't named her yet…but now I'm thinking… Fireball?"

I grinned. "I love it."

I heard my captain call me. Time to get back to the fire. I hesitated, trying to think of something to say.

Luckily, she beat me to it. "Do I have to start a fire if I want to see you again?" she asked, her eyes twinkling.

I laughed, then reached down to rub the now-purring kitten under her chin. "Well, we *are* sometimes called to rescue cats from trees."

"I'll keep that in mind," she giggled.

I smiled. "Please do."

Petronella Glover is a multi-genre author whose work has been translated into a dozen languages, including the Catalonian Romance language, where she has won two awards for Best Translated Story. A little quirky, very geeky, and unabashedly romantic, she hopes to one day visit the City of Love, find a bustling café where she can sample their hot chocolate and write her first New York Times *bestseller. You can find out more about her at* www.petronellaglover.com.

TO REACH FOR THE STARS

by Petronella Glover

I sat behind the signing table, looking at the next person in the line and plastered a smile on my face. "Hello there"—I glanced down at the child's ComicCon name badge—"Teretha. I love your spacesuit!"

The young girl beamed, visible through her handmade helmet. "Hi! Are you really an astronaut?"

I pointed to my mission patch on my upper arm. "This proves that I was on the International Space Station two years ago. I'll be rocketing back there again next month."

Teretha's eyebrows furrowed together. "But I get badges like that in Girl Scouts."

"Teretha!" her mother chastised.

I laughed. "No worries. It *is* a valid point." I pointed to the NASA badge on the front of my blue jumpsuit. "This uniform proves I work for NASA, who sent man to the moon."

I was waiting for her to say she's seen cosplayers dressed like me, too. But if anything, her eyebrows furrowed even tighter. "Not girls?"

I flushed, glancing at her mother awkwardly. "I should have said 'sent humans to the moon.'"

The girl tilted her head sideways, curious. "How many girls have been to the moon?"

I grimaced. "No woman has landed on the moon—yet." I picked up a NASA sticker, handing it to her. "But that only means you can be the first!"

Her eyes widened, twinkling happily. "That would be a-may-zing!"

I looked over at her mom to see her nod appreciatively. *Phew.* "Would you like a photo?" I asked the girl, aware the people waiting behind her were starting to get antsy.

"Of what?" she asked, frowning.

I forgot how literal children are. "Of me…I mean, of you *with* me."

She nodded her head up and down rapidly, and I gestured for her to come around the signing table. While her mom pulled out her cellphone to take a photo, I saw the most gorgeous specimen of man stride up to her, cosplaying as Captain America.

"Would you like me to take the photo for you, ma'am, so you can also be in the shot?" he asked, with the most pleasing lilt to his tenor voice.

"That would be lovely," she responded, handing the phone to him.

She darted around the table, and all three of us posed for the photo. I tried to focus on the phone, so it didn't look like I was appearing askance in the final still, but my gaze was drawn to the cosplayer's costume. In particular to how snugly the material hugged his well-formed biceps. I was not usually the one to judge a guy on physique alone, but this particular Captain actually could make America great again, just by being a poster boy for what Goodness *looked* like. Even a fictional Superhero was better than the reality that was currently leading the government.

"Moment captured," he drawled, charismatically, and I wondered how comfortable his costume was; it looked like he'd been poured into it. He reached forward to hand the phone back to the mother, then pivoted towards me.

I started when his cerulean gaze connected with my olive one, trying to put my words into a coherent sentence. "Thanks for the assist."

He inclined his head. "My first time meeting an astronaut." He reached his hand out to me. "A pleasure."

My heart did this weird sort of flip-flop as I clasped his warm hand in mine. "The pleasure is all mine." Literally.

Something flashed in his eyes, and it was if he froze for a second. Then he looked down at my name tag, a smile tugging his lips. "How appropriate."

Confused, I thanked the man, and it was as if we were caught in this weird limbo, hands still clasped.

An awkward "Ahem" from a con-goer in line bought me back to the present. I let go of the cosplayers hand, turned to hug the girl, and reluctantly turned to the next fan in line, who had a copy of my non-fiction book to be signed.

I spotted the cosplayer several other times during the first day of the Port Hamilton Military Comic-Con. Not only because of his Captain America costume, which did make him stand out but because his presence literally caused waves.

People parted like the sea as he passed by them in the Dealer's Room, his signature shield slung nonchalantly over his back while he looked at science fiction books, comics and other assorted geekery for sale. Some attendees stopped him to talk or ask for a photo with him. Usually they were women or other Avengers cosplayers, but it was sweet to notice that a surprising amount of army members—either wearing their uniform, or sporting a distinctive buzz cut—were also saluting him before they talked to him, or even as he simply walked passed them.

I had not expected the military to respond to him as if he really was Captain America: an army recruit who became a superhero through an experiment and then worked his way up to the rank of (you guessed it) captain. But these men in uniform were obviously here because they were fans of the science fiction and fantasy genre. Maybe they often saluted cosplayers who were representing service men and women.

I shrugged, dragged my gaze away from him before it could slide down and take note, again, of his gorgeous backside and the sexy line of his long tightly-muscled thighs, and started my way over to the exit doors on the other side of the large room. I was hungry (in more ways than one), and food vendors lay awaiting my appetite in the courtyard outside the old fort.

I tried to focus my mind on my commitments as an official guest of the con and a representative for NASA and pulled out my program excerpt to see where I was expected next. Not seeing any more items with my name on it, I realized I had finished my official tasks for the day before the masked ball fundraiser. I had just been on the *Conversation with an Astronaut* panel, where a lot of the audience had impressed me with their science-based knowledge behind their questions. There had only been one

Flat Earther in the audience, but the interviewer had done a top job in allowing him the floor to speak when it was his turn, then shutting him down when she realized that he had no question to ask me. He'd just wanted to grandstand about NASA being fake and that the live feeds from the International Space Station were just showing astronauts underwater in front of a green screen on Earth.

If we're underwater, how do we breathe and talk as we "float" through the capsules, idiot? I shook my head, and, reaching the fort exit, I surreptitiously gave my favorite cosplayer one last glance, seeing him spot me and smile, then I pushed the door open and darted out of the building.

Chicken, I chastised myself. I wanted to say hello again, now that I wasn't on the clock, but I didn't know what I would say after that. I have found that most science fiction and fantasy geeks are usually more liberal and enlightened in their thinking than the average human—Flat Earther excluded. That meant the attendees of cons generally made for great conversationalists, even if some of them are a little too obsessed with the fictional worlds they lose themselves in.

But what if we have nothing in common? Better the star-spangled cosplayer remains a spectacular fantasy than a disappointing reality.

I surveyed the food stand options, impressed by the Verrazano-Narrows bridge that dominated the skyline, and made my way to the pizza and pasta vendor to place my order. I just wanted a simple mac'n'cheese, but doubled the order. I needed to sate this appetite growing inside of me.

"Buying enough for two?" a sexy tenor voice behind me drawled, as I was handed my .

I flushed and turned around to see my favorite eye-candy of the ComicCon. "I'm quite hungry," I blurted out, before thinking.

Something glinted in his eyes, somehow softened by the curve of his mouth. "Me too."

I almost licked my lips. *Down boy. He is not a lollipop.* "Have you eaten yet?"

He shook his head, smile widening. "Maybe I can just take a mouthful of yours."

My imagination ran wild at the sexy image his words had caused to, ah…arise in me that had nothing to do with food, an erection threatening to tent out the front of my NASA uniform. "I'm not sure if you have another commitment," I pointed out, "but care to join me for lunch?"

"I'm all yours."

Mmmm, now wasn't that a lovely thought? Emboldened, I reached over to grab two forks instead of one, and a pile of napkins. "Anything else you want?" This time the playful glint was in my eyes, too.

His positively danced. "No, I think you have everything I need."

Hungry butterflies erupted in my stomach. I wasn't sure if I was ready for the presumed implication his words implied. I was still new to being out and considered my biracial Chinese American looks and lithe form to be more bookish than sexy. I'm not sure what made him want to flirt…. Maybe I just imagined there was a double meaning to his words.

We sat down at a picnic table with the food—him straddling the bench, so that he was facing me, and I angled towards him. For the first handful of minutes we just ate in companionable silence, our heads nearly touching as we both leaned forward to spear pasta. Then he told me he had remembered watching me do an EVA outside the International Space Station a couple of years ago:

"I loved the way you talked so calmly and educationally to your captivated audience on Earth as if you were merely replacing a fuel filter on a car and not hanging in the void of Space replacing an intricate part in a delicate science instrument, while wearing cumbersome gloves. Your casual confidence took my breath away." He scooted in a little closer on the bench to spear a couple more noodles with his fork, taking *my* breath away.

"Is the food hot enough?" I couldn't help but ask, as I watched him eat. This time any flirt that could be read in those words was purely unintentional. I was growing nervous again. He was so close now I could feel his warmth.

His eyes darted up to meet mine, as he considered my words and the slight hesitation in my tone carefully. "It's perfect. Truly. Just as it is."

My heart fluttered. I was not sure if he meant this moment was perfect, as in a great start to something new, and I need not worry if it was going well. Or if the "Just as it is" line implied that the moment would not go further than flirting, so I should not be nervous.

Again, he seemed to sense my hesitation. He reached a hand forward and placed it carefully on my mine, which was now clasping the fork a little anxiously. "There is no nee—" He suddenly leaned back, sitting up straighter and looking over my shoulder.

"Captain," came the solicitous greeting from behind me, and I watched as my lunch mate (date?) inclined his head in acknowledgment of their greeting yet dismissed them in the same gesture.

I straightened up to see two guys in full army uniform come into view as they walked passed me, passed us both, on their way to a nearby food truck. Had they saluted him, too? Did he regret being spotted with me, sitting so close?

I looked back over at my Captain America, to see him smiling at me and realized his hand was still firmly wrapped around mine, except now his fingers were stroking mine, back and forth, soothingly.

He had not pulled his hand away from me when they had approached. A good sign.

"Do the military usually salute you, call you captain, when you cosplay as Captain America? Or is this something that is particular to this ComicCon, because it is held on a military base?"

He looked taken aback, then laughed. "I should have realized you wouldn't know. I *am* a Captain in the United States Army, except I promise you I was born in 1982 and not 1920." He managed to look sheepish. "It's one of the reasons why I thought this cosplay would be so amusing; it would combine my geek side with my military side. I am one of the organizers of this ComicCon, so it gives me a little more leeway to express some bona fide geek credentials in a way that could also reflect the sacrifice and heroism of the American military."

Oh boy. No wonder I found him appealing. There was something about a man in uniform—not just how they look, but the way they carry themselves—that I have always found incredibly sexy.

An alarm went off, and the captain's hand left mine as he raised it to look at his watch, pressing a button on the side to turn the incessant squeal off. "Ah, it's nearly thirteen hundred. I have to go moderate a panel with the Gotham stars, Sean Pertwee and David Mazous."

I should have been starstruck by the names, but I was tripping over my inherent shyness, trying to

work out how to tell him I would love to not just see him again at a distance, but talk to him more.

"Tonight? At the masked ball?" the captain asked as if reading my mind. He stood up, swinging his leg over the bench.

"I'll be there," I told him, cocking my head to the side as I looked up at him. "Kinda can't avoid it. I am one of the guests of honor."

"Ah, yes. Your dance card will be quite full. Save me one?" And with that, he departed before I could answer.

I thanked the con liaison who had helped me with all the latches, zips and clasps on my outfit and looked down at myself and grimaced. Why did I think it would be smart to requisition one of the 1960's spacesuits from the Johnson Space Center to wear to the masked ball? I looked so…chunky…in this puffy monstrosity.

No, my mind informed my heart, *you look like you stepped out of the past. An astronaut cosplaying another astronaut who had actually walked on the moon is the pinnacle of cool at a SF cosplayers ball.*

"Is that a real spacesuit?" I was asked by several people in masks, the minute I walked into the vast hall.

I nodded, letting one person touch it, which then amounted to another dozen or so hands stroking the musty smelling garment.

"I can't believe this suit has actually been to space," one pimpled teen quipped, as he traced the insignia on my arm.

"So has its wearer," came the voice behind me, a lovely tenor drawl I was beginning to love. "But we can't all start petting him, too. How about we leave his suit alone, eh?"

As soon as my fans looked up to see who had spoken, half of them immediately snapped to attention, the rest—the non-military—managed to look sheepish.

I turned to see the captain and all-but-swooned He was in his full-dress uniform, the only nod to his recent cosplay as Captain America in the superhero-themed mask he wore. Gods, he was handsome. And oh so distinguished.

I felt more discombobulated by the minute, my hand plucking nervously at my ill-fitting suit.

If he noted my awkwardness, he didn't show any sign. "I have to go open the ball, and make sure I have introduced and greeted all I need to, but I'll find you as soon as I'm done."

I nodded, spending the rest of the hour trying to recapture my usual confidence. We had talked (flirted?) so easily earlier today. Why did I get nervous again?

I spent some time talking to some of the author guests at the event, one who was picking my brain for an astronaut-centered novel, until a masked, and very beautiful, Wonder Woman came up to me.

"Can I have this dance?" she asked.

I inclined my head, and attempted as courtly a bow as I could, given the spacesuit. "Teretha's mom, right?"

She laughed. "I was wondering if you would recognize me."

"How could I not?" I flirted platonically, pulling her into my arms. "I recognized a superhero in plain clothes, earlier today. You're just showing your true colors now."

We started a formal waltz, and I was relieved to realize I still remembered the steps. *One two three, one two three....*

"Not bad, Spaceman."

I glanced aside to see the captain standing at the edge of the dance floor, and nearly faltered. What is it about that confounding man that reverted me to an awkward teen with his first crush?

My crush turned to Wonder Woman. "Do you mind if I cut in?"

She looked between him and me, and stepped back, beaming. "Of course not. I need to check on my daughter anyway."

I raised her hand to my lips and kissed it, then let her go, turning back to the captain. Oh god. What do I do now? Who leads?

That question was answered within seconds as the captain stepped forward and held out his hand to me, pulling me into a waltz that was as scary as it was amazing. I had always been in the lead before now, but this charismatic man was sweeping me around the floor with an expertise that was dizzying, and so darn sexy. I wanted him.

"You make me want to reach for the stars," he murmured into my ear when the music had slowed to a stop.

"The suit has that effect on people," I replied, my heart thudding.

"No," he replied as he pulled back to look at me. His expression was earnest. "*You* do."

This time it was I who ducked my head as I blushed, letting my forehead rest on his shoulder. He pulled me a little closer, and I didn't care who was watching. His arms felt so good around me.

We stood that way for a long moment until the rest of the world intruded. Once again, I heard people talking, laughing, enjoying each other's company. The clang of champagne glasses rang in the air.

The captain pulled back, and I felt him stiffen a little—grow more formal.

Had I misread things and overstepped?

I retreated, a little hastily, but he did not let go. His arm slid down to grasp my hand. "Want to get out of here?" he asked, voice husky.

Yes!

I wasn't sure if I said anything out loud, but suddenly we were making our way through the people, his tall stature parting the crowd as I followed him, my hand still clasped in his. We left the way we entered, but before I could work out where we were going, he had pulled me down several stone hallways that were a hallmark of the old fort, the ceilings so low that he had to duck through many of the doorways.

Before long he had pulled me into a room that looked like an office—his office?—and he closed the door behind us.

He let go of my hand as I walked around the room, taking note of the military honors, dinosaur fossils—all impeccably labeled—and the statue of Captain America. Yep, his office.

I turned to see him watching me, a warmth in his eyes that intrigued me. I backed up until my thighs hit his ornate wooden desk and leaned on it. His move.

He took off his mask and walked forward until he reached me, then paused. I could see the effort he made to restrain himself, which I had first misread as a formality.

"May I?" he asked simply.

I nodded, and he swooped in, capturing my mouth with his. The kiss started out soft, then deepened until I felt the beginning of his five o'clock shadow rasp against mine. I gasped, and his hand slid up to cup my face, then slide back to the nape of my neck.

I tugged him closer, resting my hands on his hips as he angled my head and slid his tongue along my lips, asking, questing. I opened my mouth to feel him surge in as I moaned, leaning in so I could feel his dress uniform buckles scrape across my suit, catching on something.

We halted, and I laughed. His eyes were sparkling as I looked down to unhook his buckle, careful not to damage the fifty-plus-year-old suit.

When it was free, he pulled back to study me, raising an eyebrow. "Perhaps we should get you out of that contraption before we damage it?"

He had meant the words practically, somewhat playfully, but the thought of stripping in front of him soon hit us both, the twinkle in his eyes turning into a smolder.

"You will have to help me," I told him, my voice catching a little.

His hands were back on me within an instant, as I instructed him on how to unlatch this clasp and uncouple that other one. With much laughter and more than a little grunt work, we finally got me free of the spacesuit, and I was in my undershirt and boxers and back in his arms.

This time it was I who reached up to kiss him. Tugging him forward by his lapels, I nipped at his bottom lip and was rewarded by his moan and a deepening of our kiss, which soon had us both breathless. Without pulling away, he reached between us to unbuckle his jacket, and I slid my hands into it to start unbuttoning his shirt.

I couldn't get enough of him. The smell of his aftershave. His kisses. How his hands felt on me. He felt so right.

"Carter," he murmured, as he kissed his way down my neck.

"Mmm, yes?" I pushed the jacket off his broad shoulders and pulled his shirt out of his waistband.

"Can you see how your name is perfect for me?" he whispered, as his mouth moved down to my collarbone, to lave in the indent there.

My breath caught. I was distracted by his tongue, by the sudden press of his arousal against mine—both of us were hard and wanting more. He ground his hips into me.

Gods, I was finding it hard to concentrate on what he said. I pulled his shirt further apart to reveal an expanse of tightly-muscled abs. *What were we talking about?* I slid my hands up his chest in wonder. He was perfect.

I felt his intake of breath at my touch, and he lifted his head to grab my t-shirt, tugging it up until it was over my head and thrown on the ground.

He slid down my body, greedily kissing all the bare skin he could reach until he latched onto one tight, already aroused nipple. I didn't have the muscles he had—my chest and abs were as flat as a surf board and sparsely covered in hair—but if his reaction was anything to go by, he seemed just as aroused by me as I was by him.

I slid my hand into his buzz cut, holding onto his head as he teased and tweaked my nipple, before moving his mouth further down.

Nervous, I tugged gently at his head, stopping him just as his hands reached my waistband, I wasn't sure if I was ready, despite my arousal pressing hard against his stomach. This was all so new and overwhelming.

He pulled back to look at me, and then lowered himself more fully to rest on his knees. "Are you okay?" he asked.

"Yes, but…" I trailed off, trying to work out how to tell him I wanted him more than anything but wasn't ready for all that implied.

He didn't look annoyed. If anything, his eyes softened even more.

He held out his hand to me, and I pulled him up. He leaned his forehead down against mine as we both caught our breath. "I can wait," he told me eventually, gently.

Somehow, hearing those words was the sexiest thing he had said to me to date. I reached forward to pick up his dog tags, hanging down that chiseled chest of his and turned them over in my hand. I suddenly realized that I, and everyone else I met at this con, had only referred to him as the captain. Now I knew his name.

I looked up at him, surprised. "Your last name is Rogers…just like Captain America."

He grinned. "Yessir. Another reason why cosplaying as him was a given for me." He leaned forward and kissed me sensuously, teasingly—a promise of more to come. "And your first name is Carter."

I blinked, confused for a moment, then realized what he was getting at. "Like Agent Carter!" Captain America's love.

"Indeed. A good omen."

I let go of his dog tags and lightly traced a star on his chest, in the position it would appear on Captain America's suit if he wore it. I felt him tremble slightly and I looked up to capture his gaze with mine. "If things keep going as they have. I mean… well, you know…. Would you like to come to the rocket launch next month, to see me off?"

His first response was to accept my invitation. His second response was equality enthusiastic but didn't involve too many words.

Our columnist, Julie Pitzel, has been a receptionist, radio DJ, bill collector, telemarketer, administrative assistant, community college instructor, and an expediter (aka professional nag). She's been involved in the Houston writing community for many years including two years as President of a local Romance Writers of America Chapter. She writes paranormal fiction from a geodesic dome south of Houston, where she lives with her husband and a pair of cats. Most recently, her story "The Dance" was published in The Death of All Things" *anthology.*

YOU READ *THAT?* ACTION OR ROMANCE? WHY NOT BOTH?

by Julie Pitzel

I must confess I don't trust surveys. According to a recent Fandango survey, women prefer action movies to romance or romantic comedies. Huh

There are too many factors that can skew results in the direction the survey takers want. Are the questions neutral or biased? How big and how inclusive is the sample group? Are they looking for information or simply looking for corroboration?

I don't have a list of the questions asked, only a summary of the results. "Top genres" were action, science fiction, drama, and comedy. "Least popular" were romance, family and animated films, and fantasy. Were the women asked to rate the genres from favorite to I'd-rather-poke-an-eye-out? Or were they given a list of recent movies that Fandango felt best represented those genres? It's an important distinction. While many of us might say we prefer romance to science fiction, how many of us would choose *Fifty Shades Darker* over *Thor: Ragnarok?*

Did their questions include mashups? Fantasy was among the least popular while science fiction was a favorite. But many recent movies—especially those in the Marvel and DC worlds—are characterized as both. Most romances can also be categorized as dramas or comedies, so how did they differentiate between romantic dramas and dramas with no romance? Or did they? One participant might consider *The Big Sick* a comedy while another would call it a romance. To make it meaningful, we'd need to define each genre, use examples, and rig it so the examples didn't color the results.

Obviously, the questions, how they're asked, and the potential answers make a difference. However, even if the questions are well crafted, *who* is asked also makes a difference.

According to the survey 3,000 women ages 18 to 54 participated. Okay, cool. That seems like a good representative group. But maybe not. Last year Houston was home to about 557,000 women between the ages of 18 and 54. So the sample size is less than one percent of the women in Houston. When we look at the entire country, it averages to about six women per city/urban area of 50,000 or more.[*]

But let's pretend a panel of six random women represents the movie tastes of all the women in MyTown, USA. How did Fandango find the participants? Did they ask every woman buying a ticket through their website to participate or did they only ask women who bought tickets to *Jumanji*?

The age spread seems fairly standard, but it excludes the Baby Boomers. I don't know if they targeted women in that age range, or if older women don't make use of their website. And none of the results I saw broke down the responses by age. They may have had one or one hundred women over fifty responding. Basically, there's a lot of buzz about this survey, but not enough details to determine its accuracy.

Seemingly, the purpose of the survey was to find out what women want (chocolate, orgasms, equal pay…) but if they were only narrowly comparing one genre to the next, they weren't asking the right question.

Personally, I like thrillers, science fiction, fantasy, comedy, and animated films. I also like romance. I can't think of a single romance or romantic movie that could not fit within another genre. Most are either romantic comedies or dramas, but many fall in the fantasy and sci-fi arena—especially the time travel stories. And romance sneaks into movies from other genres, *Raiders of the Lost Ark*, *Speed*, and *The Terminator* all come to mind. I could easily name a dozen mystery/thrillers that include a romantic subplot, even if it didn't produce a happily-ever-after.

However, if the survey is correct and women don't want romances, it says more about current romance movies than the trends in women's taste. Romance holds the largest share of the U.S. fiction market, and those books are purchased mostly by women. Although I'm sure we don't have a direct correlation between women readers and women moviegoers, there must be an overlap.

According to the Motion Picture Association of America's statistics, the majority of moviegoers are women. Fandango's survey even backs this statistic up; women purchase more tickets and tend to be the decision makers. But the industry makes more movies for a male audience. An article in the *Business Insider* explained that after 2010 major studios drastically reduced the number of rom-coms they produced in favor of comic book movies. Apparently, Marvel and DC sell better overseas.

For the past seven years, we've been getting fewer and fewer romances with no rom-coms released by a major studio in 2017. I did a Google search for romantic movies from 2017, and had never heard of most of the titles that came up. And most that I did recognize weren't true romances with a happily-ever-after, they were romantic tragedies. Stories with tragic heroes or heroines meant to carry a message or just engineered to make us cry. There is a place for the twelve-hanky movie—sometimes we want a good cry—but they aren't *romances*.

So against this backdrop, women are asked if they would rather watch hunky men in tights fight monsters versus a two-hour sob fest. It's no wonder they chose the hunky men.

Some of the other results of the survey were that women wanted more movies with dynamic female leads, female driven stories, female ensembles, and to get away from the stereotypical women seen in blockbusters.

Most romances don't include a female ensemble but they do tend to be female driven stories with dynamic female leads. And I believe if we have strong women in any role, we'll get away from the stereotypes.

The problem I had with the survey results is that I want both action *and* romance. And based on comments I found in Facebook discussions, I think most women agree. I want my romances tied to a sleek ad-

---

[*] The 2010 Census defined 497 cities or urbanized areas with populations over 50,000.

venture where the heroine saves herself and the hero, or better, they work together to save themselves.

I've heard that it's hard to put romances on film because they require so much internal dialogue. Bullpucky! We have the opening sequence in *Up* to show that it can be done in fifteen minutes with just pictures. We have classics like *North by Northwest* and *The African Queen* that show how to blend romance with suspense and action. We have comedies like *When Harry Met Sally* or *True Lies* to show that funny doesn't have to be reduced to the least common denominator.

Unfortunately, Hollywood would rather make a few blockbusters and count on international sales than invest in the romantic comedies and feel-good movies that used to dominate the box office. And they wonder why movie attendance is going down. While many will pay to see the same movie multiple times, most of us only want to pay box-office prices once per movie. We'd go to the movies more if there were more movies that interested us.

Good romance takes effort to do right. It requires a script and plot that gives the heroine intelligent dialogue and as much or more screen time as the hero. It's not about special effects, and that makes it more difficult to market—especially to eighteen to thirty-five year old men.

I couldn't find all the data on the survey, so I can't say it's wrong or flawed. However, I think the various magazine and news articles are focusing on the wrong part of the survey. The talk is about women not wanting romance, when it should be about women wanting strong female characters. And while that doesn't have to be romances and rom-coms in every case, more female lead stories should inevitably lead to more romances.

Hopefully, Hollywood isn't going to use it as justification to deliver fewer.

Copyright © 2018 by Julie Pitzel.

Reference:

http://www.businessinsider.com/why-movie-studios-no-longer-make-romantic-comedies-2017-8

New York Times & USA Today *bestselling author Brenda Novak is the author of sixty books. A five-time RITA nominee, she has won many awards, including the National Reader's Choice, the Bookseller's Best, the Book Buyer's Best, the Daphne, and the Silver Bullet. She also runs Brenda Novak for the Cure, a charity to raise money for diabetes research (her youngest son has this disease). To date, she's raised $2.6 million. For more about Brenda, please visit* www.brendanovak.com.

LOVE THAT: BRENDA NOVAK'S EVERY OCCASION COOKBOOK

by Brenda Novak

GRILLED PEACHES

8 servings.

Each Serving: Cal, 202; Carb, 42g; Fat, 5g; Protein, 3g; Sodium, 107mg; Sugar: 26g

Ingredients: 4 medium, ripe peaches (pitted and halved), 2 tsp. cooking oil, 1 Tbsp. sugar, 1/4 tsp. ground cinnamon, dash of hot sauce, 2 and 2/3 cups no-sugar-added vanilla ice cream or low-carb ice-cream, 4 tsp. maple syrup, 8 tsp. low fat granola.

Directions: Prepare grill for medium heat. Combine the sugar, cinnamon and hot sauce. Sprinkle over peaches.

Using long-handled tongs, moisten a paper towel with cooking oil and lightly coat the grill. Prepare grill for indirect heat by using a drip pan. Place peaches over the drip pan and grill, covered, over medium heat for 2-3 minutes on each side or until tender.

For each serving, arrange one peach-half on a plate with 1/3 cup of ice cream. Drizzle with 1/2 teaspoon of maple of syrup and sprinkle with 1 teaspoon of granola.

Copyright © 2015 by Brenda Novak.

C.S. DeAvilla writes award-winning science fiction, fantasy, and romance under another pen name. She has been a romance fan since she sneaked a peek at her mother's massive historical romance bookcase and fell in love with all the characters. She reads every romance genre—as long as two people are falling in love, she'll give it a read. Her favorite authors are Jennifer Crusie, J.R. Ward, Darynda Jones, Suzanne Brockmann, Sarah MacLean, and Kristan Higgins. But she always has room for one more.

RECOMMENDED BOOKS

by C.S. DeAvilla

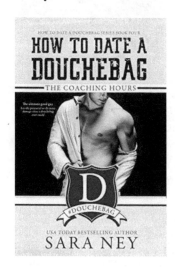

Title: ***How to Date A Douchebag: The Coaching Hours***
Author: Sara Ney
Publisher: Self-Published
ASIN: B0797ZDN7K
Release Date: February 5th, 2018

Coach's daughter saved by a nice, smart guy when she gets endlessly harassed by the wrestling team—that's the theme for the latest Douchebag series book. I absolutely love Sara Ney's deviation from her series promise that follows self-proclaimed jerks who somehow will redeem themselves. But none of the books have followed that arc exactly and it's pleased me to no end. Anabelle transfers to the University of Iowa in the hope of becoming closer to her estranged father, head coach of the wrestling team. He immediately dubs her off limits to the team and repeat-offenders take this as a challenge. It's not long before she's the target of a bet to see who can get her into bed first. The prize? Winner gets to move into the best room in the house. Except, unlike other 'bet leads to real love' stories, this one takes an unexpected turn. Anabelle instead is attracted to the nice guy who is serious about school, Elliot. Elliot is determined to finish out his year so he can be off to graduate school the next semester, but Anabelle's situation isn't one he can ignore. Realizing she is the butt of some buttheads-he-knows' joke, he lends her an open ear and also his apartment when she is too drunk to go home after a party. They soon become roommates for real as Anabelle sees part of her problem is her father not viewing her as an adult. Cue my favorite trope of roommates to lovers. This book had more than one unexpected turn at the end and I was at the edge of my seat to see what kind of revenge Anabelle would exact on these relentless "jockholes" (a term the characters use in the book to describe jocks who are jerks). After I finished this last book in the series, I immediately started binging all of Ney's other books. She can wield emotional hooks with the best of them. And I always love when writers twist tropes in really creative ways. I'm definitely a fan and Ney's books are on my auto-buy list now.

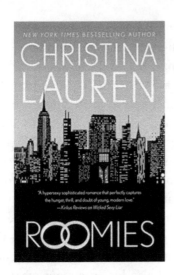

Title: *Roomies*
Author: Christina Lauren
Publisher: Gallery (Simon and Schuster)
AISN: B06ZXWGSLW
Release Date: December 5th, 2017

I fell in love with this book right from the premise: finding-her-way-in-life-aspiring-writer marries a talented street musician, so he can be a legal citizen and play for Broadway. Sounds very involved, but it's a simple love story with all the heart-fluttering anticipation of wondering if this couple will figure out they're perfect for each other or not. Holland has had a stranger-crush on Calvin, the guitarist busking at the local subway. After she's assaulted one day, Calvin steps in and calls for help. Except he runs off, leaving her with questions. She goes back to confront him but instead she continues to fall for him. Her uncle is in desperate need of a musician for his Broadway show. Sure, they're looking for a violinist, but Calvin's sound is so unique it just might fit the role they have in mind. Calvin slam-dunks his audition, only to let them down by admitting he's in the country illegally. Cue a really crazy (not to mention illegal) plan for Holland to marry him. The couple goes for it, attempting to make it as real as possible, though it gets too real and soon Holland is questioning Calvin's true motives. Calvin questions hers. And through it all readers get to witness sweet moments of these two getting to know each other, amazing dialog, and a really unexpected path to happily ever after. Christina Lauren really knocks this one out of the park and the whole book, along

with the writing style, really has a mainstream love story feel to it.

Title: *Priest*
Author: Sierra Simone
Publisher: Self-Published
AISN: B00WHGBTHI
Release Date: June 29th, 2015

Priest was one of those novels that had to be recommended to me several times before I finally took the plunge. I'd first heard of it while attending a conference where Sarah McClean was teaching a workshop. She'd mentioned the book several times during her lecture as an example of emotional investment. The book had just come out at the time and I'd quickly added it to my 'to read' pile, but then ended up pushing it aside for other books. But the recommendations kept popping up over and over. I'd been looking for a good erotic romance book to dive into (a romance sub-genre I don't read enough in), so this book came up as a possibility from another reader yet again! Okay, universe I'm listening now. So, I read it and devoured it in a few sittings. The premise is conflict driven from the set up—a priest taking confession of a stripper (though she's reformed and is an accountant now) and over several meetings they become extremely attracted to each other. The character tension is off the charts. This is forbidden romance (another favorite trope) at its absolute extreme. Do yourself a favor and don't push this one off your reading list—be smarter than I was and read it right away. It was un-put-down-able. A truly fun and forbidden romance.

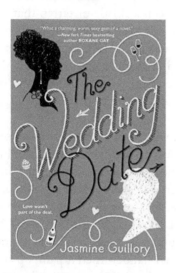

Title: *The Wedding Date*
Author: Jasmine Guillory
Publisher: Berkley (Penguin)
ISBN: 0399587675
Release Date: January 30th 2018

Debut novel, *The Wedding Date*, promised a fun read and received a lot of early praise. Guillory hits all the best romance tropes: interesting meet-cute, fake girlfriend, not the hero/heroine's usual type. Drew and Alexa are an easy couple to root for. Drew, a doctor, doesn't have time for a relationship (or so he tells himself), so once things seem to be going well he can be counted on for one thing—an easy break up that leaves him friends with his exes. Alexa works for the mayor in the California Bay Area. She is instantly attracted to Drew, but he's made his usual patterns with love clear. To highlight this, after meeting her in a trapped elevator and bonding, he begs her to be his date to his ex's wedding. At the wedding she's treated to one story after another of Drew's tendencies with women—though generally a really nice guy—he is not, repeat, not the kind of guy she can afford to fall for. Keeping things light, they cap off their weekend with mind blowing sex and leave it at that. Except neither of them can seem to contain their infatuation to one night. Both text each other and keep making plans to continue for just 'one more time.' Guillory's writing style is very quick paced. It reminded me of Janet Evanovich in her ability to keep the plot moving

and skipping all the interplay, leaving just the parts readers need to follow the story. If sweet, quick, and light is how you like your romance: this is the book for you.

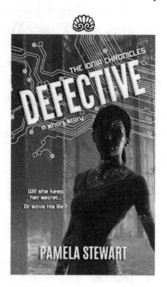

Title: *Defective*
Author: Pamela Stewart
Publisher: Self Published
AISN: B06WV93JNH
Release Date: February 10th, 2017

I'm a Star Trek nerd through and through, so any story that involves an android and human in love— I'm all in. Pamela Stewart has a series I swear was written just for a geek like me. Her writing style leans young adult: rich and filled with vivid description, though—like most recent YA offerings—her novels can be enjoyed by all age levels. *Defective* is a novella set in the same world as *Frozen Hearts*, but with different characters. Readers will be able to read this story without having read anything else in the series. Zee is on a mission to eliminate Kuta. One problem: he's a really nice guy and either through malfunction or defective programing she's finding herself falling in love with him. Zee must decide if she's willing to risk it all for love. Zee and Kuta are well developed and the story is tightly written to keep the meat of the plot intact, but also keeping the world defined enough that I felt it could be a real place. The futuristic setting in the Ionia Chronicles is lush and will leave readers hungry for more.

USA Today *and national bestselling author Anna J. Stewart writes sweet to sexy romance for Harlequin's Heartwarming and Romantic Suspense lines, but paranormal romance is her first love. Early obsessions with* Star Wars, Star Trek, *and* Wonder Woman *set her on the path to creating fun, funny, and family-centric romances with happily ever afters for her independent heroines. Anna lives in Northern California where she deals with a serious* Supernatural *and* Sherlock *addiction and spends far too much time at the movies and at fan conventions. You can read more about Anna and her books at* www.authorannastewart.com.

WARDEN OF FATE

By Anna J. Stewart

Guilt lodged in Amber MacQueen's throat as she watched her sister Nellie disappear inside *Thistles and Thorns* in search of their wayward sister Clara. As Amber was an overachiever in every sense of the word, this wasn't the type of brush-away guilt a sister felt for borrowing a sweater without permission. Nor was it the kind of guilt over having forgotten a birthday or the anniversary of a particularly nasty and life-defining break-up. Oh, no.

Amber pressed her fingers hard against her sternum and rubbed at the soreness she'd been carrying nearly every day of her life. A soreness that had gotten worse in the last few months. This was the kind of guilt that had been worn stone-smooth by years of silence. A guilt Amber could no longer swallow around without hurting her heart.

The day had come. The day she'd been dreaming of. The day she'd been dreading. And nothing, Amber knew with absolute certainty, was going to be the same. For any of the MacQueen sisters.

"Took me more than two decades, but I'm keeping my promise, Mama." Amber downed the last of the lukewarm coffee and tried to push aside the unease. "We're here. I brought them to you, just as you asked." Or at least she would, after a two-hour drive to a seaside Scottish town few people had ever heard of. Amber leaned her head against the cool window and stared out at the light dusting of snow falling on the historic streets of Edinburgh.

As much as she loved Chicago and her frenetic life as one of the top art buyers in the country, there was something about Scotland that sang to her. She'd never heard a bagpipe that didn't make her blood sing; never seen a thistle or tartan that didn't make her long to walk the cobblestone paths or climb the stone staircases of the historic city. In the three days since they'd arrived, it had been as if she'd finally come home. And something—maybe it was that guilt—began to settle inside of her.

Even as something else awakened.

A storm was coming. She could sense it. Feel it. Not a day had passed where Amber didn't feel as if she was being pushed toward an event she'd have no control over, one she couldn't predict and yet, now, sitting here, she knew the moment had arrived.

"So, what are you going to do about it?" Amber looked around her, to make sure no one was around, and flexed her hand, turned it palm up and watched as the flicker of magic danced like tiny sparks across her skin.

The magic hurt; it tugged and pulled at her, like an elastic band stretched too tight. That's what happened to muscles one didn't use, right? They atrophied and lost their strength. Obviously the same could be said of magic. Amber took a deep breath and, rather than closing her hand and pushing all thoughts of the destiny she'd been born to aside, focused on the tiny droplets of fire exploding from her fingers. It crackled like static, like the Pop Rocks she used to down with gallons of soda when she was a kid. She grinned.

Boundaries had never been anything more to Amber than guideposts; signs she was on the right path and that she should blow through expectations and barriers with as much gusto and ambition as she could muster. Watching out for those boundaries was one of the few pieces of advice she could remember her mother ever giving her.

"Mama." Amber sighed. She'd been barely four when Shona MacQueen had walked out the door and left her husband and three daughters on their own. Barely four when Amber realized not everyone stayed. Barely four when she realized it would be up to her to watch over and protect her younger sisters and be ready when the day came to tell them the truth. "What would I have become, had things been different?" Amber wondered aloud. How was it she could see that day, the day her mother had left, so clearly, yet everything else about her childhood practically blurred.

Everything except the ghostly presence of a man she had no memory of, but every hope for.

She could still hear every word Shona had whispered to her as she'd held Amber in her arms, brushed her long red curls behind her shoulder, and kissed her cheek. Words of magic and mystery and wonder. The promise of hope, and laughter, and, most of all, of love. Amber looked down at her hand, remembering the secure touch of her mother's hand as Shona had ignited the power that coursed through the veins of all her daughters. But Amber, Shona had told her, Amber was special. Amber was the link to tie them all together. Amber would be the answer that would one day bind those fighting for the greater good and start them all on a new life.

The tiny flames licking across Amber's skin strengthened, glowed. Burned. Amber waved her hand back and forth, watching the golden blue-tipped fire dance to her command. Outside, in the sludge and snow, a cab shot past and Amber yelped, closing her hand into a fist to conceal the magic once again.

What was wrong with her, playing with her powers out in the open? Ever since she'd stepped off the plane it was as if something primal had unlocked inside of her and her years of practiced control had vanished. The magic was crawling to life inside of her, anxious to be freed. Determined to be used. As if this power had a place in the real world.

All the more reason to find Shona MacQueen and settle this magic thing once and for all. The sooner she, Nellie, and Clara all got back to their normal, ordinary lives, the better. The last thing Amber—or her sisters—needed was to live the next rest of their lives with this secret hovering over them like a suffocating shadow. If, Amber reminded herself, Nellie and Clara forgave her for not having told them the truth about who—and *what*—they were.

"And that's a big if." Amber rolled her head against the back of the seat and looked forward the door to the antique store Nellie had disappeared into. "Come on, guys. I want to get this over with."

An explosion of light from inside the shop had Amber gasping and shielding her eyes. "Nellie! Clara!" She launched out of the car and raced to the front door. No sooner did her hand touch the handle than the façade shifted. The antique candlesticks in the window she and Nellie had been teasing each other about moments earlier disappeared, replaced by a thick framed print of a classic painting Amber had long considered a favorite.

The handle in her grasp warmed, but rather than letting go, Amber looked down and watched the ordinary knob transform into an elegant brass latch. Her skin went cold as the windows went glistening bright. The trim around the doorframe rippled from gray to pristine white. She looked up, the ordinary wooden carved sign was now embossed in gold and swaying gently in the morning breeze.

Amber tugged her scarf tighter around her throat as she shivered, not from the cold, and scrunched her toes in the high-heeled boots she wore beneath snug designer jeans. Just on the wind, she heard: *It is time, Amber. Bring them home. Bring them all to me. But hurry. Before you're too late. Your sisters need you.*

"Mama." There would be no reply. Just as there hadn't been every other time she'd heard Shona MacQueen's voice dancing on the air. She'd never steered Amber wrong. Despite Amber's anger and resentment at having been left behind, the permanent rolling sensation that reminded her most people couldn't be trusted, she followed her heart... and believed.

She pushed open the store door.

"Clara! Nellie!" Their names left her lips before she'd fully entered the shop. Antiques vanished before her eyes as furniture disappeared, walls rearranged themselves and displayed pictures and paintings that called to the very essence of what made Amber love art. Each was tempting in its own right, and pulled at her, drew her closer, but she had to resist. "Where are you?"

The door slammed shut behind her. Frames on their way to their display areas crashed to the floor and disappeared in a puff of smoke. The frenetic movement of spinning and catapulting objects came to a sudden stop. The silence hurt her ears.

"Hello!" Amber checked the side rooms that had somehow been caught in mid-transformation. She could see the odd combination of hers and her sister's interests: the books for Clara, the history-tinged antiques for Nellie and the beautiful artwork for Amber. Someone, Amber realized, knew them very, very well.

The magic in her blood bubbled to attention as she took cautious steps out of the hall toward the room in the back. She kept her hands relaxed, kept the flames, the magic, in reserve.

The room glowed the same blue-white as the explosion. The oddest sense of déjà-vu rolled over her, fogging her mind, tempting her memories as she stepped inside. The pristine white room held nothing inside but a solitary wooden table displaying a familiar, large burgundy leather-bound book with thick embossed imagery on the cover.

"The Bruadarach." It appeared to be a first edition of one of the books in the three-volume series Shona had left for Amber and her sisters. The stories their mother insisted Amber read, learn, and memorize. Where Amber had first learned of their magic, their legacy. And of love.

She sighed. The daydreams she'd had about those stories. The desire to be a part of it, to be a part of... him. "Full circle," Amber whispered. "Mama."

"You're not like the others, are you?"

Amber spun at the voice. The door swung closed and revealed a tall, lithe, almost skeletal young woman standing in the corner. She was dressed in white silk as blinding as the room. Her shockingly silver hair trailed long and blade straight all the way to her tailbone. Black glistened on her sharp, talon nails and over her thin curving lips. A copper amulet glowed a bright sky blue where it lay against her chest. She stayed where she was, crossed her ankles and, with a tilt of her head, smiled at Amber.

"Definitely *not* like your sisters."

"Where are they?" Amber shivered under the expression. She'd never considered what face evil might wear, but if she had to guess, this was it. There was something...vacant in the woman's obsidian-eyed stare. Something slithery and simpering as she drew her gaze up and over Amber with a disapproving click of her tongue. "What have you done with them?"

"Don't worry. You'll be with them soon." The woman let out a long breath and pushed away from the wall. Her needle-thin heels clicked hard against the wood floor.

Amber circled to keep the table between them brushed her fingers against the smooth wood of the top. She felt, rather than saw, the book quiver. Heat and fire built inside of her, simmering and smoking beneath the magic, but with each breath she took Amber stilled the rising fury. Whoever this woman was, whatever she might have planned, it was clear she was Amber's only path to her sisters.

Her sisters. Nellie and Clara needed her. It was her fault they didn't know the truth. Her fault they weren't aware of the power they possessed. She had to find them before it was too late. "Are you going to introduce yourself or do you want me to make up a name?"

The woman stopped moving and blinked. "I am Elya. High priestess of Dracha, Lord of the Forgotten Realm."

"Dracha." Amber brushed her fingers against the spine of the book. An image of a scarred-face man crossed through her mind. Darkness personified Power hungry. Determined. Insane. "I seem to remember him from stories my mother used to tell me," Amber said. "Always thought he was a bit of a coward. Doesn't surprise me he has lackeys around doing all the hard work."

"Lord Dracha is no coward!" Elya spat, sounding like the sidekick from a really bad B-grade horror movie. "He is all-powerful in his realm. And soon he will rule all the realms overseen by that fraud of a goddess."

"That would be Alastrine, I assume?" Boy, when her worlds collided they really set off a big bang "Yeah, I really don't think Grandma is going to appreciate you calling her a fraud." Not that Amber had any clue what her grandmother would think or say. She'd never met the Goddess of the Realms, but she'd lay even odds Alastrine wasn't exactly the baking cookies type of granny.

Elya's eyes widened in surprise.

"Yeah, that's right." Amber smiled around her mounting panic. She *needed* to find Nellie and Clara They were out there, alone. Maybe hurt. Or worse. "I know all about Alastrine. And the Realms. If you're so useful to Dracha, what are you doing here? In *this* world?" A world shut off from all others except through the portals stored in the storybooks her mother had created upon her escape from Dracha and his followers.

"I am the conduit through which Shona's offspring will free my Lord from his prison," Elya recited as if by rote.

Amber couldn't stop the cold fear shimmying up her spine. "You mean he sent you here to wait for us to show up. Wow. Talk about not being appreciated. How long have you been hanging around this place? Twenty, thirty years?"

Amber scanned the room for something, anything, she could use as a weapon. The brass lock rattled against the book as if trying to catch Amber's attention. But the lock stayed firm. Amber's mind flickered with recognition. Was it possible the book could read her thoughts? Was *this* the weapon she needed?

"I do my Lord's bidding," Elya stated. "I will be rewarded in this world."

"You sure about that?" One thing Amber knew about megalomaniacs like Dracha: they didn't like sharing anything—especially power—with anyone. "You're not expecting him to marry you, or anything, are you?" Amber touched a finger to the corner of the book, pressed her lips together as another image pushed its way into her mind. A castle, tall, dark stone. Shadows surrounding it, encasing it almost. Rooms. Endless rooms. Cells. Amber's breath caught in her chest. Prisoners. No. She blinked, focused her thoughts. One prisoner. In the tower. Wearing a bronze helmet. There was something familiar about the man, something heart-breakingly familiar.

It was *him*! She didn't need to see his face to know it was the man she'd seen in her dreams nearly every night of her life. *Rivalin.* Her heart soared above the fear dragging her down.

It wasn't only her sisters who needed her help.

If only Amber could be certain. Her mind flicked as a pulse of energy shot from the book into her fingers and into her mind. There, just outside the heavy wooden door that kept the helmeted man locked away, another room concealed hidden tunnels and a staircase. A way out!

But first, Amber centered herself and embraced the magic she'd ignored for far too long—she needed a way in.

"You need an intervention, Elya." Amber shifted her hand more solidly against the soft leather of the tome, ready to absorb whatever the book deemed necessary. "Dracha won't give you anything you want or expect."

"I only expect that which was promised to me," Elya said. "Wealth and eternal life in this weak world."

Amber sighed. Why did these supernatural Bond villains always want eternal life? What was it about death that terrified them so much? Why wasn't one life enough? That's what made it so precious, wasn't it? "I'm going to ask you again. Where are my sisters?"

"Where they belong." Elya glanced down at Amber's fingers lying tense against the embossed leather. "I have no way of knowing if they're alive, of course. I believe Nellie—she was the second one, was she not? poor Nellie didn't arrive in the safest of spots. But we got what we needed." Elya smiled. "Her book. And Clara's."

Amber's fists clenched, but she refused to take the bait. Anger wouldn't do her any good, not here. Not against Elya who was nothing more than a tool in Dracha's endgame. It would be of more benefit to store the rage and aim it at the appropriate target at the most pivotal time.

Let Dracha learn the MacQueen mantra the hard way: hell hath no fury like a sister scorned.

"Are you sure it's only the books you need?" Amber felt a pang of sympathy when Elya's eyes flickered like a lizard and doubt sparked. "Bad minion." Amber clicked her tongue. "I don't think you finished your homework. You were right about one thing. I am different from my sisters because I *know* all the details of our history. And I can tell you, for a fact, the books are useless without the demi-goddesses who can read them." Amber pressed her palm flat on the brass lock encasing the book. "Or even open them."

"Wait!" Elya dived at Amber as the metal restraint clicked apart and the book burst open.

Amber darted to the other side of the table, stretched her hands out as the pages flipped back and forth. *Show me where I need to go. Show me.... There! Stop!*

The book stilled and showed The Keep. The cell. The passage.

Rivalin.

An energy blast exploded up and out of the book, sucking the silence out of the room. Elya screamed and grabbed the edge of the table as her legs flew up off the ground. Amber lifted her chin and breathed in power as the wind whipped and cycloned around them. The uncertainty, the fear, the doubt she'd tamped down for most of her life was replaced with the bright, hopeful images of her sisters, lost in a magical world they'd no idea was real.

The promise that her heart, finally, would be filled. Elya might think she had something to fight for in Dracha's name, but nothing was going to get in the way of Amber and the man she was destined to love.

"Ah!" Amber caught Elya's wrist as the other woman lost her grip and started to fly away. Elya cried out, tried to tug herself free but the undertow was too strong. Amber was too strong. "Where do you think you're going?"

With the power of her magic supporting her, Amber yanked Elya forward until they were nose to nose; Amber with her feet solidly on the ground and Elya, half flying.

The fear the eldest MacQueen sister saw in Elya's eyes told her what she had to do.

"Since you're such a fan of your boss, how about you introduce me?" Still holding Elya's wrist, Amber climbed up on the table.

"Not this way!" Elya resisted as Amber pulled her with her.

"I think being at Dracha's side is what you really want, isn't it, Elya?" Amber's eyes narrowed as resolve stiffened her spine. "Let's go."

Without another thought, she jumped into the book. And dragged it and Elya in behind her.

How long had it been since he'd slept, Rivalin wondered? How long since he'd eaten food? Drank water or wine? Spoken his own thoughts. How long since he'd been…alive?

Rivalin of the Western Realm, warrior of old, leader of countless battalions, escorted what was left of Dracha's first line of soldiers into the great stone hall to stand before Lord Dracha. He stood there, silent, as his mind screamed against the silent prison he'd been locked in. This place always smelled like death to him. Rotting and fetid, clinging to his senses to the point of normalcy. The Forgotten Realm was known for torturing its prisoners in the cruelest way possible. Whatever they treasured most, whoever they loved most, was the first thing to be ripped away upon their arrival.

That Alastrine, the goddess he'd sworn fealty to when he was barely a boy, had cast him and his friends out still stung.

Given what he'd lost, Rivalin couldn't imagine what Keane and Bowen had taken away from them. Until earlier tonight, he'd believed them both dead as they'd been separated immediately after their exile. He'd grieved for them, to the point of wishing himself to join them. Seeing them again, watching them as they battled with the other resistance fighters, determined to put an end to Dracha once and for all, had awakened that dormant obligation he'd buried long ago.

Had he a heart left, it would have swelled in relief upon discovering Keane and Bowen lived. Instead, Rivalin found himself overcome by the need to call out to them, to beg them to please put an end to his suffering and kill him, once and for all.

But the plea had been a silent one, stopped by the spell that kept the honorable man Rivalin was locked away in his own mind, hidden behind the cloak and sword of the heartless mercenary he'd been turned into. A puppet Dracha could force into doing his every whim.

Regret and anger swarmed inside of him, a furious whirlwind that spun every moment he breathed into one of agony.

How many moons had turned since Lord Dracha's bronze-tipped spear had pierced his heart? A heart that was only held together now by the magic Dracha cast; a magic that rendered Rivalin powerless against his new master. He had been made into an enforcer, one who had no say over who he meted out punishment to; who he attacked. Who he killed. His body was not his own. His heart was destroyed. His mind was fading.

Only his soul kept him barely holding on.

That and the life-long image of a woman without a face, haunting his dreams.

From behind the bronze helmet Dracha insisted he wear, Rivalin's eyes shifted to the three marble podiums on the dais. Two held metal-clasped books Dracha had long been searching for.

Without the third, these would remain useless, deadly even as they'd turn any unworthy who opened them to ash.

Those books, all three of them together, were the only way Dracha would ever return to Alastrine's world. They could open a portal long believed dormant, but the magic inside of the tomes was more powerful than anything else in the Forgotten Realm. Which meant opening a portal wasn't the only thing they could do.

This Rivalin knew for certain. Since he'd encountered the first book, he'd recaptured part of himself. Regained control, however slight. He had awakened from the mind-numbing trance he'd been put under so long ago. Which was the only reason he was grateful to have to report his failure in defeating the rebels to Dracha in person.

The longer Rivalin could be near those books, the stronger he would become.

Only then could he break the spell binding him to Dracha. Only then could Rivalin finally find peace.

"You called a retreat." Dracha set his favorite jeweled goblet down with far more care than normal before he turned his grotesque face to Rivalin. Older than the seas themselves, angrier than the volcanic fire that raged beneath the Keep, Dracha, the one time personal guard to the Goddess Alastrine displayed every drop of darkness inside of him with a cruel set of his jaw and the never-blinking stare of his liquid amber eyes. Eyes that were now locked on Rivalin with such disapproving intensity, Rivalin's fellow soldiers ducked their heads and shifted away. "How is retreat better than surrender?" Dracha asked in a deadly quiet tone.

"They have the pharentas on their side, Lord Dracha." Rivalin spoke without wanting to. "A witch controlled one of them. A witch rumored new to this realm. It was either retreat or lose what was left of your troops."

"The old warrior Rivalin saw retreat as weakness." Dracha rested his elbows on his knees and leaned forward. His burnished pharenta hide boots squeaked as he shifted on the throne he'd made out of the bones of other warriors he'd defeated in battle. "Perhaps you are not as courageous as legend would have us believe." He addressed the other soldiers whose gazes were all cast downward. Dracha's black-eyed

priests and priestesses, however, stood vacant eyed and staring from their positions behind the throne. Nothing phased them. Nothing moved them other than the will of Dracha and his magic. "Perhaps it is time to find another First." Dracha reached for the spear still stained with Rivalin's blood.

If only. Rivalin's body tightened to attention and his chin jutted out. "I am yours to command, Lord Dracha. Do as you wish."

Rivalin wished he could roll his own eyes at his own statement. Not only had his voice and thoughts been replaced by a simpering sycophant, he often sounded like a complete idiot.

But Dracha wouldn't kill him. If Rivalin believed that, even for a moment, he'd have done whatever he could to evoke Dracha's wrath. Rivalin was too visible a symbol of Dracha's power. To destroy that which he had created with the darkest of magic would go against the very ego that kept Dracha breathing—the magic Rivalin was certain was stored in the bronze spear.

Destroying that spear was the only way to secure his release from this after-life. He was sure the power in the spear was the only thing keeping his heart beating, but all he wanted was oblivion. Silent, unending, eternal oblivion. And yet, no one would kill him. No one *could* kill him. Not while Dracha possessed that spear.

Rivalin focused his attention back on the books that had fallen from the sky. His hand twitched, at his own volition. In the prison of his mind, Rivalin gasped. What was left of his heart pounded with hope. He was so close. So close!

"The men say they recognized some of the Outsiders," Dracha stated. "Did you, First?"

"Bowen and Keane, yes." His spoken betrayal was yet another spear to Rivalin's chest and he tasted bile in his throat. Would that he could cut out his own tongue. "Rumor is they have recently found mates. Flame-haired witches. Perhaps those who arrived with the books."

"Perhaps, yes." Dracha stroked a finger down the side of his misshapen face. "It is something to think on. I want a new battle strategy in place. If the Outsiders are now willing to meet us head on, it means they've grown in numbers. They are not as frightened or intimidated as they once were. We must find a way to discourage hope. What word from our spies in the *Cosanta Baile*?"

"Nothing in recent days," Rivalin said as the fragments of his heart twisted in regret. The *Cosanta Baile* was a refuge, home, and marketplace for those banished from the other realms. Families lived there. Mothers, fathers, children. The elderly. Anyone deemed, for whatever reason, to be unsuitable to inhabit the realms under Alastrine.

Not that Alastrine herself was responsible for the banishments. No, that was the secret Rivalin had uncovered upon his, Keane, and Bowen's return from hiding Alastrine's only surviving daughter Shona in the parallel world of men. A journey that had sealed his and his friends' fate. The goddess's priests had been corrupted by outside forces; bought off by those seeking the power and influence held by Alastrine. Those who had become allies of Dracha.

It was that discovery Rivalin was convinced that led to their banishment. Somehow her advisors had convinced Alastrine that Rivalin and his friends had failed, that her daughter Shona was not safe, but dead. Not that Rivalin had the chance to tell Keane and Bowen about the conversation he'd overheard. Their so-called trial had lasted less than a blink of an eye before they'd been cast into the Forgotten Realm. A banishment that was irreversible and final. Unless….

Rivalin's gaze drifted back to the books.

Unless a portal connecting the Forgotten Realm to Alastrine's world could be re-established. Which was exactly what Dracha was counting on happening if the three volumes of *The Bruadarach* were reunited and under his control.

"We must rid the *Cosanta Baile* of sympathizers," Dracha mused as a servant boy refilled his goblet. A servant boy who carried the haunted look of suffering on his pale, waxen face. "Or perhaps we need to be rid of the *Baile* entirely. I want a plan of action put into play within the day. I want their homes, all sense of security and safety, destroyed. They must learn that anyone who chooses to take up arms against me will be made to suffer the consequences."

"Yes, Lord Dracha." Rivalin bent his head and stepped away. He called his men to attention, watched them file out of the hall and head mindlessly to the sleeping quarters in the lower levels.

The man Rivalin wished he still was raged as his body walked away. What he wouldn't give to drive that spear deep into Dracha's throat and rid the worlds of his poisonous ambition. Even now he could feel their last conversation fade into nothingness. There was little Rivalin himself could retain as it filtered into the nothingless creature that controlled his body. Like short term memory loss while he could grasp the threads of knowledge, his mind was fading more every day, and he would lose them again.

His body had become nothing more than a vessel for violence dictated by a man who had neither the inclination nor compulsion to put himself in danger.

While the soldiers wound down the stairs, Rivalin went up to his own room, a prison cell with a small window overlooking the world he reluctantly helped to control. He set his weapons and shield by the door, as usual. He lit the candle on the table that held nothing more than an empty plate from which never ate and a glass from which he never drank. He sat at attention on the edge of the rickety wooden pallet bed, hands on his knees, as the night hours crept close.

Exhaustion he couldn't describe draped over him Rivalin tried to force himself to relax, but other than the most recent second of control over his hand, his spine remained stiff, his shoulders tight as he waited for his next call to action. If only he could close his eyes, for a few moments, sleep for a brief few seconds….

His lids flickered closed for an instant. His chin dropped forward slightly.

Rivalin tried to keep calm, craving that escape more than he wanted to admit, but he'd just gained another fraction of control over his body. He forced himself to take a deep breath. Ah…there. He could feel himself drifting off…so close. So…close….

From a distance he heard a low whistle, like that of a boulder being catapulted into the sky. The sound grew louder, drew closer and against the side of his face, through the small window, he felt the warmth of flame lick his skin.

The wall beside the bed exploded in. He flew through the air and crashed back against the door as debris and ash rained down and around him. The pain of cuts and bruises barely registered. Rivalin coughed, waved his hand in front of his face as the image of a iridescent figure stepped out of the rubble and smoke.

Not just a figure, Rivalin realized as he struggled to get his bearings. A woman.

Not just any woman. It was…*her.*

Parts of him he'd believed long dormant awakened in a flash. She was stunning—more stunning than she had been in his dreams; dreams he'd abandoned when adulthood had descended. But she was here, with her unsettling, familiar green eyes and a lush body encased in the oddest clothing he'd ever seen. The fabric covering her legs seemed painted on; dark, and durable and accentuating every curve. A splash of white flashed beneath the shiny coat and rough scarf that bore singe marks along the edges. Her otherwise pristine pale face carried a smudge of ash across one cheek.

"Whew!" She tossed her head from side to side that sent her hair cascading behind her back in a flood of tousled red waves. "Now *that* was a ride." She opened one hand and released the arm of another woman who slumped unconscious into the debris. "Hey, there, handsome."

Her voice. Something he long believed dead stirred to life inside of him. He knew that voice. He knew that silhouette. He'd seen her, felt her, touched her in his dreams. Dreams he'd let himself forget.

There was no hint in her expression that she was surprised to see him. If anything, she looked incredibly pleased with herself and approving of him. She hitched one hand against her hip and it was then he saw the book. His pulse hammered heavy in his throat. The third tome!

Intrigued and unnerved, Rivalin could only manage, "Who are you?", then was shocked the words were allowed to leave his lips.

"I'm Amber MacQueen. I'm here to rescue you."

Her smile made his head spin. Desire hit him square in the stomach and moved lower.

She studied his shocked reaction carefully, head tilting. "Sorry. Always wanted to say that. Let's see what's beneath the helmet." She crunched her way through the rocks and debris and dropped down in front of him. "You sleep with this thing on?" She knocked a knuckle against the side of his helmet.

"I don't sleep." Rivalin's response shocked him. Other than commanding his men and talking to Dracha himself, his master's spell prevented him conversing with anyone. Unless….

His gaze flickered from the woman to the book she set on his lap.

"I'm sorry to hear that. Let's get this off of you, shall we?"

"No, it will not…" Rivalin's protest faded as the weight of the bronze lifted from his head. For the first time since he'd felt the hot spear pierce his chest, Rivalin could breathe. He drew in a long, clear, cold breath and let it out in what sounded to him like a strained laugh. Until this moment only Dracha had the power to remove the helmet, but this woman… oh, this woman! She was his dream come true. Rivalin reached up and touched her face. Never before had he felt skin so soft, or saw anything as beautiful as this Amber MacQueen. "Amber."

As wrong as his life had become, he knew everything about now, and her, felt absolutely right.

"Nothing wrong with your hearing." Instead of pushing his hand away, she moved her face into his touch, like a secar wild cat nuzzling him for attention. "Rivalin."

The sound of his name sent an odd, forgotten tingle through him. "You know me?"

"Oh, I know you. You're one of the three warriors who hid my mother. Bet you're glad I'm here to get you out of your prison cell. Should have realized you'd have gotten yourself captured trying to defeat Dracha and his minions. If you're okay to walk, we need to get moving. I have to find my sisters."

Sisters. Red-hair. Green eyes. *Shona…* Rivalin's breath halted in his chest. No wonder this woman seemed so familiar.

"You good to move?" She asked again.

He didn't know if his hand on her face was a fluke movement of personal choice. He stretched his legs, just to know he could, and answered "Yes!" with more enthusiasm than he believed she expected. He didn't know whether to be surprised or mortified when she wedged herself under his arm and helped him to stand. Dust and pebbles rained off his ripped and worn uniform. Before he could retrieve the book, she had it back firmly in one hand while Rivalin placed the helmet back on his head.

The elation at seeing her, that sensation of freedom, evaporated when he gestured to the prone figure on the floor. "What about her? She's hurt."

"She's fine. Just passed out." Amber waved his concern away with her hand. "She's Dracha's problem now."

"You know of Dracha?"

"Yep. And while he sounds like a charming individual, I'd rather wait to meet him when I'm prepared. Don't look so shocked there, Riva." She patted a solid hand against his chest, arched an approving brow before she headed to the door. "I've got this. Just have to find our way out. Unless you know of a better way?"

He knew every inch of this Keep, from the top of the spire to the raging fire pits that kept the towers heated. He could easily get the two of them out without being seen or found. But this time when he opened his mouth, the words froze in his throat, stopped by that same invisible force that had kept him prisoner for countless cycles.

Terror locked around his chest and squeezed. This woman, this Amber, was in far more danger than she realized.

From me.

Rivalin had to get her out of here. Now. Alone. Without him. Except his evil possessor, his other voice, wouldn't surrender. Wouldn't let him warn her.

His binding also wouldn't let him help her by telling her the way, but it appeared he could still talk around that restriction. As long as he didn't actively help her, his binds had loosened with her, or the book's, presence. "You know a way out?" Even as he said the words he heard the sound of footsteps pounding up the stairs. The rattle of swords and armor chilled his blood. Her quick words and impulsive attitude would be no defense against those who blindly followed Dracha. There had to be a way to protect her.

She patted the book in her arms, let it drop open and scanned the image she found. "Oh, yeah. Come on." She shoved open his cell door and peeked outside. "Coast is clear."

Such odd phrasing Rivalin thought as he retrieved his weapons and shield from the now decimated cell and followed her down the dank stone hallway to one of the rooms across the way.

"There's a hidden passage in here." She looked over her shoulder at him and motioned with her head to follow. "Quick. They're coming."

He saw the flash of his sentries rounding the corner as she hauled him in behind her and closed the door as quietly as possible. She leaned against it, peering out the tiny opening into the hall as she pressed a hand against the metal latch and lock.

Smoke and flame erupted from her fingers. The smell of hot metal burned the back of his throat as the lock melted into the wood and sealed the door shut. The amusement on her face made him wonder if she thought they were playing some kind of game? "Hold this." She shoved the open book into his hands.

He started, expecting to be turned to ash, just as one of his men had upon discovering the first book in the forest. Except nothing happened. The book lay still and silent in his hands.

Amber glanced up from where she was digging her fingers into the cracks between the stone in the wall. "What's wrong? Too heavy?"

"No." Rivalin tried to shake off his confusion. He heard his men gathering outside the door, but they made no move to break in. What was happening to him? The book warmed beneath his touch. Was that a warning? Or a welcoming? "We have to hurry."

"Tell me something I don't know. That is the last time I pay fifty bucks for a manicure." She slipped her fingers down and around the mortar lines. "Ah! There you are." One of the stones softened beneath her touch. One big yank and the giant stone moved back and exposed a narrow, dark, putrid passageway. "You first." Her eyes watered as she pinched her nose closed. "I need to close up behind us."

"You are a witch." A witch who might just be his salvation.

"Demi-goddess, apparently. Although I appreciate the sentiment." Amber patted a hand on his back as he moved past her. "Into the chute, Fly Boy. I've got my sisters to find."

Now what?

After what amounted to a slippery stagnant water slide combined with steep, crumbling stone stairs, Amber waded through the endless tunnels of knee deep water and tried not to think about the rat (at least she hoped they were rats) carcasses and other *stuff* floating around them. Using the bare hint of light ahead as a beacon, she finally stopped at an enormous iron grate and stared out into the darkness. The putrid water that had seeped into her boots, soaked her jeans and custom leather jacket. She could feel the cool air blowing from outside, but for some reason she wasn't cold. Maybe it was because the magic inside of her was finally burning free.

Or maybe it had something to do with the seriously hot man behind her. Amber blew out a breath and widened her eyes. Boy, her imagination hadn't come close. The book's description of Rivalin had been cursory enough for her to fill in the blanks, but one thing was for sure: genetics and nature loved this man. She'd always understood the appeal of tall, dark, and handsome in theory, but for whatever reason, she'd always hooked up with fair-haired men. Standing face to face with Rivalin—or in her case, forehead to chin—had produced more fireworks inside of her, in mere minutes, than the going-through-the-motions relationships she'd endured over the years. That she'd put sex and dating on the back burner for the past few years must have been fate's way of preparing her for him.

As if *now* was the time to dwell on how long it had been since she'd been set to boil.

"We've got a problem." She motioned Rivalin forward, then regretted it instantly as he took up nearly every inch of space between her and the wall. He'd put that bronze helmet of his back on as if it were some kind of security blanket. How he could move so effortlessly, so quietly, in that heavy black leather uniform of his, being the size he was, baffled her.

The heat of him radiated toward her, warmed her, and sparked a light inside of her that had been dormant and ignored for too long. She wobbled on her heels, her legs shaking and trembling under the strain of stooping over. Rivalin lay a hand on her arm to steady her.

Amber pressed her lips together to stop from whimpering. His hand might as well have been a branding iron. Voices echoed from beyond the grate, bouncing off the walls of the keep on the other side.

Damn! The soldiers were already patrolling the perimeter of the keep. She thought she'd have more time to get out of the building, but whoever ran these soldiers knew what he—or she—was doing.

She hugged the book close and tried not to feel disappointed when it provided no new information. No images. No forcing itself open. No doubt it was as exhausted as she felt.

"Do you know where you are going?" Rivalin asked.

"We need to get into the cover of the forest." Amber angled her head and pointed to the line of thick, blossom-drenched trees more than fifty yards away.

"And once there?" Rivalin asked.

Amber frowned. What an odd question to ask. Where was the man she'd read about? The warrior known for his ability to wing it. A master strategist who had a talent for going with the flow. Maybe he was just out of practice. Who knew what he'd suffered while he'd been locked in that cell. "We'll play it by ear. You okay?"

"I am fine." His voice carried the faintest hint of strain. "Given your actions upon your arrival, I assumed you had a plan for escape."

"I did. They didn't factor into it." She slipped her fingers through the grate and shifted closer. Three men in heavy looking uniforms, not unlike Rivalin's, had stopped at attention a few yards away on either side of the tunnel. "You have any ideas?"

"Charon."

"Charon?" Amber whispered, with a shake of her head. "Wrong story, bud. This isn't the River Styx and this better not be the passage to the underworld." No way was she ready to say "Hi" to the afterlife.

"My olappa can outrun any other creature in this realm, other than a pharenta."

"Right. Pharenta." Some kind of winged dragon-like creature if memory served. The three-legged creatures had always reminded her of a flying tripod. "This olappa of yours, it's like a horse? Can she carry two of us?" The very idea of riding a horse with this man made her cheeks flush.

"*He* can carry the weight of three grown men."

"Or one of you," Amber mumbled. "So, yeah, okay. Great. Where is he? Did they put him in his own cell?"

He hesitated briefly before answering. "He is in the stables by the drawbridge."

"Meaning on the opposite side of where we are? Awesome." Clearly she wasn't great at winging things.

"I can retrieve him and return to claim you." Those dark eyes of his glimmered in the dim light of the tunnel and made her shiver.

"Yeah, sure." Amber swallowed hard. *Claim her?* "Sounds good to me. I'll find a way to get rid of those guys out there then."

"You cannot do that." Rivalin gripped her arm, the leather of his gloves squeaking.

"Why?" She glared at him. "Because I'm a woman?"

"Because all of Dracha's men are connected by a magical tether. We—they know when one is under attack. The rest will arrive to defend or avenge them."

"Great. Military low jack. What's the range of that so-called alarm system?" She pointed to the three shadowy figures. "How long would we have before reinforcements arrive?"

"Two, maybe three minutes."

"I'll give you ten before I let them have it." She flexed her right hand repeatedly until a steady flame of fire danced across her palm. "No. I'll keep this." She hugged the book tighter when he reached for it. "You better get moving. If you aren't back in that time, I'm leaving without you."

Rivalin inclined his head, the corner of his mouth twitched. "No. You won't."

Damn. They'd known each other for a matter of minutes and he could already tell when she was lying. "Put it to the test, Riva. Get going, already."

"Riva." He jerked as if she'd slapped him. "No one's called me that in years."

There was something in his expression. Grief, maybe? Sorrow? Longing? Whatever it was struck Amber straight in her core. She lifted a hand to his face, cupped his…helmet. The tips of her fingers brushed against the smooth, worn metal. Before she could think about it, before she could think anything, she lifted his helmet up and leaned forward to kiss him.

The world faded beneath the feel of him. The taste of him. Softness beneath the strength, surprise beneath the control. Was it impulse? Or was it desire? Or maybe it was the longing to connect with the man who she only now realized had been a part of her from the first time she'd seen his name on the page. Whatever drove her, whatever inspired her, she knew that this moment, this man, this kiss, had been fated long before she was born.

It must have taken a moment to dawn on him, however. Maybe she'd shocked him, caught him off guard, but how could a man like him ever be taken by surprise? It was as if he froze, then, in the next moment, his hands had come up to capture the back of her neck, pulling her toward him as he angled his head and pressed her lips open under his. She tasted his hunger as his tongue swirled around and tempted hers into a kiss that erased all others from her memory. The strength of him surrounded her as she breathed him in: leather, sweat, and heat that might never be properly stoked except by her.

This…this was what she'd always believed a kiss should be. All encompassing, all consuming. And the magic inside of her agreed, roaring through her blood, through her body, as the storybook warrior named Rivalin did indeed claim her. She'd waited twenty-nine years to be kissed like this.

It had been worth the wait.

"Why?" He whispered against her lips when he ended the kiss.

"Why what?" she teased.

"Why would you kiss me?"

"You looked like you needed it." That was a lie. She'd needed it. More than she'd needed her next breath. She pressed her fingers against his mouth and wished they were anywhere other than where they were. "You looked sad." While she, on the other hand, had never felt more exhilarated in her life.

"I am not. Not anymore."

But he *did* look lost. Or maybe dazed. Amber rubbed her thumb across his lips. "We need to get out of here, which means you need to go. My legs are falling asleep and I'm going to need them to take those guys out."

His eyes flickered in the moonlight, then she lowered his helmet down again. "Be careful," he told her solemnly. "I'll be back."

Amber snorted. Now who was spewing movie quotes? Still, she watched him slink back down the passage and disappear into the darkness. Amber gnawed on her lower lip and tasted him again. The man could give lessons to a concubine. As expected as he was, as exciting as she found him, she couldn't shake the sensation something was off. She couldn't define or explain it. The man she'd read about, dreamed about, was almost a contradiction to the one she'd discovered in that cell.

Give him a break, she told herself. He'd been held prisoner by Dracha. Who knew what he'd been through for goddess knows how long? Torture and imprisonment could do lasting damage to a person's psyche, even a man as strong and loyal as Rivalin of the Western Realm. No wonder she'd felt the need to kiss him. He needed to be reminded of some of the good things in life.

And kissing Rivalin had most definitely felt good.

She glanced down at her watch, at the glowing hands. The second hand was ticking backwards. No, forward. Oh, backwards, again…great. She didn't even want to think about the money she'd spent on the thing only to have it not withstand a trip to a parallel magical world.

"Nine minutes and counting, bud." Amber leaned her head back against the damp, moss covered stone wall and began to count.

❖

"First!"

Rivalin grasped the saddle horn after cinching Charon's saddle. The olappa took a step back, its solid form ruffling beneath Rivalin's touch. "Lord Dracha."

Rivalin screamed inside as his body turned to face the man lumbering toward him. Every synapse in Rivalin's mind, every cell in his body fired as if trying to reboot itself. Control ebbed and waned. At times he felt like himself; others…like now? The control slipped like water through his fingers. The only thing keeping him tethered to reality was thinking of Amber. Of her kiss. And how…*alive* she'd made him feel.

"You have the intruder?" Dracha demanded.

"She waits for me by the back passage." Revulsion slithered through him. Was there no way to stop himself from betraying those he should be protecting? "I let her believe she was rescuing me from imprisonment."

"Then she trusts you?" Dracha looked impressed.

"Yes."

"And the book? Does she have it?" He reached a gnarled hand toward Charon, who shied away and snorted.

"The book?" Rivalin tightened his hold on the reins for fear his olappa would offend Dracha. Not that Dracha would injure the animal. He couldn't without causing the same injury in Rivalin, but predictability wasn't Dracha's best attributes.

"The third issue of *The Bruadarach*."

An image of the tome sliced through Rivalin's mind like a knife. He shook his head. Once. And screamed silently in pain for it. But, for the first time since he'd been cursed, he'd won the battle to stifle his response. "She arrived with someone. A silver-haired woman in white."

"Elya." Disgust coated Dracha's voice. "The priestess I sent to one of the parallel realms. Useless drone, obviously. I will learn more about these women of the books once she has been tended by the healer. She will tell us all we need to know."

Not if Rivalin had anything to say about it. If he couldn't help Amber himself, if he couldn't protect her, then there was only one solution: he had to get her to Bowen and Keane. With them, she'd be safe. What happened to him after that wouldn't matter. "What are your orders?" Falling back under the control of the spell eased the fiery pain coursing through his body.

"Mind the woman," Dracha said. "See where she goes. Who she meets. Learn what powers she possesses and what weaknesses she has. Given the power it took to invade the Keep in this way, she's more formidable than those who have arrived before her. Keep her close. And when it is time, you will bring the women and the book—if you find it—to me."

"Sir." Rivalin bowed his head and wished for death.

"When this is done, we will celebrate in the realm of Alastrine."

"And what of the women?" What of Amber?

Dracha made a dismissive gesture. "Their connection to the books aside, they are valuable. If not to me, then no doubt to one of our allies. We will earn more collateral, not to mention good will, by offering them up for purchase—after we bind their magic."

"And if they're of no use to anyone?" Rivalin forced the question out.

Dracha's lips stretched into a sickening smile. "Then they'll be of use to me. "

"Sir." Rivalin swallowed the nausea rising in his throat and gripped the saddle so tight his fingers went numb. The idea of Dracha ever putting his hands on Amber ignited a fire inside of him. One that had nothing to do with magic and everything to do with possession. All the more reason to get

Amber to his Bowen and Keane. He'd be tracked and traced by Dracha, but somehow, someway, he would find a way to keep her safe.

And make sure Dracha never got a hold of that book.

Rivalin mounted Charon with ease and welcomed the odd sense of peace that often overtook him when riding the beast. It was truly the only time he ever felt free. Despite Dracha's orders, despite the potentially treacherous journey ahead, Rivalin sagged in relief as he urged the creature on. Through the gates, across the drawbridge, around the perimeter of the keep and through the men who parted to give him clear passage, Rivalin rode.

Amber. Her name brought both pleasure and pain. He didn't want to remember what it was to feel alive, to have desire strike so hard he would do anything to make her his. Yet the feel of her, the taste of her, the smell of her sweet skin that permeated even the dankness of the tunnel beneath the Keep, had awakened something within him that made fighting possible. He'd nearly given up. But her arrival, her presence, her touch…she'd given him something to live for. But being with him, that was impossible. He had to keep his distance, no matter how much he wanted her. He had to keep her safe from the one person who could do her the most harm.

Himself.

There *had* to be a way to break this curse; to break Dracha's hold over him. His fragmented memory would work against him. Did he remember anything of importance? Would Bowen or Keane even believe him when he told them about the spear? About the curse?

It couldn't matter. One way or the either, he was done hovering between life and death. It was time to choose. Once and for all.

He thought he'd prepared himself for what would come next, for watching Amber fight her way free of the tunnel and grate. Even before he rounded the corner, he heard the hissing blast of fire that left all three men screaming before the clang of the metal gate hit the rocky soil.

Rivalin pulled up hard on the reins and brought Charon skidding to a halt before a wind-and-fire-swept Amber. Glorious Amber, he thought and blinked himself free of the dazed stupor the sight of her caused.

She may be descended from the Goddess Alastrine herself, but she was, without a doubt, a power in her own right.

Without a word, he stretched out his hand. She locked her fingers around his arm and hooked her foot into the stirrup. He swung her up and behind him, felt the book wedge between them as she gripped his arms and squeezed. "I'm good. Go!"

"Okay, we can stop for a few minutes." Amber held out as long as she could, but between the book pressing into her ribs, the constant jostling, and her empty stomach, she needed a break. This small stream beneath the glow of a grove of (what Rivalin called) Farrengold trees was the excuse she'd been looking for.

"We should keep going." Rivalin craned his head around to look behind them. "They may follow still."

"Yeah, well." She grabbed hold of Rivalin with one hand and kicked her leg back and over and dropped to the ground. Her entire body cried out equally in pain and relief and, clasping the book to her chest, she rocked back and forth. "I can't feel my butt anymore. I need to stretch." And figure out where the hell they were.

Well, other than in one of the most beautiful settings she'd ever beheld in her life. The buttercup-type flowers of the Farrengold trees flickered like tiny lanterns, casting the usual constant darkness of this realm into a silvery haze of light. The greens of the plants and surrounding flora gave way to blues, reds, pinks, and other glistening colors that put any science-fiction or fantasy movie to shame.

As she looked toward the stream, the branches bent closer, lighting her path as if sensing when she needed guidance. She could smell scents that reminded her of honeysuckle and jasmine amidst the thickness of tree trunks the size of a small car.

She'd lost track of how long they'd ridden, lost in the wonder of this night-eternal penal colony. Lost in the closeness of the man she'd loved nearly all her life. But not lost enough to forget she was here for one reason only: to find her sisters.

All that beauty and wonder aside, Rivalin aside with the book having gone silent, she could say without a doubt that they were most definitely lost.

Charon chuffed, moving back and forth as Rivalin dismounted and removed his helmet. The creature's iridescent scales reminded Amber of a dragon's. His brilliant silver tail and mane were as soft and malleable as liquid mercury. Intrigued, Amber set the book on a large rock beside the stream and cautiously approached the animal who had been going full-out from the moment they'd left the keep. You are a beauty, aren't you?" Amber whispered as she held her hand out to the creature's rounded nose. "Our horses have nothing on you."

"Be careful." Rivalin caught her arm and stopped her from petting Charon. "He's possessive and bonded to me."

"That's right." Amber had forgotten. "It's a soul connection between you, isn't it? If one of you dies, so does the other." In a storybook, it seemed romantic. In reality? Amber blinked back hot tears.

"We are one, yes." Rivalin flinched, but instead of pulling her away, he moved in behind her and covered her hand with his. Together, they stroked the side of Charon's face. Charon blinked slowly and turned his head. For a moment, Amber swore the creature was looking directly into her own soul. Good boy," Rivalin whispered. "She's a friend."

Amber felt the tension in Rivalin's body as he spoke. As if he didn't quite believe what he was saying. "I am a friend," she said. "Even though we've never met before today, I've known you all my life. I know I'm safe with you." She glanced over her shoulder and smiled up at him. "There's a reason you were in that keep when I arrived. We were meant to find one another. Fated, one might say?"

His jaw tightened, as did his hand around hers. "I am not worthy of that devotion, Amber MacQueen. Do not mistake mutual desperation for anything substantial."

"Mutual desperation?" Amber arched a brow and took the blow to her feminine wiles in stride. All the fuzzy warm thoughts that had accompanied her through the woods vanished beneath his harsh words. "Is that what that was, back in the tunnel?"

"Yes." He bit the word out with more than a tinge of irritation.

"Okay." She took a long, deep breath. "Wow. Misjudged that by a mile." She clung to the humor that shielded her from the sharpest pain. "So you're

not into me. Noted." She pulled her hand free and walked to the stream.

"I did not mean to offend." Rivalin did not follow and instead moved closer to Charon and pressed his forehead to the creature's. "This is a complicated world, Amber. We are in a complicated situation. I will help you find your sisters, but no more. There cannot be anything beyond what there is in this moment."

So much for her being good with signals. How a man could kiss her like that and not want more? She must be out of practice with more than just her magic.

"You do not agree?" Rivalin asked when she didn't respond.

Amber bent down to scoop water into her hand. "I said I felt safe with you. That wasn't some protestation of undying love." She'd kept that part to herself. She'd long given up hope of finding anyone to spend her life with. Not only because she was incredibly independent and distrustful, but what man was ever going to understand, let alone accept, that she was descended from a goddess and possessed magical abilities even she couldn't comprehend? Besides, who was to say there wasn't more of her mother in her than Amber ever wanted to believe?

The decision had been an easy one, no doubt because in the back of her mind, in the deepest corner of her heart, she'd known there would always be Rivalin.

But it was time to face the truth. Despite her devotion to the stories of *The Bruadarach*, there were no such things as fairy tales.

The water tasted crisp and fresh and she continued to drink. If for no other reason than to give herself something to do. One kiss and she'd been willing to follow him anywhere, especially if anywhere had anything resembling a bed. "Do you know where we are?" He was right. This was about finding her sisters. That was all.

"Another day and a half journey north will bring us to *Cosanta Baile*."

"Is that where Nellie and Clara will be?"

"It is a place to start," Rivalin told her. "It is the sanctuary for all those sent to this world. It is protected from most magic. Even Dracha's."

"Any chance you've got anything to eat in that saddle bag of yours?" Amber's stomach growled and she pointed to Charon.

Another hesitation. "I did not have the chance to stock provisions."

"Right." Something shifted inside Amber. Something that felt unsettled. Why couldn't she pinpoint what was bothering her about him? "Guess water will have to do then." She resumed drinking until she thought she'd float away. "What about you?" She gestured to the stream as she dunked her scarf into it and bathed her face.

"I am fine." Rivalin's tone was once again sharp, detached. Cool. "We should keep moving."

A branch snapped in the distance.

Amber dived for the book, rolling toward Rivalin as the forest around them exploded with hooded figures. Rivalin drew his sword as he reached to pull Amber behind him.

"These aren't Dracha's men." Amber's wide eyes scanned the tree lines as they became obscured behind countless dark-hooded figures.

"No, they are not," Rivalin said.

"Then who—"

"Amber?" The soft female voice broke through the darkness as the men surrounding them eased back and pulled their weapons away.

"Nellie?" Amber watched, stunned, as her middle sister, red curls flying, pale face glowing, emerged from the trees.

"Amber, thank God!" Nellie ran toward her and threw her arms around her, laughing and crying and rocking her back and forth. "You're okay! When we saw you heading for the Keep we were afraid Dracha and his men—"

"You're making me sea sick," Amber managed, with a laugh. Relief surged through her and nearly drove her to her knees. She squeezed Nellie even harder. "Are *you* okay?" Still clinging to the book, she stepped away from her sister. "What on earth are you wearing?"

"Battle armor?" Nellie grinned and gave a bit of a curtsey. "I can ride a pharenta. Or, I guess, she'll let me ride her." She glanced sideways, realizing her sister was not alone. "Um. Who's this? Hello." Nellie peeked around Amber to where Rivalin stood with his back to them. "Amber, you want to introduce us?"

"Sure." Amber took her sister's hand and tugged her closer. "Nellie, this is—"

"Stop!"

The barked order had Amber jumping, but when she looked at Nellie, she found her sister rolling her eyes in all too familiar way. "Really, Keane? I think we decided I can take care of myself."

"Keane?" Amber echoed as she watched the tall well-built man with broad shoulders and a scarred face close in. Another man followed, bigger, fairer, more handsome, but far more intense than Keane. "That would make you Bowen."

"Nellie, step away." Bowen placed himself between the women and Rivalin, who turned around. "Amber, you, too."

"What's going on?" Amber demanded as Nellie grabbed her arm and pulled her away. "No, wait. You don't understand. You don't recognize him with his helmet on, do you? It's—"

"We know exactly who this is." Keane drew his sword and aimed pressed the edge against Rivalin's throat. "Welcome home, Rivalin."

Rivalin hissed as Keane's blade drew a thin line of blood.

"I don't understand." Amber looked to her sister for help. "That's Rivalin! He's one of you."

"He *was* one of us," Bowen countered with no hint of emotion. "Now he's Dracha's First. Which means it's time for this traitor to die."

He'd been shackled by the best friends he'd ever known.

Steel and chains clanged as Rivalin was pushed along the torch-lit corridor of the citadel Keane had taken possession of; the Citadel he ran the resistance out of. The Citadel that was shielded by a magic neither Dracha nor Rivalin had been able to penetrate.

While Amber had ranted and raged during the long trek to the compound that served as base and sanctuary for those following Keane's resistance against Dracha, Rivalin had remained silent. What argument could he make in defense of the indefensible? He knew the magical bounds on him would not let him defend himself—to explain himself. And nothing Keane or Bowen told her was a lie. He *had* become Dracha's First. He led the charge against those Dracha deemed enemies. He'd called for the death of countless people, innocent or not. There wasn't a punishment suitable for the crimes he'd committed, not the least of which was betraying the oath he'd sworn to Alastrine and his fellow warriors.

Had their roles been reversed, had either Bowen or Keane found themselves in the service of Dracha, Rivalin would have swung his sword and been done. That his former comrades in arms saw fit to escort him to a prison cell themselves was only further proof they were far better men than he'd ever been.

Bowen pushed the heavy wooden door at the end of the corridor open and stood back. Keane stood at Bowen's side, doubling the uncomfortable silence stretching among them.

They didn't push him. Didn't shove him to the ground or chain him to the stones. In fact, as Rivalin stepped inside the oddly large cell, he found it wasn't a cell at all, but a room with the barest of comforts. But comforts, nonetheless.

A real four poster bed for the sleep he'd never fall into. A lighted fireplace for the warmth he'd never feel. A bowl of fruit he'd never eat.

And a window overlooking the outside world he'd no doubt never step foot in again.

Far more than he'd expected. Far more than he deserved.

Bowen and Keane stepped in behind him and, after ordering his men away, Keane closed the door and tossed Rivalin's helmet onto the bed. Bowen waved his hand. The manacles around Rivalin's wrists fell away and clanged to the floor.

Guilt and shame engulfed Rivalin, from toe to head. Every action he'd taken since arriving in this realm slammed back at him, robbing him of whatever life still coursed through his veins. How could he ever make up for all he'd done? All he'd failed to do?

How would he stop Dracha from killing them all?

"What happened to you?" Bowen stood before him, looking older than he had the last time Rivalin had seen him. His hair was longer, his face carried more scars, but his eyes, the eyes that had always seen far more than anyone was ever comfortable with, pierced him sharper than Dracha's spear ever could.

Rivalin said nothing. Not only because the words got stuck behind the spell, but because he had no explanation. How would they ever understand or believe?

"You've killed dozens of my men," Keane said in a tone that sent unusual chills down Rivalin's spine. Keane had always been the light-hearted one of their trio. The jokester, the one they could count on to relieve the tension or pressure. The deadly look in his friend's shining eyes now spoke of the responsibility he'd taken on as leader of The Outsiders. And the pain he felt at Rivalin's betrayal. "Men, women, children. All dead either by your order or your hand. You've turned your back on all we are, all we were. How? Why?"

Rivalin stood where he was, fighting against the evil rising inside of him. Somehow, someway, he had to make amends, but that would only be possible if he could tell them the truth!

"Amber told us she found you in one of Dracha's cells. That she helped you escape. That you helped her." Bowen moved in, fiery sparks of magic shooting from his fingertips. "Is that true?"

The darkness inside Rivalin roared to life and tried to push him back into the silent prison of his mind. His fisted his hands, leaned over and squeezed his eyes shut. He couldn't allow another lie to slip from his lips. Not with Amber's safety, the book's security, and his friends' lives at stake.

"Is it true?" Bowen demanded.

"No!" Rivalin dropped to his knees as the fire inside of him raged. "Not. A. Prisoner. But…Not. Free." He forced his chin up to look at his friend and begged him to hear him. "Spell." He drew in a breath that scraped his lungs like the talons of a pharenta. Then did the only thing he could think of. He pulled open his black tunic and exposed the sunburst scar covering the expanse of his chest.

"What spell is this?" Keane crouched beside him, lay a hand on Rivalin's arm and for a fraction of a moment, the pain roaring through Rivalin subsided. "What did he do to you? Bowen?" Keane looked to their friend and, in that moment, hope flared inside of Rivalin.

"Let me see." Bowen moved in, bent down and grasped Rivalin's face between his hands. "Let me see, Rivalin." The desperation in Bowen's voice acted as an almost balm against Rivalin's non-existent heart. Was it possible…would they believe him? "Stop fighting and let me in. Drop the barriers. All the ones you've built around your mind. Just let them fall."

Rivalin let out what he could only describe as a sob as he fought against the magic encasing him to surrender to his friend's order. All these endless days, months…years? All the control he'd struggled to maintain, the fragile grasp he kept on his soul…. He did the only thing he had left to do: he put his faith in Bowen and let go.

"What do you think they're doing to him?" Amber gnawed on her thumb as she paced the fire-lit room she'd been escorted to. It wasn't exactly five-star quality, but it had a medieval charm that soothed the ragged edges of her mood. No one was listening to her; if anything they were humoring her, as if a trip through a dimensional portal somehow robbed her of her intelligence and ability to be logical.

She scanned the room for the hundredth time since Nellie had arrived. A beautiful wooden bed, a mantle and hearth that took up half the stone wall. She'd washed up in the tub on the other side of a modesty screen and reluctantly discarded her damaged clothes for those she could have bought at a high-class Ren faire. She'd opted for trousers and a loose-fitting tunic rather than the waist-cinching, bosom boosting contraption Nellie had poured herself into. The modest table that sat beneath an oversized window displayed a variety of food and drink that, at the moment, made Amber's uneasy stomach churn.

The Rivalin they saw wasn't the man she knew. The man she'd helped to free. The man she'd kissed.

Kissed. Amber blew out a breath. He must have scrambled more than her hormones given how confused she felt. Had one not-so-simple kiss changed the trajectory of her life? She knew, dammit she *knew*, the man she knew and loved since childhood was in there.

Loved? Amber scrubbed her hands over her face. What insipid, ridiculous fairy tale had she fallen into?

"Bowen and Keane will do whatever they feel is necessary." Nellie poured a cup of wine and settled into one of the two chairs near the window. "This isn't easy for either of them. Clara was with Bowen when he first saw Rivalin ordering Dracha's troops. She said he was devastated."

"Where is Clara, anyway?" Amber had been beyond disappointed, and was still more than a little worried, that their youngest sister had yet to make an appearance here at what Nellie called the Citadel.

"She took the women and children to the *Cosanta Baile*," Nellie said. "Don't worry, she's safe there. Bowen would never let anything happen to her."

"Bowen." The man could put an action movie star to shame. "So, what? He and Clara are a thing like you and Keane?"

Nellie's cheeks flushed the same red as her hair. "Um, a bit more, actually." Nellie sipped her wine. "They're married."

Amber stopped pacing. "What? Like *married* married or married as in we-are-trapped-inside-a-storybook-and-it's-all-a-fairy-tale married?"

"Near as I can tell, it's all real." Nellie shifted on her chair.

"She's been gone a few hours! How on earth…oh, right." Amber snapped her fingers as the first pangs of envy struck. "We aren't on Earth, are we? And it's been longer than hours for the two of you. You're serious? Clara got married?"

"Bet you can use this now, huh?" Nellie brought over a cup and pushed it into Amber's hand. "She's happy, Amber. Happier than I've ever seen her. And he adores her. Remember all those nights we used to dream about our happily ever afters? The men we talked about; what we wanted. She found him." Nellie hesitated. "And so did I."

The men Nellie and Clara had talked about while Amber had kept her feelings about Rivalin to herself. "Don't tell me you got married without me, too."

Nellie shook her head and offered a sympathetic smile. "No. Keane and I aren't quite there yet. And Clara getting married was, in a lot of ways, *because* of Rivalin. With Bowen and Keane heading out to meet another group of resistance fighters, she wanted to be certain he'd come back to her. They had a beautiful ceremony by the lake behind the Citadel. Only Keane and I were there."

"Clara's married." Amber sank into the chair across from where Nellie reclaimed her seat. As hurt as she was not to have been at the ceremony or a part of the decision her baby sister had made given the world they'd fallen in to, she supposed she understood. "Will she stay here? In this…ah, book?" What was she saying?

"Don't know." Nellie shrugged and reached for one of the odd purple fruit-looking things on one of the plates and bit in. "We haven't gotten that far. We only knew it was a matter of time before you showed up, so that's what we've been waiting for."

"I'm that predictable, am I?" She drank some of the wine that tasted of oversweet honey and the hint of citrus.

"The two of us disappear in a weird little shop in Scotland and you don't come after us?" Nellie rolled her eyes. "Please. Speaking of that shop, I take it you met Elya."

"Oh, I met her." Amber smirked. "Brought the psycho with me, too. Last I saw her, she was lying in a heap on the floor of the cell where I found Rivalin. She's Dracha's problem, now."

Nellie sat up straight. "Elya's here? In the Forgotten Realm?"

"Uh-huh. Why?" Suspicion had her setting down her glass. "What else don't I know?"

"I don't think there's enough hours in the night to fill you in on everything. I might have to write a book. I'll be right back."

Before Amber could say another word, Nellie ran out of the room, calling for someone named Erian.

A headache niggled behind Amber's eyes. Maybe it was the lack of caffeine, but more likely her system was on maximum overload. How was it she was the one who knew everything about their heritage, about their magic, but it was Nellie, and obviously Clara, who had settled into this world as easily as walking across the street? In the hours since they'd left her they'd fallen in love. Clara had gotten married.

What was happening to her life?

"Rivalin." Amber pressed a hand against her chest and the pain that struck her heart. The ache she'd been feeling for so long finally had a name. But it was an ache that was getting worse. Bad enough to make her wince. In the distance, she heard Charon screech into the night. "They're hurting him."

Amber raced out the door, the flat soles of her stiff boots slapping against the stone as she ran down the corridor to the stairs. "Nellie?" She kept going down, down, down, until she reached the opening to the main hall where she found her sister amidst the group of men she assumed had been part of the forest brigade. "Where do they have him? Rivalin?" Amber demanded. "I need to see him."

"You cannot interrupt his questioning." A rough looking man laid a hand on Nellie's arm, his silver hair glimmering against the torches lit around the room. "Keane and Bowen left strict instructions—"

"They're killing him." Amber's mind raced as she looked at him. "I've seen your face before. What's your name?" But his name didn't matter. Because she knew who he looked like. She knew who he was.

"This is Erian," Nellie hastened to explain as she came to Amber's side. "I'll explain in private, Amber, I promise. Just, please—"

"Take me to see Rivalin. *Now.*" Amber cut Nellie off and ignored the flash of pain in her sister's eyes. "Or I'll tell all of them what I know."

"Oh, Amber." Nellie sighed, but she looked back at Erian who had stiffened his spine. "This is about so much more than you and Rivalin."

"This isn't about me and Rivalin," Amber shot back. "This is about them killing a good man. Do you hear that?" She pointed to the door where Charon let out another heart-breaking screech. "That's his olappa. If this keeps up, they'll kill him, too."

"They're soul bound," Erian confirmed, when Nellie turned questioning eyes onto her sister. "It can't be helped."

"The hell it can't!" Amber advanced, palms open, flames erupting in her hands. "Where is he? Tell me!" The men surrounding Erian drew their swords and shifted to instant attention. "You tell me or I'll blow you all into the next realm." She'd done it to the soldiers at the keep. A dozen more wouldn't stop her.

Erian didn't move. He simply arched a silver eyebrow over tightly drawn features and waited.

"Amber, stop this." Nellie came up to her. "Rivalin's not worth it. He betrayed them. Betrayed all of them. It's what Rivalin would want. Keane told me before all of this started. He wouldn't want to live this way."

Amber couldn't believe what she was hearing. "You're condoning murder."

"I'm condoning that which I think will keep these people safe. He's one of Dracha's soldiers. His First soldier. I'm sorry, but Rivalin has crimes to answer for."

The ache in Amber's chest increased as she realized she and her sister were on opposite sides for the first time in their lives. The idea she'd have to choose between Rivalin and her sisters made her physically ill. But all the more determined to fix this. "Take me to him or I'll find him myself." And if she had to burn the place down to do it, she would.

"Seriously?" Nellie's eyes went wide.

"Why won't you trust me?" Amber demanded.

"Like you trusted us with the truth about who and what we are?" The edge in Nellie's voice proved that more than just their location had changed. She wasn't the same innocent, free-spirited Nellie she'd been before she'd stepped into that store. "How long have you known about Mom? About our grandmother? About our magic?"

"Long enough that you have every right to be pissed at me," Amber agreed. "Are we really going to have this discussion while a man is being tortured to death somewhere in this castle?"

"Citadel," Nellie muttered under her breath. "And you're right. Now isn't the time. But we will talk about this."

"Awesome. Looking forward to it." Amber turned back to Erian and lifted her hands. "Are you going to take me to him or not?"

"She won't change her mind," Nellie told him.

"At ease." Erian stepped out from among his men. "Continue with the plans," he told his men. "Keane will not be pleased," he told Amber and Nellie.

"Ask me if I care?" Amber countered. "There's more to this than Rivalin's told anyone, I'm certain of it." How she was so sure, she couldn't explain. She'd known Rivalin for hours and yet…she'd known him forever. "And I'm sorry I threatened you about your sister."

"Was she alive when you last saw her?"

"She was breathing," Amber admitted. "Obviously she got the creepy eyes in the family. Silver's a much better look." The image of Elya's empty jet-black eyes would haunt her for weeks.

Erian frowned.

"I told you, she's alive," Amber added.

"That's no guarantee she'll stay that way," Erian said stiffly, as he led them to another descending staircase across the hall. "Especially after I get my hands on her."

"Boy, not a lot of forgiveness in this realm, is there?" Amber said. "Going to torture her yourself or leave it to Keane and Bowen?"

"Amber, enough." Nellie grabbed her arm and swung her around. For the first time in her life, Amber saw Nellie in a full rage. "You've been here a few hours. Stop acting as if you know and understand everything. You don't."

"I know that nothing you or Clara could ever do would ever make me want to kill you." Amber grabbed hold of the walls as Erian came to a halt. He turned and looked at her, and for a moment Amber regretted her words. "Touch a nerve, did I?"

"Do not presume to know anything about my life or family, Amber MacQueen. And be grateful I know Clara and Nellie as well as I do. Otherwise, I might judge you by the same measure as I do Dracha."

"The same measure as Rivalin?"

"Oh, for God's sake, Amber." Nellie waved them on. "You're hardly the poster child for truth and honesty. How about you see what's going on with Bowen and Keane before you go passing judgment on anyone."

"I don't have to see. I can feel it." Amber hunched over to ease the pain in her chest. "It's like they're setting him on fire from the inside."

"Wait, what?" Nellie grabbed her arm when they reached the landing. "You can feel what they're doing to him?"

"Yes." Amber steeled her expression to leave no doubt. "And no matter what he might be guilty of, he sure doesn't deserve this. He's down there?" She demanded of Erian, pointing down the hall.

"Last door on the left." He stood beneath a torch and motioned in that direction. "From here, you are on your own."

"I'm going with—"

"You will not." Erian moved in front of Nellie to stop her from following. "I will protect you as I protect Keane. If Amber wishes to see this foolishness through, that is up to her. But you will not be a part of this until Keane says. I have pledged this oath, Nellie MacQueen. I will not be deterred."

As irritated and angry as Amber was at these men for what they were doing to Rivalin, she had to admit there was something admirable about the way Erian stayed true to his word. And his loyalty to Keane.

"I'll be fine, Nellie." Amber nodded. "Erian's right. This isn't your fight." She stepped closer and looked Erian directly in his silver eyes. "It's mine." With that, she left both of them behind and headed for Rivalin's cell.

Rivalin didn't know how much longer he could withstand Bowen's mental exploration of his mind. He could feel his friend pressing in on his thoughts, around the edges of his fears and forgotten dreams. But nothing Bowen did eased the darkness swirling inside of him. A darkness neither of them could pinpoint and destroy.

He'd accepted the pain, even as it coursed through him like a raging river of fire, up and down, over and around, scorching every internal inch of him before beginning again. Bowen and Keane's voices glazed over him, barely brushing his consciousness as he struggled to remain upright against the strong pull of blessed unconsciousness.

"I can sense something's there, but I can't lock onto it." Bowen's voice echoed like a fog in Rivalin's head. "Whatever magic's been used, it's beyond anything I've ever encountered."

"Then maybe you should let me try."

Amber. No, Rivalin wanted to call to her. *Go back. Stay away.* He didn't want her near him anymore, not when he couldn't control his actions or even his thoughts. He could withstand all he'd done up until now, but to hurt Amber or cause her pain? There would be nothing worse for him than that.

Raised voices, angry voices, floated over and around him, followed by a stoking of fire he could see through the fog of darkness clouding his vision. Rivalin cringed against Bowen's loud protests. He didn't want them fighting. Not over him. Not when it wouldn't do any of them any good. Rivalin needed his friends to protect Amber, to make certain she and the book didn't get near Dracha. But how to tell them…how to convince them he was worth fighting for?

"You're killing him." Amber's voice soothed the fire in his blood. "You're killing Charon. You're killing me."

Killing…her? Rivalin shoved away the grief and self-pity and forced himself up onto his knees, shaking his head as if that could clear his thoughts.

"I can feel the battle raging inside of him," Amber whispered before her fingers stroked the side of his face. "He's in there, the man you know. Beyond the magic and the evil. I promise you, the Rivalin you trusted with your lives is somewhere inside."

Rivalin's vision cleared. He blinked, blinked again, and the stunning red-haired vision of Amber shifted into focus.

"Hey there, handsome." She was kneeling before him, the magical fire she possessed burning bright in one open hand as she traced the side of his face with the other. She remembered that Clara's husband had powers akin to her own. "Bowen, take my hand." She held out her flame-kissed one.

"Are you sure?" Keane asked him, as Bowen moved in.

"To hurt me is to hurt Clara." Bowen cast determined eyes on Amber. "I do not believe she would ever knowingly cause her sister pain."

"I wouldn't. Although, I *am* a bit ticked I wasn't invited to the wedding."

Bowen grinned, a quick flash of humor that eased Rivalin's mind, before he took Amber's hand and doused the flame.

Or so it seemed. The second Amber and Bowen's hands connected, and she moved her other hand onto Rivalin's chest, he collapsed. Convulsions overtook him, dragging him to the very edge of consciousness. He heard Keane's cries, Amber's order for Bowen to maintain his hold as she moved over Rivalin, pushing her hand more firmly against his chest. He could feel her pulse hammering against where his heart would have beat, had he still had one. Felt the magic of her seep into him, trailing and winding through his system to hunt out the darkness.

Amber bent over to whisper in his ear. "Let it happen, Riva. Let the magic happen. Don't fight me." Her lips brushed his cheek. "Let me in."

The heat in his body subsided as the tremors subsided. That controlling force that had been his constant companion, ever since Dracha pierced him with that spear, shattered like glass under the weight of his desire to please her. His Amber.

For a moment, everything stopped.

He stopped.

Then he took the deepest breath of his life. He opened his eyes.

And saw only Amber.

"Hey." She smiled at him.

Was there ever a more wondrous sight than this woman lying before him? He lifted a hand to her face, as if seeing her for the first time. Because it was the first time his mind, his thoughts, his soul, wasn't shrouded in darkness.

"There you are, Fly Boy."

"Should have realized that would work," Bowen said as he released Amber's hand and shook the magic sparks free. "Clara reignited my magic, and Nellie gave you back your sight, Keane. Stands to reason Amber was Rivalin's salvation."

"What a poet you are, Bowen," Amber said, without looking away from Rivalin. The hand pressed against his chest shifted and she frowned. "What's this?" She shoved his tunic open and stared down at the expansive scar.

"That's where he was stabbed," Bowen told her. "I saw it happen. After that water demon got a hold of Keane."

"Your heart. Does it hurt?" Amber pressed her fingers against the wound. Rivalin caught her hand, brought it to his lips and kissed the inside of her wrist.

"I don't have a heart any longer. Dracha destroyed it with his spear." Or was he wrong? An odd ache had settled inside him, around where his heart had once beat in chest. His stomach growled, and his eyes went wide.

"Someone's hungry." Keane's strained smile didn't quite reach his eyes.

"I'd forgotten..." Rivalin sat up, the wonder in his voice astonishing even himself. His limbs tingled. His head ached. He could feel the stiffness in his fingers that came from years of wielding a sword. All sensations he'd lost until now. "I can't remember the last time I ate anything. Or felt anything but pain." He kept hold of Amber's hand, afraid that if he let her go the darkness would return. "I—" He saw the doubt on his friends' faces and knew, with or without the spell, nothing could change what he'd done. He'd betrayed all he stood for, all he and his friends stood for. It was because of him they were in this realm in the first place. "There's much I need to tell

you." So much came flooding back, his head began to spin.

There was something...something important. Something vital he had to tell them, but the words, the ideas, floated past his mind and into the ether of fog.

"When was the last time you slept?" Bowen asked as he held out a hand.

Amber shifted away as Bowen helped him to his feet. Rivalin swayed against the dizziness, but even with that and the hollow feeling in his stomach, he felt better than he had in forever.

"I can't remember," Rivalin admitted.

"Let's get some food into you, then let you rest," Keane suggested. "We can talk later."

Rivalin nodded and headed for the bed where his helmet lay.

"No, not here." Amber grabbed his hand and tugged him close as she picked up his helmet and tucked it under one arm. "You'll come to my room. If that's all right?" She asked Keane.

"You will watch over him?" Bowen asked. "You will take responsibility for him?"

"The spell's been broken," Amber said. "You felt it break. I know you did."

"He's right to be concerned, Amber," Rivalin told her. Her defense of him warmed him in the best of ways, but they couldn't be too safe. He drew her to him, under his arm, and felt the rest of his world shift back on axis. His salvation, in more ways than one. "We can't be sure of anything where Dracha and his magic are concerned. Until we are, I shouldn't be left alone."

"Oh, well, in that case." She grabbed the arm looped around her neck and held on. "Let me lead the way."

"Bowen wants to head out for *Cosanta Baile* first thing tomorrow." Nellie pushed a cup of fragrant warm tea into Amber's hands. "He's anxious about Clara."

"I thought she was safe there." Amber stared into the cup, stifling the constant urge to yawn. While sleep appealed, she knew Rivalin needed it more than she did. And the man did take up nearly the entire bed. "Are you going with him?"

"Yeah." Nellie sat on the arm of the chair Amber had pulled beside the bed hours before. "Keane's staying here. Erian and Trevelyan, too. If you need anything, you only have to ask them."

"Keane maybe." Amber managed a weak smile. It's probably best I avoid Erian for the foreseeable future, seeing as I almost outed him."

Nellie sputtered something of a laugh.

"What?" Amber frowned. Was there anything to laugh about?

"That's just funny. He's already…out, in another way." Nellie grinned. "Him and Trevelyan. On again, off again, but currently on."

"Okay." Amber shrugged. "You'd think he'd cut me a break, being new to this place and all."

"Knock it off. Whining was never a good look on you. Erian's a good man, Amber. He's been a good and loyal friend to Keane. You can't blame him for being suspicious of Rivalin. Not after all he's done."

"No, I can't." Amber continued to watch Rivalin sleep, the first time he seemed at peace since she'd met him. The scar on his chest made her own hurt. The brutality of it. His heart had been destroyed and yet…that which made him Rivalin, the boy, the young man, the warrior she'd read about all her life, was still in there. She could feel it. Feel him. That he'd survived at all was a miracle. Or was it magic? I *can* resent the hell out of the fact you won't trust me about him."

"And how should I feel about you not telling me about Mom and all…this?"

Amber would gladly take anger over the defeated resignation she heard in her sister's voice. "How was I to supposed to tell you and Clara about our legacy? Growing up, even the mention of her would break Dad's heart. I saw it in his eyes every time I said her name. Believe me, I wanted to tell you what I knew. Coming to Scotland, seeing her, it seemed a less painful way."

"Dad's been gone five years, Amber. You've had more than enough time to find the words."

"I did what I thought was best." Amber swallowed the tears burning the back of her throat. As much as she'd worried about seeing their mother again after all this time, the revelation that Amber had been lying to Nellie and Clara for the past two decades was going about as well as she'd expected.

"You did what was easiest on you. And I understand why," Nellie added quickly. "You've carried a lot

on your own between us and Dad. But none of that changes the fact that you lied to us by omission. And let's face it, all this?" She waved a hand around the room, in the middle of a Citadel, located in a magical world stored in a book. "It would have been nice to have a clue before we were literally dropped into it."

"I know saying I'm sorry won't cut it." It wasn't just Nellie and Clara struggling with these newfound powers. Amber had done all of them, her mother included, a disservice by ignoring the abilities they'd inherited. How much of this could they have prevented, how much more could they have stopped, if they'd fully embraced who and what they were?

If Amber hadn't given in to the fear of being different. Of just wanting a normal life. Despite living part of hers in a dream-shrouded secret.

"You're right. Sorry doesn't change anything." Nellie drank her own tea and glanced over at Rivalin who hadn't moved since he dropped off. "I have to admit, having talked to Keane—"

"You talked to Keane about this?"

"I talk to Keane about everything. That's what people who love each other do."

"Suddenly you're the Dr. Phil of supernatural relationships."

"Don't get all bitchy because you've fallen for the bad boy of the trio." Nellie's glare was accompanied by a pointedly arched brow. "And no, I'm no expert on relationships, just what works for me and Keane. He's it for me, Amber. He was it the second he dragged me out of that lake and saved my life. He did that blind, by the way. That earned him serious bonus points."

"Don't think I want to know what he gets for those points," Amber tried to joke.

Nellie grinned as he cheeks went bright pink. "Next girls' night, you'll hear all about it. All this is my way of saying that even though we've got all this out in the open, that doesn't mean everything's peachy. I love you, Amber. And I appreciate all you've done for me and Clara, but if you're going to choose him over us, with barely a second thought? You might want to consider that maybe you're not in as much control of the situation as you think. This isn't some fun Dungeons & Dragons world. It's real. With real people who are going to get hurt if we make a mistake."

"You know he's not evil." Nothing Nellie or Keane, or Bowen or Clara, could say would ever convince her otherwise. Just as her sisters had found the men they'd been fated for, so had she. So what if hers came with extra considerations? "I know you don't have reason to trust me, after what I've done—or him, after what he's done—but I know, in here." She pressed a hand against her heart that seemed to beat only when Rivalin looked at her. "I've seen his face, heard his voice, for as long as I can remember. He's a part of me, as much as Keane is a part of you and Bowen belongs to Clara. I *know* he's on our side, Nellie. He won't betray us. I need you to believe me on that."

"I hope you're right." Nellie pursed her lips as she plucked the mug out of Amber's hands. "Because if you're wrong, a lot of people are going to pay for it."

❖

Rivalin awoke to a string of oddly grouped words that he couldn't decipher. Given the emphasis Amber gave each phrase, he assumed she was cursing. The sound made him smile.

He opened his eyes in time to see a plate drop out of her overfilled hands and shatter on the stone floor. "Son of a—" Amber glanced over her shoulder. "Oh, hey." She grinned. "Guess I woke you up. Sorry."

"I'm not." He propped himself on his arm and watched as she reorganized what looked like a feast on the small table beneath the window. As hungry as he was, there was no mistaking the unease on her face. "What's wrong?"

"Nothing."

He might not know much about where she came from or the life she led, but he had no doubt she was lying. He pushed himself up and back against the headboard, trying to remember who had undressed him and when. Hopefully not Amber, as that was something he'd have preferred to be awake for. "Amber. Come here."

"Just give me a second—"

"Amber." He softened his tone, breathed her name.

"Fine." She sighed, set everything down, and came over to sit on the edge of the bed. He patted the space closer to him. She inched up, then again until she was close enough for him to smell the citrus soap she'd used.

She gave him a quick glance before concentrating on the frayed hem of the cream-colored tunic she wore. "Did you, um, sleep okay?" She tucked her hair behind her ear. Silky, flame-colored hair that he'd been resisting the urge to capture in his hand to tug her to him.

"Tell me what's wrong."

"I'm just worried. About Nellie and Clara. About what happens next. To all of us. To this world. To our lives."

"You've had a lot to deal with, coming from where you do." She'd lulled him to sleep with tales of her life, her sisters' lives. The odd, unfamiliar world of men she'd come from. The world he'd spent only moments in. "You're scared of me. Aren't you?"

"Of you?" Amber asked, surprised. She tilted her head, shifted around and took hold of his hand. "No. No, I'm not, actually. That's what's so strange. There's nothing inside of me that doubts you, Rivalin. Nothing." She weaved her fingers through his.

"I don't know how you can, when I can't even trust myself." How he wanted to accept the solace she offered in the way she held his hand. "I'm not sure I know what it feels like to be in control of my own actions anymore. My own thoughts." They said confession was good for the soul. Given that his soul—and maybe his heart, if it still existed—was all he had left to save at this point, it was worth a shot. But Amber ducked her chin and remained silent. "Tell me what you're thinking."

"Oh, I'm not sure you want to hear it." The nervous laugh was a complete contraction to the kickass woman he'd escaped the keep with. "I guess I've just had a lot of time to think about things, and you and me and…oh, hell." She shoved her free hand into her hair and tugged hard. "You know what? I'm just going to say it. I've known you forever. And yeah, we really just met yesterday and all, but I saw you before I ever came to this world. I can't remember a time I didn't know who and what you are."

"And what am I?" He wasn't entirely sure he wanted to know.

"Amazing. Determined. Dedicated. Powerful. Dangerous." She added with that saucy grin of hers. "The first time I read *The Bruadarach* I couldn't imagine a world where you didn't exist. I wanted to be with you, know you. I couldn't wait to grow up and tell you that you were—that you *are*—everything I'd ever want or need in a man. This all sounds so silly, now. Silly teenage fantasies, I guess."

He couldn't resist any longer. He caught a curl of her hair between his fingers, reveled in its softness as it wrapped around him. "Tell me."

"You really don't want to know. Trust me." She held up a hand, absently igniting and rolling some flames across her fingers, and then she extinguished them, rolling her eyes. "And I don't know if Mama knew what would happen when I finally read those books, but I do remember her saying we'd find everything we'd ever want between the pages. And I found…you. And now, I've actually found you." The way she waved a hand from his toes to his head set his entire body on fire. "And I'm so on the record as hating that whole "you complete me" line of bullshit men have spouted on screen—"

"What men have spouted this?" The idea of Amber with other men—any other man—coiled a knot inside of him.

"Oh, in movies and…never mind. The point is, I know, in here." She pounded a fist against her chest. "That you're the man from that book. Whatever's happened to you since you came to this place, it doesn't matter to me. Because my heart tells me despite it all, the spells, the torture, you're the man I've always…loved."

"I see." He'd heard the words throughout his life, from different people, but until this moment, until they were spoken by this wondrous, brave, uncertain, fully-clothed woman, he'd never accepted it. And he'd certainly never believed it.

But did he now? Doubt crept in around the odd surge of affection sweeping through him. Was he capable of love when he didn't possess a heart? Was what he felt for her just the desire to be with her, to touch her. To possess her? Or was it…more?

"Yeah, well," she continued, unaware of his thoughts. Her brow furrowed, and she pinched her lips together. "There you have it. I know it's totally off and doesn't make any sense. I mean, Nellie thinks I'm batshit crazy, and who knows what Clara will say when she hears about this. About you. It certainly doesn't make any sense to me…. Oh, man." She scrubbed a hand over her forehead and smiled so awkwardly, so radiantly, that it sent a spear of desire straight to his soul. "I guess this is the real me, now. No more secrets. I just thought you should know. Not that you have to say anything. You had already told me that the kiss we'd shared was just mutual desperation, and you didn't want me or—"

Rivalin kissed her. As much as he adored the sound of her voice, the need to kiss her, reassure her, hold her, make love to her, overrode any reason, any trepidation. Any spell that had been cast upon him. She gasped into his mouth as he hauled her over him, pressed her lips open and dived in. He didn't need any more words; didn't want them. He only wanted her. And given her response, the feeling—and desire—was mutual.

"Okay, that's a better reaction than I'd hoped for," she responded, when she'd dragged her mouth free so she could catch her breath. "Holy hell, but I've waited a long time for this." She grabbed hold of his hair and straddled him. After taking a moment to look into his eyes, eyes that finally felt like his own, she kissed him again. "Mmmm, wait. Hang on." She continued to cling to him with one hand as she looked over her shoulder at the door. "Just want to make sure…. Damn. No lock."

He followed her gaze, seeing the door did not, indeed, have a keyhole or a latch.

"I wonder." She twisted and aimed her hand at the chair she'd spent the night in and sent it rocketing across the room where it wedged beneath the handle. "Huh." She pulled her hand back and smiled down at the residual sparks emanating from her fingers. "I'd prefer not to be interrupted. If I burn you, you'll let me know, right?" She pressed her hand flat against his chest and curled her fingers inwards, scraping his skin and making him tremble.

"I'm not entirely sure I'll notice. Amber…" He kissed her again. Softly, slowly. Completely. And waited until he felt her melt into him before he slipped his hand beneath the fabric of her shirt. "I'm yours."

She slipped her finger between his lips and rotated her hips as his hand pressed into the curve of her spine. "Best response ever."

"It's quiet," Amber whispered later as she snuggled into Rivalin's side. She'd thought him asleep, had reveled in his slow even breathing, but then his hand had moved against her and she'd looked up to find him watching her, an oddly dazed expression on his face. "I guess Bowen and Nellie have headed out to *Cosanta Baile.*" She smoothed a hand over the scar on his chest. The scar that pulsed warmly beneath her touch.

"Keane did not go with them?"

"No." Amber flinched. She didn't want to go into the whole who trusted whom saga again. "At least, that wasn't the plan. Maybe, if we eventually leave this room, we'll find out for sure."

"What is the plan?" He stroked a finger down her spine and made her shiver.

"Um. Not really sure. I only know what *my* plan was." She kissed him and settled into the crook of his arm. "I've always been a single-minded kind of woman."

"Hmmm." He pressed his lips to her forehead. "I'd say you excel at multi-tasking." He caught her wandering hand in his. "Is the book safe?"

Amber frowned. "Yeah. Keane had Erian lock it away." She lifted her head and looked into his now-somewhat-intense, handsome face. "Why?"

Rivalin shook his head. "Old habits. It's important we keep that book as far away from Dracha as possible. We can't allow him to open that portal to Alastrine's realms."

"Uh-huh. I wouldn't worry. Erian strikes me as the type of man with multiple tricks up his sleeves. Plus, he'd give his life for Keane. He'd take protecting that book as seriously as he does protecting Nellie."

"That is good to know. Do you think they expect us to join them in the hall anytime soon?"

"I think they expect me to keep you under lock and key." She rested her chin on his chest and grinned. "Unless you feel like taking a walk."

"I do not." He slipped his arm around her waist and rolled her under him. "I don't want to be anywhere other than where I am."

"Works for me," Amber squeaked as his mouth trailed down her throat, between her breasts, and… lower. "Definitely works for me."

❖

Rivalin shot up in bed, dislodging a sleepy and clearly cranky Amber. What time was it? What day was it? What—

He looked to his side as Amber pushed up under the blankets. How long had he been asleep?

"What's going on?" Amber mumbled.

Panic seized Rivalin's throat. New thoughts, memories that weren't entirely his, were fogging up his mind. Making love to her again, and remembering it, but not really being there during it….

The images flashed through his now-conscious mind.

And other thoughts…or were they memories? Dracha's men were marching, riding. Carrying torches and who knew what else on their way to—

His pulse slammed against his skin and pulled him out of bed. "Where are Keane and Bowen? I need to talk to them."

"What?" She shoved her hair out of her face and pulled the covers around her. "Rivalin, we talked about this when you asked about the book. Keane's here, but Bowen and Nellie are on their way to—"

"*Cosanta Baile.*" Dracha's plan to attack! "We have to stop them!"

"Okay, you're starting to scare me." Amber got up and followed him behind the privacy screen where he found clean clothes to wear. "What's going on?"

"Dracha's men are marching on the sanctuary, as we speak. They may even be there already." He shoved what looked like one of the dresses Nellie wore, minus the intricate lacing, into her hands. "Get dressed. And tell me what we talked about." He didn't remember talking about Nellie and Bowen.

"Okay." She draped the dress over her head and retrieved her underwear from the floor. "We'll tell Keane. He'll find a way—"

"Amber, listen to me." He swung around and grabbed her by the arms. Hard. "I didn't ask you about the book. Or about Nellie and Bowen. Do you understand? Whatever conversation you had"—he took a deep breath as fear rose in her eyes—"it wasn't with me."

"What do you mean it wasn't with you?" She glanced to the bed as her face lost all color. "The spell," she gasped. "The spell hasn't been broken, has it? You're not you?"

"I am me…." He caught her face between his hands and looked pointedly into her confused eyes and knew he couldn't lie to her. "Now."

She shook her head and backed away. "How do I know that's true?"

"Because you know when I'm lying. Just as I know when you are. It's me." Why couldn't she see? How could she not believe him now, when it mattered most?

"But I *didn't* know last night—when we had that conversation you said was not with you." The devastation glistening in her eyes hollowed him.

"Listen to me. I—no, the magic compulsion in me—was distracting you, while we were both half-asleep. But deep down, if you thought about it, you would know." He had to believe that. *She* had to believe that. "I didn't tell you everything I should have. I couldn't." Not because the spell wouldn't let him, but because he was afraid to see this exact expression on her face. "Back at the keep, Dracha ordered me to go with you, to do whatever you said. Whatever you wanted. While he made plans to attack."

"What do you mean whatever I wanted? You mean…*that?*" Amber pointed to the bed. "Don't you tell me you didn't want that. I *know* you did." Her hand sparked with angry, red hot fire.

Good. He needed her angry. He needed her focused. "Of course I did. But we weren't alone…that second time."

"Are you saying I had some weird supernatural three-way with you and…" She covered her mouth and wrenched herself out of his grasp. "Don't you dare tell me Dracha, because I don't have time to puke right now."

"It doesn't work that way. Exactly. It was me you were with, Amber. I promise, it was always me. It just means the magic compulsion was turned on to ask the questions he needed answers to, so I don't quite remember them. I would never hurt you. I would never let *him* hurt you."

"Him, who? Because if it's Dracha in your head—"

"It is not. You have to trust me. We don't have time now." But Rivalin was past the point of being able to believe anything. "Shoes." He pointed at her feet as he pulled on his boots. "We have to tell Keane to warn the others. They have to evacuate *Cosanta Baile* before it's too late."

❖

They spotted the smoke in the air.

"Hold on!" Keane ordered Amber as he angled his pharenta Sera, the three-legged dragon-like creature, to drop and circle the perimeter of the *Cosanta Baile.*

Amber looked behind her, to where Rivalin rode with Trevelyan. Whatever suspicions Keane and Erian still held about Rivalin, they'd set them aside upon the revelation that the sanctuary of this realm was under immediate threat by Dracha.

"It's not Rivalin's fault," Amber yelled into Keane's ear, but she couldn't be certain he heard her. His attention was entirely focused on the makeshift town that was engulfed in flames, screams, and howls of despair. Fear mingled with anger and sorrow as Amber gripped Keane's tense arms. This wasn't fun anymore. "We're too late, aren't we? Nellie. Clara."

"We don't know that." Keane shook his head once and increased Sera's speed. "I won't believe anything, one way or the other, until I see her."

Sera dropped to the ground in a rustling of feathers and scales, just outside the walls of the village. Keane dismounted as the other pharentas landed around them, their riders falling into formation without a word. "Fan out!" Keane ordered, as he helped Amber down. "Gather the survivors and then begin tending to the wounded. Rivalin, with me!"

Relief surged through Amber, until she realized Keane's request had more to do with him wanting to keep an eye on his friend, than trusting Rivalin had nothing to do with the attack. But if he had, why would he have said something within the time frame that allowed them to save some people, at least? Why would he have wanted to warn those who lived here? The thinnest thread of doubt wove around her strained heart.

"Amber." Rivalin came to her side, but rather than taking the hand he offered, she hugged her arms around herself and squeezed. Out of the corner of her eye, she saw his jaw clench.

"I need to find Nellie and Clara." The smoke continued to plume, fires raged, the crackle of people's homes and livelihoods evaporating into the darkness. Whatever haven this place had been, it was turning to ash before her eyes.

"You stay close to me," Keane ordered her. "Trevelyan, take charge out here. Triage area, a place for the dead. Understood?"

"Go." Trevelyan waved his scarred hands to move them on before shouting to some of the others to follow him.

Amber shivered, amidst the flames, as she entered the *Cosanta Baile* behind a strident-looking Keane. He showed no emotion on his stoic face, but held his sword in a fist so tight his knuckles had gone white in the night. She could hear Rivalin walking behind her, felt him move away as a young man cried out from beneath a collapsed structure.

"Go with Keane," Rivalin shouted, when she debated staying with him. "He'll keep you safe."

She didn't care about being safe. How could she, when no one was safe. The panic and screams surrounded her. Children cried out for their parents. Parents shrieked in desperation for their offspring. Dozens of men lined up at the central well to fill buckets of useless water as the buildings continued to burn. Women tossed children out of windows into the waiting, desperate arms of those below. The wood of market stalls snapped and collapsed. Fabric caught and burned in colors of the brightest blue and orange. A wind whipped up and sent the fires spreading faster and carried dying voices along its wake.

"Do you see them?" Amber yelled at Keane as he scooped up a terrified toddler.

"Not yet." He pointed to the ground where a man lay with a spear in his back.

Movement beneath the dead man had Amber clutching her dress and dropping down to push his body over so she could reach the baby he'd cradled in his arms. Tears of anger and fear mingled with the soot and ash of the fire streaming down her face. The infant's deafening screams etched themselves onto Amber's soul as she hurried after Keane.

"There! Nellie!" Keane yelled and pointed across the way. "She's alive."

"Keane!" Nellie screamed. She pushed a rag into the hands of a woman kneeling beside the man they'd been tending to. "Bowen's in there! Miranda and Clara are trapped!" She raced over to him, but instead of throwing herself into his arms, she pulled the child from his grasp. "He thought his magic would be enough." Nellie turned stunned eyes on Amber. "But it isn't."

"I've got them." Keane glanced at Amber, who heard the doubt and fear in his voice, before he plunged into the flames.

"Take her." Amber pushed the crying infant into Nellie's already full arms. "I've got to help him."

She made it almost to the dwelling before the building in question began to crumble. "Keane! No." Amber screamed and held her hands out in front of her face to shield herself from the explosion.

In an instant, silence descended. The fires stilled. The buildings halted mid-collapse. The entire world around her froze, even as the people around her continued to move.

"Amber." Rivalin ran up behind her. "What's happening?"

A heavy vibration pulsed against her open palms. A force pressed in on her, around her. Inside of her. She shook her head, unable to speak. Unable to think. Other than to know.

"This is me." She shifted one hand and the flaming roof of the structure Keane had stepped into began to right itself as the flames extinguished beneath the weight of her thoughts. "This is my magic. Clara and Keane are inside. Get them out." She yelled over her shoulder, uncertain how long she could keep the structures standing. Her arms ached. Her blood boiled, but she held herself still, shifting her attention to the other structures as people came screaming out.

People gathered behind her, dozens upon dozens racing toward her for safety. They fell silent, clinging to one another, clinging to her, and as they did, Amber's power strengthened. She gained more control. Beyond the quiet sobbing and tears, overtaking the now-muted roar of the flames, she could hear the magic rushing in her blood.

She nearly sagged in relief when she spotted Rivalin carrying an unconscious Clara, followed by Keane, who had an old woman thrown over one shoulder. Bowen stumbled clear behind them, his pale hair and face coated with soot and grime. He cast a grateful look at his friend as he helped him lower his wife to the ground.

"We're clear!" Rivalin yelled at her and, with a blink of her eyes, Amber released that building. It crashed in on itself. She shifted her focus, turned in a slow circle, waiting for others to clear the other structures before she released them, too. Finally, gradually, the fires died back. The people stood safe. Once again, she found Rivalin, Bowen, and Keane watching her.

She trembled from head to toe. Tears streaked down her face as the magic in her blood exhausted itself.

"It's enough, Amber." Rivalin dived for her and caught her in his arms as her legs folded under her. He cradled her, guiding her down as she leant into him. "You did enough."

But did she? "Clara? Is she okay?" Amber choked.

"She's alive," Rivalin whispered into her hair. "Thanks to you, we're alive."

But not everyone was. Amber squeezed her eyes shut, but the images of the dead followed her. If only she'd been faster with her magic. If only she'd realized sooner what she was capable of. If only—

She looked up at Rivalin. If only….

Was this her fault? Had her determination to save Rivalin, to prove he was worthy of their trust, given Dracha the opportunity to attack? Had her desire to be with Rivalin, to believe only in him, exposed those she loved to this danger?

"Let me up." Amber pushed free of Rivalin's embrace and stood on her own.

"Amber…"

"I need to see my sister." She shoved him aside and raced to where Clara coughed and wretched her lungs free in Bowen's arms. "Clara." She dropped to her knees and caught Clara's chin in her hand. "It's me, Amber."

"Where the hell have you been?" Clara choked as she drew in a raspy breath, clawing at Amber's dress to drag her into a hug. "I was afraid I'd never see you again."

"I know the feeling." Amber clung to her youngest sister until Clara pushed away and shifted around to where Keane knelt over the prone body of an older, white-haired woman with braids down the side of her face.

"Miranda?" Clara reached out for the woman's hand. "Keane? Is she—"

"She's gone." Keane sat back on his heels and tilted his head back to gaze into the endless sky. "I'm sorry, Clara."

"No," Clara sobbed and fell forward. "No, she can't be. She can't be!"

"Clara." Bowen locked his arms around her and drew her back against him. "She's at peace."

"She shouldn't be at peace, she should be here! With us. And her children and grandchildren. Oh, Bowen, they didn't know." Tears poured out of Clara's eyes and trailed down her cheeks. "They didn't even know who she was!" She turned her face into his chest and sobbed. "And now they never will."

"Clara." Amber laid a hand on her sister's head and wished she understood her sister's pain. But she understood love when she saw it. While Clara might not have been in this realm for long, it was clear she'd fallen in love with more than Bowen.

Bowen. Amber shifted her gaze over Clara's head to Bowen, who turned steely, dark eyes on Rivalin. She knew that look. She understood that stare. That anger. That rage. "Bowen, no." She grabbed his arm. "Now isn't the time—"

"Did you know about this?" Bowen yelled as Amber spun to face the man she loved. "Did you *do* this?"

Rivalin stood among the people who had run to Amber for protection. Heads taller, shoulders wider, his sorrow stronger. His sword now drawn. "I tried to stop it. He told me about the plan, yes, but I didn't remember. Not in time." He let go of his sword and let it fall to the ground. "I was too late. I'm sorry."

"What are you talking about?" Bowen demanded. "How did he do this? The sanctuary is supposed to be protected against his magic. Tell us how he did this!"

"I don't know!" Rivalin bellowed.

Amber rose to her feet, nausea rolling over her as she caught the flash of uncertainty in Rivalin's eyes. No. Not uncertainty. Deception. And guilt. "You're lying."

Rivalin shook his head. "Amber, please."

"You *do* know. Or at least you suspect. Was it you? Your…other half?" Had she been wrong? Was he capable of such destruction? Such…evil? "Is that what this has all been about? Using me to get to them? Finding a way in so you could help Dracha do this?"

Rivalin's eyes went cold. "No."

Amber's chest tightened. She wanted to believe him. But how could she when all she could feel swirling inside of her was heart crippling doubt?

Nellie pushed her way through the crowd that had fallen silent once again. The baby in her arms had stopped screaming. The child holding her hand continued to sob.

"I've only ever told you the truth, Amber," Rivalin continued. "Even when I didn't want to. And I'll tell you the truth now. While I am guilty of many things, I did not do this."

"Amber," Nellie moved toward her, but Keane caught her arm, held her back.

"But you knew it was going to happen. You knew this was what he planned."

"Don't do this, Amber. I didn't remember until now."

Amber stepped closer, stood directly in front of him, placed her foot on his sword and looked into his eyes. "Tell me how they broke through the protection magic."

He reached for her, but she moved away. "What does it matter now? The damage is done. Their families don't need the added shame—"

"Traitors." Keane murmured. "You're saying there were traitors living here, helping him. Planning this?"

"They did what they thought they needed to survive. Just as you've done. Just as Bowen's done." Rivalin lifted his chin. "I only know that Dracha chose his people with great care. People he knew would do anything to protect their families and save their own lives. Not that it matters." He glanced to the side. "They're all dead. Those who helped him. All of them."

"Tell me who they were!" Bowen demanded.

"Why? So you can interrogate their families?" Rivalin blasted back. "Their wives, their husbands? Their children? What are you going to do, Bowen? Shove yourself into their minds to uncover all their secrets? How are you better than Dracha, then?" Rivalin challenged. "I may have failed in every other respect, but I will continue to protect those I can." He tapped his head, grimacing. "It was kept from me until now, so I couldn't warn you in time, but now I know who was responsible. And they will not betray anyone ever again. They've already paid the ultimate price for their treachery."

"Not all of them," Keane seethed and Amber's stomach soured.

"That is not your call to make," Bowen added.

"No, it would have been Miranda's." Clara spoke for the first time. "Rivalin is right. The damage is done. Too many lives are already destroyed. If he says the threat is gone, I believe him."

"Believe him?" Bowen looked at his wife as if he'd never seen her before. "You don't even know him."

"No, but I know you. And I know Amber." Clara swiped the tears from her face. "And I can see how much you both care about him, despite how angry you are. You're letting your emotions get the better of you. All of us are which is exactly what Dracha is counting on." She turned to her sister. "Amber, is Rivalin telling the truth now? Do you believe him when he says those responsible are gone?"

Amber searched Rivalin's bereft face, steeling her heart against the sadness in his eyes. Whatever doubt she'd picked up, whatever hesitancy, she sensed none of it now. He looked back at her without flinching. "Yes, he's telling the truth this time."

Rivalin closed his eyes.

"Then let's move on." Clara urged her husband. "If you can't forgive the man he is now, forgive the friend you remember, Bowen. These people need our help. Not your rage. Miranda wouldn't want this. And I don't either."

Amber's heart stuttered. When had her baby sister become the wise one?

"Fine. Go." Bowen stood up and helped Clara to her feet.

Rivalin took a step forward. "I can help with—"

"We don't want your help!"

Amber's heart shattered as Rivalin bowed his head. He picked up his sword and backed up while what was left of the people of *Cosanta Baile* parted for him. She watched him head out of the village, and it was only when he passed through the entrance that she realized her mistake. "Rivalin, wait!"

He stopped, but kept his back to her as she ran after him.

"Rivalin." She caught his arm but couldn't make him budge. She stepped around and in front of him and wished she could take her accusations back. Wished she'd never doubted him. "Why couldn't you remember about the spies? We could have stopped this."

"I told you earlier. The spell was never broken, Amber." He brushed a finger down the side of her face. "He kept it from me. The memory of my orders, and what I had overheard about his plans. He made me believe I was free. Dracha might have loosened the reins, but no matter what I do, no matter how hard I fight him, he's still in here." He tapped his temple. "He's lurking. Waiting to use that which I care most about against me. He's done that with Bowen and Keane, with the people I swore to protect." He touched his heart. "And now with you."

"Rivalin, no." Why couldn't she find the right words? "I was wrong." The only time he had *chosen* to lie, had been to protect the innocent families of the spies. Every action he'd done that was bad, or not helpful, had *not* been of his own choice. That was a distinction they all should have focused on before now. The darkness in Rivalin was not there with his permission. Rivalin would have only done good, if it had been his choice. "We can fix this. We can find a way to break the spell—"

"There is no breaking the spell, Amber. There's only ending it. And that's something I have to do on my own." He brushed his fingers against her face. "That spear destroyed my heart. It stole all I was and all I could ever hope to be. Now I can only pray there's enough of my soul left to end this once and for all."

"What are you talking about?" Alarm now mingled with the concern she felt for him. "What do you mean end this once and for all?"

"Amber." His lips curved in a small smile as a light caught in his eyes. "Had I heart left it would be filled with you. Thank you for reminding me what I've always been. And what I'm meant to do." He brushed his mouth against hers. "I love you. May you live a long, happy life."

"He's going to do something stupid." Amber paced by the windows of the great hall, Rivalin's helmet clutched in her hands. It had been hours, maybe even a day, since they'd returned to the Citadel. Bowen, Keane, and their resistance fighters. Dozens upon dozens of survivors from the attack. Food was being prepared while sleeping quarters were being arranged. The ghostly echoes of the sparsely occupied castle had faded beneath the chatter and sorrow-filled cries of her grandmother's people.

"See to the plans," Keane ordered from his place at the long, wooden table by the roaring hearth. His men vacated the room leaving him, Bowen, Trevelyan, Nellie and Clara in strained silence. "Amber?"

Bowen stood behind Clara, his hands resting lightly on her shoulders as she continued to swipe tears from her cheeks. "What did Rivalin say to you before he left?"

"Why? Do you even care?"

"Amber." Nellie sighed. "Don't make this more difficult than it already is. You can't blame Keane or Bowen for reacting the way they did. People died. Innocent people."

"People are still dying," Clara added, referring to those still succumbing to fire related injuries.

"Why did Dracha attack the sanctuary?" Amber asked the question she'd been mulling for hours. "Why now?"

"To cut our numbers down," Keane said. "To stop others from joining the resistance."

"But he first attacked when Rivalin was with me at the Citadel. He didn't use his First in the attack, which would have meant a larger casualty number. And we now know he could have forced Rivalin to kill, because he's still in control of his body; he just gave Rivalin the *illusion* of free will. But he hasn't tried to control him again. Instead, he let him watch the disaster at *Cosanta Baile* unfold, like some form of torture. Why?" Amber shook her head. "There's something we're missing here. Something we aren't seeing. I don't think this was about attacking the *Cosanta Baile*. It can't be, otherwise he would have done this ages ago, before anyone even thought about creating a resistance."

Bowen's hands stilled. "Go on."

Encouraged, Amber ran her fingers along the edge of Rivalin's helmet. "This spell Dracha cast on him, what does it do exactly? Do we know?"

"It turned him into an automaton," Nellie said as she poured herself a cup of tea. "Like the Walking Dead only unkillable."

"Exactly." Amber nodded. "So why would Dracha have let Rivalin go with me in the first place? He knew Rivalin wouldn't be trusted by us once Dracha made sure he could not warn us. He knew this was only going to end one way, especially after he attacked the sanctuary. What was he hoping to gain?"

"He didn't gain anything other than…" Keane's gaze shot to Bowen. "We cut Rivalin out completely. We banished him. Again."

The fear that had been spinning inside Amber picked up speed, gained a focus. "So he did the only thing he thought he could do to protect us. He went back to Dracha. To end the spell."

"Break the spell you mean," Clara said.

"No." Amber shook her head. "No. He said he was going back to end the spell and that he was the only one who could."

"He's going to kill himself?" Nellie exclaimed.

Amber nodded as the realization hit her, her heart breaking.

"But how does that help Dracha?" Bowen asked, "To send him to us, only to then entice him back in order to kill himself. That would break the spell—and he would lose his First, his most powerful warrior."

"Not quite." Erian spoke from where he stood in the doorway leading into the catacombs beneath the Citadel. "Rivalin is about to do something very, very stupid. Come with me. All of you. You need to see this."

Amber and the others trailed behind down the curving stone staircase into the torch lit passageways that smelled moldy and dank. Erian's shadow guided them into a large, circular room filled with thousands upon thousands of books, rolled pieces of parchments, and odd torches that glowed but didn't burn.

"Something Amber said when she first got here reminded me of something." Erian ushered them inside and retrieved an enormous thick book from a table in the center of the room. "Elya's and my grandmother was a sorceress. One who devoted her life to Alastrine and her family. When we were children, I remember her telling us the story about a spell used to enchant enemies. The greater the hatred for the spell caster, the tighter the bond. Amber, you said Elya had black eyes."

"Yeah." Amber stroked her hand over one of the books. Dust and grime coated her fingers. "Creepy black eyes. Didn't seem human."

"Because what's taken up residence inside of her isn't. She's being used as a host by a creature sympathetic to Dracha's plan. We've known all he wants is to overtake Alastrine's realms. He can only do that with creatures that can't die. But these creatures can't survive in our world, not without a human host. They're energy. Dark matter. Smoke. And I'm betting all the soldiers fighting for Dracha, Elya included, have been taken over."

"That would explain why, after thirty years, she looks younger than me," Amber said.

"She was an old woman with me," Clara said. "Can these things shift form?"

"Absolutely, but not easily. It steals their magic. Weakens them. Only by returning to this realm can they be recharged by the magic trapped here."

"And I brought her back," Amber whispered. Had she condemned his sister to a fate worse than death? "I'm so sorry, Erian."

"You couldn't have known." Erian said.

"Can you break that spell?" Trevelyan asked his partner, resting a hand on his arm. "Is there hope of saving your sister?"

"The only way to break the spell is by casting Dracha out of this realm. Once he's no longer in control of the Forgotten Realm, the magic he's used here will die. Everyone should be set free."

"Including Rivalin?" Nellie asked.

"No." Erian grimaced. "Dracha is using him for something else and I think I've found out what." He shifted to the table behind him and unrolled a decaying bit of parchment. "That spell that destroyed Rivalin's heart. It left a starburst pattern, you said." He turned the paper around. "Does it look like this?"

"Yeah, exactly like that." Amber felt Keane and Bowen move in on either side of her. "What does that mean?"

"It means the spell hasn't been completed yet. What do you know about the books, Amber? The books you and Clara and Nellie brought through with you?"

Amber glanced at her sisters, who both shrugged. "You're the one Mom told about all this," Nellie said. "We're still clueless."

Amber tried to condense thirty years of memories quickly. "The gist is that when all three books are together, they can open the portal to their place of origin. But the books can't be read or touched by anyone other than the three of us."

"Or someone connected to you," Erian revealed. "You said you've always felt connected to Rivalin. Was he able to touch the book?"

She thought back to their "escape." She nodded.

"You knew he was in pain when Keane and Bowen were questioning him. He's a part of you, like Clar on is part of him. The book recognizes him as such; it didn't turn him to dust."

"One would hope she isn't destined to die when he does," Clara said.

"I think their connection is stronger than that," Erian said. "It would have to be for her to have felt as strongly as she has about him all these years. And I think, after last night, you're probably more connected to him than ever."

Amber felt her face flush. "You think sleeping with Rivalin created some kind of magical bond?"

He nodded gravely. "One that makes him capable of reading those books, which is what Dracha wants to do most. The attack on the *Cosanta Baile* wasn't about stifling the rebellion," Erian told them. "It was about creating a wedge so big between Rivalin and the rest of us that he believed he had no choice other than to return to Dracha and end the spell. He went back to destroy the spear."

"Because he thinks it'll kill him."

"Which would be the something stupid, right?" Amber tried to joke even as she felt Keane place a comforting hand on her shoulder. It was all she could do not to muster all her magic, grab Charon, and ride to Rivalin's rescue.

"Incredibly stupid," Erian said. "Dracha can't complete the spell himself, or open the portal to Alastrine's realms without aid. He either need all three of you, with your magical goddess blood and your books, *choosing* to help him—or it has to be an act of self-sacrifice, meaning only Rivalin can complete it. The second Rivalin destroys that spear, whatever remains of his soul will disappear. It will leave all of his thoughts, all his knowledge, about everything he's ever done, every person he's ever known, intact. He will become a magical shell no one can destroy. A shell that will have enough magical power to use the books and be able to open that portal at Dracha's behest. Dracha will become unstoppable, and Rivalin will be lost to us for good."

"Man, karma has a serious bitchy side to her," Nellie muttered. "We asked for this, didn't we? Turning on him the way we did?"

"We have to stop him," Bowen whispered with a desperation that both warmed Amber's heart and chilled her to the bone. "But how? Why should he

trust anything Keane or I tell him. This time it's we who betrayed him."

"You wouldn't have brought us down here if you didn't know already," Amber said to Erian who was already retrieving another rolled parchment. "What do we need to do?"

"Not *we*." Erian handed her the scroll and the book she'd brought with her from her world. "*You*. You're the only one who can stop him, Amber. And by stop him, I mean kill him."

Rivalin had lost track of the hours he'd waited, hunkered in the woods outside the tunnel, where only days before he and Amber had escaped. When he finally approached, he found that the grate hadn't been replaced. Dracha expected him to come back. To sneak back in the way he'd left.

As if Rivalin was going to do anything Dracha wanted him to do.

Hand poised on the hilt of his sword, he began the trek around the Keep. The soldiers he'd once commanded descended on him like flies on a corpse, but he brushed them off, shoving through and past them. Either Dracha would drive that spear into him and end his suffering, or Rivalin would do it himself. Regardless, he'd rid Dracha of his most prized weapon and hopefully, Goddess willing, protect Amber and the others from Dracha's final scenario.

It wasn't Dracha, however, who waited to greet him, but the silver-haired woman who had arrived with Amber. She wore a uniform of blood red and moved far less gracefully than Rivalin would have expected. The black, vacant eyes shimmered with resolve as she turned to lead him into the Keep, down the hallway and into the cavernous hall where Dracha sat upon his bone-encrusted throne.

"You've returned at last." Dracha's voice carried a hint of lightness Rivalin couldn't recall ever hearing before. "Come for this, have you?" He motioned to the spear as the woman took her place at his side.

"End this, once and for all." Rivalin pushed the words beyond the barriers in his mind. Since leaving the sanctuary, a calm strength had overcome him. A control that surpassed even that provided by the tomes sitting untouched across the room. The spell might still be intact, but he could still find ways around it.

"Oh, I plan to." Dracha waved his hand and the books rattled against their bindings. "Did you bring the last tome?"

"I did not." And he'd paid the price for it, with the branding-iron hot pains shooting through him the closer he got to the Keep. He had been ordered to return with the sisters, and the last book, and he had failed. Still, the only thing he had on his mind was destroying that spear. That purpose had helped him fight the compulsion to return for the magical tome.

Dracha's fists clenched. "You will return to the Citadel and reclaim that book."

"He doesn't have to."

The voice that echoed behind Rivalin, throughout the room, terrified him more than a bronze spear ever had. "Amber." He spun around and found her standing in the open doorway, Bowen and Keane standing on either side of her. Nellie and Clara, and Erian and Trevelyan, came in behind them.

And in Amber's hand…

The third tome.

"What are you—" Rivalin's voice was cut off. Pain sliced through his torso and he dropped to his knees, unable to catch his breath.

"Leave him be, Dracha!" Amber advanced after passing the book to Bowen, who—with Nellie and Clara—ran to the dais to claim the other two tomes and stacked them on the floor, one on top of the other, on top of the other.

What was happening?

Rivalin dragged his gaze back to Amber. She wore the black uniform of one of Keane's resistance fighters and on her head, covering that brilliant flame-red hair, Rivalin's helmet. "I know what you're thinking, Dracha. But I'll tell you, here and now, you won't be returning to Alastrine's realms."

"Are you sure about that?" Dracha dropped then kicked the spear over to Rivalin. It rattled against the stone floor. "You know what you have to do, First. You know that breaking that spear is the only way to protect them. Do it and I'll let them live."

Rivalin groaned as he reached for the spear. Why would the Dracha give it to him so easily, *and* say he could use it to protect them? He'd expected to have to use the light Amber had brought into his life to help him fight against the darkness binding his soul, in order to claim the spear and blessed oblivion.

But now the spear had just been handed—or rather thrown—to him.

He was sure Dracha didn't want Rivalin to break the spear—the source of his power over him—but when he nudged the darkness wrapping his mind in a vice, there was no compulsion to protect the weapon. So what did that mean, then?

Then he realized Dracha was now up against *three* powerful goddess-born, and their partners. Dracha would use him against them, make him *seem* to be on their side, then take them by surprise. Again.

This was just another ruse.

He remembered all the deaths that had been caused by his hand. Bowen's parting comment haunted him. If he didn't kill himself, Dracha might turn him against his own friends. He remembered his promise to Amber, that he would never hurt her.

He didn't have a choice. Not when it came to protecting the woman he loved.

His fingers brushed against the blood-stained hilt of the spear. The wood warmed beneath his touch. Amber's foot landed hard on his hand.

"Do it and I'll make your afterlife a living hell," she said.

"Amber," he gasped. "What—"

She bent down, brushed a hand down his cheek. "I need you to trust me. I need you to trust us. All of us. Please." She pressed her lips against his. He tasted her tears, felt the fire of her magic. "I love you." She picked up the spear and removed the helmet.

"Amber?" What was happening? What was she…?

She looked him straight in the eye. And drove the spear into his chest.

Rivalin gasped. He choked. She pulled the spear free and threw it to Bowen as she rounded on a surprised Dracha.

Rivalin coughed, dragged in ragged breaths and spewed blood as he fell onto his back and stared up at the ceiling. The darkness closed in. The blood rushing through his veins slowed. His breathing started to fade.

"Bowen?" Amber's shouted question echoed in the hall as Erian and Trevelyan raced over to Rivalin and hauled him to his feet. He tried to speak, to beg to plead with them to help Amber, but his voice was gone. His legs refused to hold him up; he had no strength left. He could feel whatever life remained inside of him draining, drop by drop.

"Ready!" Bowen yelled back.

Through the fog in his mind, Rivalin watched as Bowen handed the spear over to Clara, who held it out to Nellie. Together they grasped the spear and held it over the books.

"Do it!" Amber yelled.

"No." Rivalin's protest sounded more like a grunt as Clara bent to place her hand against the brass lock on the top *Bruadarach*. The one Amber had brought through. It threw itself open beneath her touch. "You can't let Dracha—"

Amber whipped around. "Save your strength!"

His strength? Rivalin might have laughed if he didn't think it would kill him. The hole in his chest continued to ooze blood, drenching the stone floor as it seeped beneath and into the cracks.

Dracha's face stretched into a sneering smile, his eyes flickering with amusement and triumph as he looked at the sisters. "I never thought I would get all three of you together, opening a portal willingly. That was why I had pinned my hopes on this pathetic shell of a warrior. You're only doing that which you're fated to do. What you were *always* fated to do."

"I know." She pointed to the discarded helmet. *That* showed me. Everything you used to control Rivalin, all those thoughts and plans that passed between you both, I've seen them. I've heard them." She moved closer to him. "I *know* them. And I've changed them."

Dracha shook his head. "You're stalling. If you do it now, the magic binding Rivalin will dissipate as soon as I leave this world; you could try to save him." He glanced over at his First, his eyes gleaming to see so much blood. "End this now. Open the portal."

"Be careful what you wish for."

Rivalin slumped forward. *Amber. Hurry.* He couldn't hold out much longer. His chest, behind which his heart had once beat, seared with pain.

She started, looked over at him, as if she'd heard what he'd said.

Slowly, Amber stood up straight. Lowered her hands. And smiled.

The Keep rumbled around them. Bowen and Keane were suddenly at Rivalin's side, Keane taking

Erian's place as he hurried to his sister. Elya stood frozen beside the throne, her body trembling as if fighting off an infection. Her brother caught her around the waist as her knees buckled.

"Last chance to change your mind, Dracha," Amber yelled as a riotous roar encompassed the hall. She raced up the dais to join her sisters as an eerie silence fell.

Dracha turned, just as Amber joined her sisters in grasping the spear. Together they twisted it around, aimed it.

"No." Dracha's whisper echoed in the hall.

"Now!" Amber yelled. Together, the three women plunged the spear into the heart of the open tome, and straight through it into the second and third. And set them all to screaming. The tomes burst open, the light and power inside exploding up and out and around. The world screamed.

Or was it Rivalin? He couldn't be sure.

Dracha gasped, threw his head back and looked up as the whirling, spinning portal he'd plotted and schemed and killed to access opened above him. Dracha laughed, but as Rivalin looked back to Amber and her sisters, he saw Amber smile. And he understood.

While Dracha looked up into the slowly forming portal, Amber, Nellie and Clara released the spear and stretched out their hands, moving as one to descend and surround him. The stones beneath and around Dracha's feet trembled and crumbled. They dropped away to reveal the fiery volcanic pit of swirling rivers that cascaded far beneath the Keep.

Dracha stretched his arms up and laughed, ready to embrace the universe he was determined to claim as his own.

The portal above them expanded until it encompassed the entire ceiling. Filmy, floating, shimmering darkness sparked with the stars and planets Rivalin had only read about in books. Dracha's feet lifted off the ground as he began to float up.

"Hey, Dracha!" Amber yelled as the skin-scorching wind blew her hair back and reddened her face. "Wrong way!" She drew her hands down hard.

The last of the stones fell away, leaving Dracha hovering in air, caught between this world and the next.

Amber walked to the edge of the stone circle. Heat blasted up from the depths, flames licking at Dracha's feet and legs. His face contorted as realization dawned. His eyes flashed. His hands whipped out as if to lock around Amber's throat.

"Just so you know," Amber said. "This is a one-way trip." She glanced at her sisters. "Let him go."

Nellie and Clara lowered their hands.

Dracha hovered for another moment then, without a sound, he dropped straight to hell.

The shadows, the smoke demons, all he'd controlled and commanded, shot free of their hosts and followed.

The portal above them closed with a quiet *wumph.*

The stones at their feet reformed as the second portal closed.

The hall went silent.

"Is that all it took?" Nellie flipped a smoking red curl behind her shoulder and huffed. "Seemed a bit anticlimactic if you ask me."

"Yeah, two portals, multiple dimensions. Totally ordinary." Clara grinned. "For a MacQueen woman."

Rivalin groaned and pitched forward. But he didn't fall.

Not only had Keane and Bowen held on, but Amber was now there. Touching his face, his arms, his shoulders.

The pain, the fire, the burning, was gone. Exhaustion crept over him as he pulled his feet under him. Amber ripped open his tunic to examine where the spear had pierced him a second time. The wound was closing beneath her touch, and as it did, his mind became his again.

All the darkness. All the barriers. The despair, the fear, the anger. All gone.

He was blessedly, thankfully, at peace.

Amber caught Rivalin's pale face between her hands and pressed her lips to his. "You good?" Her voice sounded raw to her own ears. Fire and damnation did that to a girl. Never in her life had she been so terrified. Or so confident. She knew this moment would come.

"I've been better." Rivalin choked. "And I've been a hell of a lot worse, too."

"The lengths I'll go to for a date." Amber wrapped her arms around him as Bowen and Keane stepped away. "Hang on, I've got you." She staggered under

his weight, but she was held up by her sisters. "You and I are going to have a serious talk about self sacrifice. You hear me, Fly Boy?" Once she was able to let go of him long enough to lecture him. For the time being, she was happy to have him as is.

"Whatever you say."

"Sounds like a match made in heaven to me," Clara said. "What about Elya?"

"I've got her." Erian called from beside the throne

"Erian?" Elya choked as Trevelyan headed over to help. "What happened? What's going on?" Her silver eyes scanned the room as if she were coming out a trance. "The last I remember I was—oh!" She caught sight of Rivalin. "You were there. In the court of Alastrine. You'd overheard the priests plotting her murder. They cast you out before you could warn her They cast both of us out."

"That's right." Rivalin blinked as if recalling a new memory. "You tried to help."

Erian wrapped his sister in his arms and held on tight, before holding out his hand for Trevelyan.

"So that's what happened?" Bowen demanded of Rivalin while Amber helped him over to the steps of the dais. "You tried to stop—"

"Alastrine's assassination." Rivalin shuddered. "I don't know what happened after that."

"I think I do." Clara was headed out of the hall "You aren't going to believe this, but I think…Oh my god. You have to come see this." She waved them over, holding out her hand to Bowen.

"You want me to carry you?" Amber teased, once everyone had gone. The world righted itself. All the worlds. Because all of them were where she belonged, as long as she had Rivalin.

"Maybe just for today." He kissed her. "I can feel my heart." He took her hand and pressed it against his chest. "It's the most amazing sensation. Almost as good as this." He kissed her again "There are no words."

"Sure there are." Her grin made him laugh. "Give it a shot."

"I love you. I think I always have."

"Fate's funny that way. I'm hoping it'll take a bit of a vacation now, though. I need a break."

"Amber!" Nellie yelled from outside.

"Guess we'd better see what's going on," Rivalin said

"Unbelievable," Amber whispered as they stepped outside into the sunshine. "After all that, and not a moment's…holy hell. Or is it heaven?"

"My thoughts exactly."

The sun beamed down on the Forgotten Realm. The sky had gone clear. The dark stone of the Keep had been transformed into shimmering, shiny silver. Dracha's soldiers removed their helmets, blinked free of the black, endless eyes, as if seeing for the first time.

People wandered out of the forest, dazed, laughing, smiling. All the survivors of the attack. All those who had stayed behind in the sanctuary to begin the rebuilding. All of the rebels who had fought side-by-side with Keane to defeat the evil Dracha brought upon their world. And there, standing before them all, a woman clad in shimmering, sparkling white and gold.

With flame-red hair and green eyes.

Rivalin's legs trembled again. "Alastrine."

"Ala—huh?" Amber balked at Rivalin's revelation.

His people knelt, all of them, before the Goddess of the Realms—even Bowen and Keane—while Clara, Nellie, and Amber remained on their feet, staring, dumbfounded at their grandmother.

"Amber," Rivalin whispered. "Let go. I need to—"

"You do not." Alastrine's voice floated over them as she strode toward them. "Rise, Bowen. Keane. For I do not deserve your fealty. Not until you have my apology." She touched them each on the shoulder and drew them with her to the sisters. "And my undying gratitude. Nellie. Clara." Alastrine cupped each of their faces in turn. "Amber. What wondrous women you are."

"Hey, Grandma." Amber's lips twitched.

Rivalin groaned. Keane and Bowen ducked their heads, but not before she saw them smile.

"We have much to talk about. All of us," Alastrine told them. "But not today."

"What happens now?" Nellie asks. "Where do we go? What world—"

"Nellie, hush." Keane circled around her and wrapped his arm around her waist. "She'll tell us."

"No, I won't tell you." Alastrine said with a smile. It is not up to me to decide what your life is, from this moment forward. You have all done as you were meant to in ridding the realms of Dracha and his darkness. And for that, I will give you whatever you ask."

"Our families?" Bowen asked, as he reached for Clara and drew her over to him. "My parents, brothers and sisters?"

"Are all well in your realm. As are *all* of your families. Those responsible for your banishment have been removed from power and are no longer an issue."

"Bet they didn't get the fire pit though," Nellie rocked back on her heels.

"Indeed not," Alastrine nodded with a glimmer of amusement in her eyes. "What is it you want, my beautiful girls?"

"Mom." Clara spoke first, startling herself, apparently, as she cast surprised eyes to Nellie then Amber. "We'd like to see our mother."

"Agreed," Nellie and Amber said together.

Alastrine bowed her head and removed a trio of amulets from around her neck. "These will allow you to travel between all the realms under my rule. All you need do is wish yourself there and you, and whoever you hold close in spirit and in reality"— she glanced down at Amber and Rivalin's clasped hands—"will be with you."

"Our own personal portals." Amber clasped her amulet in her palm. "Cool."

"And for you three." Alastrine opened her hand and offered three braided gold bands. "I believe you will find a use for these."

"Bride's family usually pays for the wedding," Amber said. "Just saying." She laughed when Rivalin gave her a quick, tight squeeze. "I'm guessing as a goddess, you do a pretty mean reception."

"Should you choose it, we would be honored to host your bindings in my realm. And celebrate the return of my family." Alastrine turned toward her people. "Those of you who wish to return with me may do so. Those of you who wish to stay, this realm will now be under the watch of Erian. Your new Warden."

"Hot damn." Nellie reached around and nudged Erian. "Score! You got your own realm!"

Erian blinked as if not quite understanding. "Your highness?"

"You and Trevelyan have earned it." She offered another pair or rings. "Loyalty is always rewarded."

The goddess turned to Elya. "There is a place for you in the temple when, and if, you decide to return."

"Thank you."

Amber wasn't so sure that was going to happen. The poor girl—and she could see now that she was still a girl in the way she clung to her brother—looked beyond frazzled. No doubt a lot of soul-searching was in the cards for the young priestess.

"Trevelyan," Alastrine said. "I would appreciate your help with the fire demons and pharentas in the other realms. Perhaps you would be of assistance?"

"I would be honored." Trevelyan nodded.

"Then, I will see you all soon." Alastrine gave them a final smile before she vanished.

"Guess that means we can go home—for a while," Clara said. "I can't even begin to figure out our living arrangements now."

Bowen pulled her close. "My home is wherever you are."

"Perfectly said," Keane echoed. "I've had enough magic for a while. How about you show us your world?"

"How about we all do?" Amber looked to Rivalin for his assent, then nodded to her sisters. They each closed their hands around their amulets. A cool wind rushed around them, a gentle tug spun them, and a moment later, they found themselves on the edge of a small valley. The took in the dusting of snow over a field of blooming—

"Since when does heather and lavender bloom in the middle of winter? And hey!" Amber let go of Rivalin and stretched out her arms to spin. "My clothes are back." She kicked out one foot. "My boots! Hallelujah, my boots!" Her eyes went wide as she caught sight of Rivalin in jeans and a heavy cable knit sweater. "Oh. My. Grandma really knows how to make up for past mistakes. You feeling okay there, Fly Boy?"

"I feel," he took a deep breath, "alive."

"I'll bet. Nellie? Clara?" She looked over to her sisters, who seemed to be having the same reaction to seeing Bowen and Keane in Earth street clothes, as Amber had to Rivalin. "Boy, if we ever have kids, they'll have hit the genetic jackpot."

"Kids sound good," Clara whispered, earning a kiss from Bowen. "I like the name Miranda, for a girl."

"As do I," Bowen agreed.

"Anyone know what happened to the car?" Nellie asked as they turned to look into the valley.

"We can worry about that later." Amber's delighted gaze landed on the cottage below. Despite it being winter, and the snow falling all around, the cottage and land surrounding it appeared to be in its own patch of perfect summer sunshine. Flowers and flora of all kind encompassed it, trailing over the roof, down the trellised walls. A small stable sat beyond it, and, in that moment, two familiar magical creatures appeared.

"Charon," Rivalin whispered, a delighted smile spreading across his face. "And Sera."

They could hear Charon's chuff from a distance as Sera took flight and soared toward them. "I might have cast an extra thought for them," Amber explained, spotting Keane's overwhelmed and grateful expression.

"Amber? Is that—" Clara pointed to the woman emerging from the house. Familiar red hair, she was barefoot and wore a simple flowered dress in hues of yellows and blue. She stopped in the garden, shielded her eyes, and after a moment, she waved.

"Mama," Amber whispered.

"Shona," Rivalin said.

The dread was gone, the fear and doubt left far behind in a world of magic and wonder. It all made sense now. All the pain and anger she'd felt for the woman who had left them behind. She understood so much more; what had been at stake. And how difficult it must have been for her to leave her children. None of that mattered now. Amber's heart had been refilled with the unending feeling of peace and love.

For the man at her side, and the woman in a house that waited for them in a Scottish valley.

Beneath a Farrengold tree.

Copyright © 2018 by Anna J. Stewart.

CLOSING EDITORIAL

by Lezli Robyn

A Tina and I have ended yet another issue with more than enough love to get us through cold summer months....

Yes, you read correctly: I wrote cold. It's been an unseasonably chilly spring on the East Coast, and if it weren't for all our authors warming me up with their stories, I'd begin to despair we'd ever experience any heat this coming summer.

But you see, that is the amazing thing about romance stories. I don't just mean they get you all hot and bothered with steamy love scenes (although they do that, too!). But love stories help show us that there is warmth in this world, in people, and that is enough to thaw the coldest spring.

While I'm sad to say goodbye to Anna J. Stewart (just for now!), next issue we'll be delighted to welcome back L. Penelope, with yet another story in her Before I series and Petronella Glover has sold her first story to us that does *not* involve astronauts—although there will be a mermaid or two.

If the thought of frolicking on the beach isn't enough to warm your toes (or tails!), Alice Faris' delightful *Pregnant Girl's Guide to Falling in Love* would be enough to thaw any cold heart, and we can't wait to reveal who we're interviewing next!

Until next time. Love well, my dear readers.

CPSIA information can be obtained
at www.ICGtesting.com
Printed in the USA
BVHW01s2026020918

526239BV00031B/343/P

9 781612 424149